Fate accomplished

The terribly mutilated body of a man is recovered from the wreckage of a car involved in a night-time collision with a freight train. Not only is the body initially identified from documents as being that of an unemployed waiter named Johnson – known to have died months earlier and now apparently miraculously resurrected from his grave to die once again – but it is also diagnosed this time as having died violently hours before the collision.

Detective Superintendent Rogers's critical thinking leads him to a correct identification of the body as that of an eminent consultant in obstetrics and gynaecology with a reputation for lusting after any woman who is not his wife. The subsequent post-mortem findings persuade Rogers that the body had been driven to the rail crossing and left there to be hit by the next train to come along.

A detachable moustache of artificial hair, an expensive nightdress on a bed and a woman missing from a cottage rented for adultery, the gossip and opinion of inquisitive neighbours, all point to the gynae-cologist's regular indulgence in a liaison that risks professional ruin.

To compound a harassed Rogers's problems, a subsequent death at the deserted cottage appears to have no connection at all with the death he is already investigating.

With the help of the crisp and demanding Sister Morag Anderson, Rogers fights his way through the defensive protocol of hospital politics to a dramatic and violent denouement.

Also by Jonathan Ross

The blood running cold (1968)
Diminished by death (1968)
Dead at first hand (1969)
The deadest thing you ever saw (1969)
Here lies Nancy Frail (1972)
The burning of Billy Toober (1974)
I know what it's like to die (1976)
A rattling of old bones (1979)
Dark blue and dangerous (1981)
Death's head (1982)
Dead eye (1983)
Dropped dead (1984)
Burial deferred (1985)

Under the name of John Rossiter

The murder makers (1970)
The deadly green (1970)
The victims (1971)
A rope for General Dietz (1972)
The manipulators (1973)
The villains (1974)
The golden virgin (1975)
The man who came back (1978)
Dark flight (1981)

Jonathan Ross
Fate accomplished

Constable London

First published in Great Britain 1987
by Constable & Company Ltd
10 Orange Street, London WC2H 7EG
Copyright © 1987 by Jonathan Ross
Set in Linotron Plantin 11 pt by
Rowland Phototypesetting Ltd
Bury St Edmunds, Suffolk
Printed in Great Britain by
St Edmundsbury Press Ltd
Bury St Edmunds, Suffolk

British Library CIP data
Ross, Jonathan
    Fate accomplished – (Constable crime)
    Rn: John Rossiter   I. Title
    823′.914[F]   PR6068.0835

ISBN 0 09 467450 7

I

The locomotive and its string of wagons sang an iron progress through the darkness of the night, the single beam of its headlight showing only the glistening of wet rails and the taut wires of slashing rain. Sitting in his cab and nursing the controls of the straining diesels in the engine room behind him, the driver squinted his eyes to see beyond the rubber wipers sweeping distorting water from the thick glass of his windscreen.

He saw the car across the single line suddenly in the blurred fringe of the headlight, saw through its side window the bowed head of its occupant. Even as he lifted his feet from the deadman's pedal, pushing the brake handle to its emergency stop and reaching frantically for the horn valve, he knew that nothing he could do would halt the locomotive and its thousand tons of roadstone-loaded wagons from smashing into the car.

In the few heart-stopping seconds before the impact, his brain threw up tiny coloured pictures of the woman suicide his locomotive had decapitated; later, the group of line gangers, unheeding of his approach, that he had ploughed into, and the same horror and fear he had then felt returned to him. He shouted a useless warning that died in the blaring of his horn as the buffers slammed into the car, driving it along the track in a grinding of rending metal and a spraying of sparks that lit up his cab; then, incredibly, the car riding up over the nose of the locomotive to hang momentarily upside-down, shattered and twisted, against the windscreen. In the acuity of frightened vision he had caught a brief glimpse of a pale face flattened against splintered glass before the car fell sideways into darkness.

When the locomotive ground to a halt he remained in his seat, shaken and distressed enough to vomit on to the metal floor of the cab.

Given a man of a tall solidness equipped with black hair, a handsome wedge of a nose, brown eyes that could darken in

5

easily provoked irritation, an amiable enough mouth and a generally cynical disbelief that mankind held in itself much evidence of saintliness, these would fit the physical character- istics and the persona of Detective Superintendent George Rogers in his 37th year. That the professional part of his mind had the disposition of an inquisitive ferret was his own not completely accurate assessment.

Having convinced himself that brightly-plumaged birds were by no means the sweetest singers – he had the peacock and parrot in mind – he mostly, and always when working, wore charcoal-grey suits, white shirts and muted ties, considering even polychromatic male underwear to be a symptom of either latent effeminacy or egotistical flamboyance.

Being firmly in the category of the not-wholly-unfortunate men whose discontented and carping wives had left them or thrown them out, he was able occasionally to tranquillize the deprivations of his solitariness with those usually no longer discontented and carping women who had left other husbands.

Now in the assemblage of concrete and glass boxes called the County Constabulary Headquarters, his office much too like a soundproofed monastic cell with soulless metal and plastic furniture, his communications equipment of cables and electric impulses keeping him remote from his staff and the rest of the force, he was for probably the first time glad of it. The late morning sun, entering in golden stripes through the venetian blinds, made blue the layers of smoke from his meerschaum pipe which had been clenched almost continuously between his teeth since arriving at the office and starting on his unloved administrative chores. Not the most self-approving of men, in his more rational moments he thought it an oddity that he should choose to pass so much of his time with a piece of vulcanite and magnesium silicate stuffed with burning vegetation sticking out of his mouth.

Committed by his purchase of flight tickets and a booking deposit with an auberge in the *quartier Montparnasse* of Paris to an autumn break with a librarian – Katherine, divorcee, no children, an obsessive interest in the life and writings of Gustave Flaubert, in tall men with their own teeth and no

6

ambitions towards marriage, and months away from being discontented and carping – he was dealing with the paperwork on his regimented desk for a departure in two days' time. It meant that he would scowl his disfavour should any person carelessly get himself, or herself, shot, strangled or otherwise done to death in his bailiwick before then. Indeed, he would regard with irritation any other interruption to the clearing of his desks.

As if he had invited his own come-uppance, the green telephone on his desk rang. Its number was unlisted, given to only a few, and its ringing usually meant looming trouble and having to do something about it.

'Rogers,' he said into the mouthpiece, wishing that he had unhooked it earlier and left it lying incapable.

'I think we've a problem, old George.' Rogers recognized the voice of Dr Wilfred Twite, graduate in morbid pathology and the somewhat slapdash dissector of bodies at the Abbotsburn Hospital.

'Oh, we have? Such as?' he said cautiously.

'That chap Johnson you sent in.' For a man with even a shared problem he sounded excessively cheerful. 'I'd like you to see him.'

'You would?' To confess his ignorance of that wasn't in Rogers's book, and he dug unsuccessfully into his brain for a dead Johnson he should know about. 'What's the problem?'

'Not over the blower, old chum.' Twite was, as Rogers knew, quasi-paranoiac in his belief that every call he made from the Pathology Laboratory was listened into by a switchboard operator in the pay of local journalists. 'It isn't a hundred per cent certain yet, but enough for you to get yourself off your rectum and down here.'

Rogers replaced the receiver, his black eyebrows frowning. Who the hell was, or had been, Johnson, anyway? Why hadn't he been told? Or had he been and it had not sunk in? Was he losing his touch, his mind drifting into a confused amnesia? He retrieved from the mass of papers in one of the four desk trays a hitherto unread CRIME AND INCIDENT RETURN sheet for the preceding night. This he would normally run through as a matter of routine when he got around to it, for he would have been advised at the time, on or off duty, of anything serious enough to warrant his attention or involvement.

It contained among its miscellany of burglaries, shopbreak-ings, thefts, offences of indecency and domestic disturbances resulting in violence, an entry that read, *FATAL TRAFFIC ACCIDENT. Dhugal Gordon JOHNSON, Hidden Cottage, Gorres Lane, Alwick. 11.20 p.m., Wednesday, 21st October. Collision with freight train (Driver J. Lander) at Madbrook Farm crossing. N.O.P.I. Inspector Orriss.*

It was clearly the uniform department's job and, endorsed *NOPI*, one with no other person involved. With the cause of death obvious and non-criminal, Rogers was puzzled that there could be any problem that Twite felt necessary to refer to him and not to Inspector Orriss who, admittedly now off duty and probably in bed, had dealt with the accident. But a foreboding of inescapable involvement was growing in him and he thought about Katherine, about eating unworriedly and leisurely in Parisian cafés and his 8.15 a.m. flight on Saturday. Just short of heaving something smashable against the wall, he said, 'Damn and bloody damn!' to what seemed an unsympathetic pile of yet-to-be-read crime files.

2

Although Rogers had a healthy man's dislike of hospital wards and a fear of hypodermic needles being stuck into him, he approved the exterior of Abbotsburn Hospital. Guessing that it had been built when its medical staff was required to deal with not too much more than bloody fluxes, smallpox, the plague, blood-letting by leeches and the twisted ankles of sedan-chair carriers, he saw it now as a flaking brick and slate island stuffed full to its fourth floor with suffering humanity and surrounded by the continuous din of fuming traffic and plastic-bag-carrying shoppers.

The Pathology Laboratory was a ground-floor annexe to the main building and a conveniently short walk from the basement mortuary and body store. Twite was in his office, waiting for the detective and smoking one of his scented cigarettes with an offhand disregard of the General Medical Council's proscription against them.

He was a short man, nourished to fatness on the *haute cuisine* of the town's only four-star restaurant, with parts of his amiable face covered by an incongruous Mexican-style moustache and sidewhiskers. By Rogers's standards colourful in his dress, he wore a brilliant turquoise silk tie and breast-pocket handkerchief with an Oxford-blue shirt and chalk-striped suit, managing to look as though he ran a male boutique on the side.

'What's your problem, Wilfred?' Rogers asked after they had each ritually enquired of the other's well-being. 'This chap Johnson doesn't seem to be mine.'

'I'm sure he is,' Twite said, beaming. 'About as sure as I am that he was dead long before the train hit him.'

Rogers stared at him. 'I knew it,' he muttered. 'I bloody well knew it.'

Twite looked surprised. 'You did? How?' Speaking with the cigarette in his mouth, ash dropped on to his lustrous tie.

'No, not that. I just knew you were going to bugger up my few days off.' Rogers shook his head in frustration. 'Tell me, what *did* kill him?'

'Ah! That I don't know and that's your problem, old chum. Why he died, I do know. He bled to death from a rupture of an artery; the abdominal aorta.' He raised a pudgy hand as Rogers started to speak. 'His collision with the train chopped him about pretty badly and he's in a bit of a mess. But you'll have to see him in order to get the picture.'

'I'll try not to throw up,' Rogers said, tongue-in-cheek, although he knew that, even discounting what the train might have done to the unfortunate Johnson, being in a mess would be true of any corpse examined by Twite, wielding as he did his chisel, saw and scalpels with cavalier recklessness.

Walking with him across the yard and down the ramp to the mortuary, his anticipated lunch only an hour away, Rogers

9

could now think of his abandoned paperwork with regret. Expecting one day to be felled in his stride by an impatient God, he always saw any mortuary as a possible destination for his own body with somebody like Twite hacking away at his inner machinery.

Windowless, it was all white tiles, cold shadowless light and the pervading smell of formalin and dead flesh. Its décor – shelves of glass jars and enamelled bowls of leached organs and pieces of tissue, plastic containers of coloured fluids on a bench, a hand wash-basin with elbow-operated taps, iron pipes around the skirting and a steel and glass wall cabinet of fearsomely glittering instruments – gave it all the homely cosiness of a butcher's shop. Two stainless steel necropsy tables stood side by side in the centre. On one of them, a hose hanging down on it and dribbling water, lay the naked body of what had been a man.

Twite, after fitting on his parchment-coloured rubber gloves, slapped the body on its chest as if greeting an affectionate friend. 'He's going to be all yours, old chum,' he said cheerfully to Rogers, 'so you'd better get to know him.'

Rogers filled and lit his pipe as an air deodorant as he took in what the outer aspects of the body was supposed to tell him. He saw the dead Johnson to have been a sinewy man of about 45 years with light brown hair, wet now and plastered to his skull, his horribly distorted and mutilated face clean shaven. The eyes staring sightlessly at the ceiling were the pale-blue of a dead fish and the cut mouth showed four teeth to have been broken off. His hands, the nails well kept, bore no signs of having been used in manual labour. Apart from the gaping incision from throat to groin made by Twite and left unsewn, the chest and arms were ugly with multiple lacerations as though caused by jagged metal, the wounds extending to a lesser degree to the legs.

Rogers took the pipe from his mouth and, to anaesthetize his nose against the raw smell, sniffed smoke directly from the bowl. 'Immensely illuminating,' he said drily. 'I can guess that he's dead, but otherwise I can only see what happened in the accident.'

'An oral thesis then, in simple terms for you,' Twite said with a friendly disrespect for Rogers's understanding. 'When it's supported by the lab you'll shout me a slap-up dinner at the *Provençal*.' He poked a rubbered finger at the dead man's chest. 'These lacerations, despite their appearance, are relatively superficial, more or less only skin-deep with no ribs broken or the internal organs behind them damaged. Those on the face and head about the same, and I found pieces of glass in some of them.' He put a finger in the open mouth and pushed down on the lower jaw. 'A blow here that broke four teeth and loosened others, which would have been more painful than dangerous if he'd been alive. None of the external injuries would be likely to cause death other than, perhaps, by prolonged bleeding or shock brought on by a sudden huge loss of blood. Only that couldn't happen, for dead flesh and tissue don't bleed unless with the small amount of blood already left in the arteries and veins, and all the indications are that he was dead long before the train hit him.'

Slapdash as Twite might be with his scalpel, Rogers had to accept that he was wholly competent in his diagnoses. 'But you're still waiting on the lab tests to prove it,' he pointed out.

'To confirm it, believe me,' Twite replied. 'It isn't much, but you've noticed the post-mortem staining and contact lividity on the left side of the trunk and limbs?'

'Yes, and agreed. I don't think he would have been left in the car long enough for that to develop. How long would you guess at?'

Twite pushed out his bottom lip to indicate uncertainty. 'Difficult, old chum,' he said. 'It depends such a lot on external temperatures. Two hours? Three? And certainly not developed sitting upright on a car seat. And I'm not saying that was how long he had been dead, only that he was lying on his side for approximately that time.'

'How long had he been dead then?'

Twite shrugged his fat shoulders. 'As there's no marked hypostasis from his sitting in the car, not a lot longer. Put an hour on at the most.'

'You did say a ruptured abdominal aorta. Definitely not in the smash-up?' Rogers guessed that the pathologist was now intending him to work for what he could get. It was all good professional fun.

'It could have been, but it wasn't.' Twite pulled aside the stiff flesh of the belly, exposing the interior and causing Rogers to step backwards and puff furiously at his pipe. 'This,' he said as if showing the detective an interesting work of art, 'was caused by a non-penetrating abdominal violence which mashed up the stomach, the transverse colon and the small intestine, rupturing the aorta in the process. He could have died in seconds from the loss of blood alone. That he was alive immediately prior to the blow causing it has to be, because a massive bleeding needs a live pumping heart.'

'Guessing wildly, would his being run over by a car produce that mess?' Rogers asked.

'Certainly it would. A car, bus, lorry, van – anything on wheels except a bicycle. I've dealt with similar cases – road accidents, that is – though not associated with a burst aorta. Compression from any heavy weight would cause that sort of damage.'

Rogers had been scrutinizing the dead man's legs. Immediately below each kneecap was a wide horizontal depression, suffused with a pink stain, into which Twite had cut to expose the bone. 'What about these?' he asked. 'Were they done at the same time?'

'Yes, they were. And certainly by something harder than a tyre, because I found comminuted bone fractures immediately behind them. Those and a corresponding crushing of the calf muscles.' He smiled genially at Rogers as if to say 'Sort that one out, old chum' and began removing his bloodied gloves, careful of his immaculate shirt cuffs. 'Incidentally, you've noticed the size of his whacker, eh?'

'In passing,' Rogers said airily, 'and only not envious because I'm sure that being oversized there can mean being under-developed in the intelligence.' He was more interested in a small gouging out of tissue on the outer side of the right shin, more over the calf muscle than the bone. 'What might have made this?' he asked.

'Same as, because it's bled,' Twite said. 'Pressure, or even a

12

blow, from something hard and, I'd guess, with an edge to it.'

Rogers, using the span of his thumb and forefinger as a measure and carefully avoiding contact with dead flesh, moved his hand over the body. 'Approximately twenty-four inches between the base of the stomach and the kneecaps,' he said grimacing. 'That seems to knock out any idea of his having been run over by a car.'

'Foxing, isn't it?' Twite seemed happy to have Rogers shoulder the problem. 'I did think about him banging his shins against the car's fascia, but that wouldn't explain the crushing of the calf muscles. Or would it?' Having removed his gloves, he lit a cigarette and let the smoke drift from his mouth, watching for Rogers's reaction.

Rogers didn't show one. '*And* he'd have to have been un-belted,' he said. 'Are you also going to say that impact with the steering wheel couldn't possibly explain the compression in-juries?' While not prepared to dispute them, he was no more inclined to accept the pathologist's conclusions as absolute and infallible than he would his own. Facts could misrepresent causes and deepen the thick fog which usually enveloped his initial investigations into violent deaths.

'In my opinion, unlikely,' Twite replied with a little less assurance. 'Too wide an area of compression for a start, although I wouldn't bet you another dinner on it.' He moved over to the wash-basin and started to scrub his hands.

'I'm grateful,' Rogers said sardonically. 'So let me sort it out from my point of view. We have a man here whose car was hit by a train at about 11.30 last night. In heavy rain, incidentally, when I imagine visibility was minimal. His body was brought here and you examined it this morning. You then found that he was already dead at the time of the accident, having died as a result of a ruptured artery in his belly caused by a forceful compression some three to four hours before it. That means death could have occurred between 7.30 and 8.30 yesterday evening and, presumably, somewhere else but at the crossing. It also means that somebody – almost certainly somebody connected with his death – drove his body there and parked the car on the rails knowing that it would be hit by the next train to come along.' He was guessing, being still in ignorance of the details of what had happened and unwilling to admit it to Twite. 'However he died or was killed, it seems that the circumstances of it would be an embarrassment for the somebody who left him there; hoping, I imagine, that he'd be sufficiently smashed about to suggest that to be the cause of his death.' He thought about that, then said smiling, 'He certainly didn't anticipate the deductive brilliance of my pathological friend. Why *did* you do a post-mortem on him, Wilfred? You wouldn't normally with such an obvious traffic accident.'

Twite shrugged, apparently relieved of whatever problems his examination of Johnson's body had given him. 'I hadn't anything brought down from the wards and I needed to keep my hand in. I was bored, too. It's as simple as that.'

Rogers scrutinized again the body, wishing fancifully that, like the priests of the old Roman gods, he could read in entrails the answers to his questions. The slightest doubt about the causation of a violent death made it his professional responsibility, a responsibility that overrode any officially irrelevant and trivial arrangements he might have made discreetly, such as accompanying an attractive woman called Katherine to a low-profile auberge in the *quartier Montparnasse*. To compound his feeling that life had taken on a greyish tinge, he wasn't much looking forward to his lunch either.

3

Rogers ordered what he would normally consider a derisory lunch of bouillon from the canteen on the basis that it would contain no bits and pieces likely to provoke subliminal off-putting glimpses of what he had seen in the mortuary. When he had finished he killed the taste of it by lighting his pipe, then read through the preliminary accident report by Inspector Orriss that he had retrieved from the Divisional Superintendent's office.

Orriss, on the 10 p.m. to 6 a.m. night tour, had received a telephone message from the Rail Traffic Manager at 11.47 p.m. to the effect that the down-line freight train No 33117 had, twenty minutes earlier, collided with a car standing across the line at the Madbrook Farm crossing. Arriving at the scene with PC Harness he had found the wreckage of an Austin Cambridge saloon, registration number 1032HNL, at the side of the line about 200 yards west of the crossing. The locomotive and wagons had stopped a further 400 yards beyond it. The car was badly damaged with the bodywork gashed and crushed in, the two offside wheels torn off and later found near the point of impact at the crossing. The body of a man was in the driving seat, wearing his safety belt which was still intact. Although it was impossible for him to open any door of the car to remove the body, Orriss was able to reach through the broken window and ascertain from the absence of a pulse that the man was dead. Having been sent for, a detachment from Fire Brigade Headquarters had arrived at 12.20 a.m. and removed the body from the car. It was then taken by ambulance to Abbotsburn Hospital where, having been examined and confirmed dead by Dr Aherne, Duty Casualty Officer, it was placed in the mortuary.

There was more about the driver of the train having been badly shocked and unable to give a coherent account of the accident, that the headlight of the locomotive had been examined and found in good working order. It had been raining heavily at the time with extremely poor visibility and the crossing to the farm was uncontrolled, access to it, and to nowhere else, being from the B8014 road. The previous train, a local passenger, had passed over the crossing at 10.09 p.m. when no obstruction had been observed.

Inspector Orriss had taken possession of the driving and registration documents identifying the car's owner as Dhugal Gordon Johnson, sending PC Harness to Madbrook Farm to enquire if the occupants knew Johnson; which they did not, neither having had any visitor nor expecting one. Owing to the damage caused to the car, left at the scene for any further examination thought necessary, Orriss had found it difficult to decide in which gear it had been when the collision occurred,

15

although there was no indication that it had been other than in neutral gear and stationary. The ignition key was intact and in the 'off' position. The possibility that the death was suicidal was being enquired into. Sergeant Ray of Moorfield, in whose section Alwick lay, had been sent to the address given on the driving documents. He had received no reply to his knocking, calling there later with the same result. On the assumption that the dead man had lived alone, enquiries would be continued to trace any relative or associates.

While Orriss's report had been done without knowing the result of the post-mortem examination, his suggestion of suicide might be a near-credibility. But not, Rogers knew, one committed by sitting in the path of an approaching locomotive. He could not disregard, however, the possibility of an unusually grotesque means of suicide hours previously and its attempted concealment in the collision by a second party to whom it would otherwise have been a serious embarrassment. Or, he thought, an accident or circumstance necessitating a face-saving camouflaging of it such as – and he dredged into a previous investigation of his for an example – where an otherwise respectable married man and deacon of a local chapel had carelessly died from a heart attack in a prostitute's bed.

He examined the dead man's clothing which he had brought back with him from the mortuary. The suit, of good quality brown worsted and hand-sewn, was wet with muddy smears and ripped in several places. There was neither visible blood staining nor any dirt mark identifiable as a trace from the tread of a car's tyre. The tan soft-calf shoes were obviously, despite the mud and scratches on them, large cheque bespoke.

The documents retrieved by Orriss from the car were all current, the driving licence being endorsed *Replacement*, the vehicle registration document dated seven months earlier. Rogers noted that Johnson had public-spiritedly signed the donor card attached to the licence, authorizing his organs to be used for transplantation should he die in an accident. A frustrated bequest, he thought, now that Twite had had access to them.

Other items retrieved from the body by the inspector were a

leather wallet containing bank cashpoint and cheque cards and £127 in notes, a cheque book, a costly looking gold moon-phase watch, a gold finger-ring, bifocal spectacles in a case, a brass Yale-type key with a tag numbered 3 and an ancient mortice lock key. There were five stubs in the cheque book – interestingly issued by a Birmingham bank with no branch office in Abbotsburn – each made out to M. O. Barrington for identical amounts of £140, each for the first day of the preceding five months.

Nothing of which told him much, other than that he remembered the Cambridge as a car that had dropped out of production in the 1960s with a registration number matching it, and not quite appearing to fit the expensive clothing and gold hardwear, and the picture he had formulated in his mind of the dead man. A man who, so to speak, had forced himself and his affairs on Rogers and who would be the subject of a probing he would possibly not have attracted when alive and doing his own thing.

After advising the Divisional Superintendent that he and his staff need no longer concern themselves with any enquiries regarding Johnson, he put into effect a computer name check, arranged for the clothing to be taken to the Forensic Science Laboratory for examination and then sent a patrol car to find his second-in-command, Detective Chief Inspector David Lingard, strongly suspected of spending his rest day at the High Moor golf course. Rogers could think of no civilized reason why he himself should suffer alone.

Deciding on a quick visit to the Madbrook Farm crossing, about six miles from his office, he left a note for Lingard to await his return, then drove his car out into the warmed-up air of the countryside. Channelling his professional resolve to a definite objective was minimizing the frustration of his probable missing out on the *quartier Montparnasse* which, he supposed, would still be there another day; and lightening by just a fraction his foreboding that Katherine would decide to go it alone, bumping adventitiously into a lecherish roué of incredible charm with time on his hands and an encyclopaedic intimacy with the writings of Gustave Flaubert.

Turning into the farm road – less a road than a muddy lane – he noted that it was clearly signposted *Madbrook Farm Only*, the railway line crossing it 300 yards from its entrance. Parking his car at what he considered a safe distance from what had proved to be so dangerous a crossing, he climbed from it into the autumn-crisp sunshine coming from the rural over-abundance of sky that invariably made him feel smaller and more solitary than he actually was.

Diamonds of shattered safety-glass and twisted strips of chromium-plated metal were scattered between the rails on the crossing, indicating the point of impact. The car lay on its side further along the line, its nose buried in a thicket of small bushes on the sloping embankment. Walking to it, Rogers took in what it must tell him. The passenger side of the mauve-coloured bodywork had taken the force of the locomotive's impact, showing that the car had been facing towards the distant and invisible farm. Caved in, the front passenger door missing, the metal shell was split and gashed, scored and filthy with infilling from the track, its underside brown with advanced body-rot. The two wrenched-off wheels had been laid behind it.

The interior was reduced to a narrow confusion of compacted seats, a chewed-up instrument panel and a steering wheel that had been pushed sideways through the window glass of the driver's door. That the dead Johnson hadn't been crushed to a paper-thin flatness seemed to Rogers to have been a lesser miracle. He could find no evidence of bleeding in the inside wetness, but that meant little in a tangled mess of metal and upholstery. If there were, it should be found by the laboratory scientists he could have called to examine the car. The finding of any fingerprints might, he thought, be out.

He was certain – almost certain – of two things. Accepting Twite's diagnosis of an earlier death, the body of Johnson had been driven in the car to the crossing, almost certainly in the dark, strapped in the driver's vacated seat and left there to whatever happened when a locomotive hit a relatively small heap of rusting metal and dead flesh. The crossing being to Rogers a comparatively long way from civilization, and eight miles from Alwick, it would be necessary for the disposer of a dead body to have transport back to somewhere. Which probably meant another car and an accomplice to have driven it there. He recrossed the lines and walked the length of the lane and back, looking for any record of its coming and going, not too happy about the mud and cow manure plastering his shoes and socks. Unless he was badly astigmatic, there was nothing, the night's rain having washed away any tyre marks or footprints there could have been.

Starting his car and doing a necessary three-point turn with difficulty in the narrow lane, Rogers considered that it wasn't the most fact-ridden investigation with which he had been saddled, even extending to his being clueless about the cause of the victim's death. People who got themselves killed, he muttered to himself, could at least be bloody unambiguous about it.

4

Detective Chief Inspector Lingard was waiting in Rogers's office when he returned to it, standing at one of the windows and apparently engrossed in an entrancing view of grey rooftops and the more distant gasholders and concrete high-rise flats. Lingard was what would have earlier been called a dandy, a Beau Brummell of fashion with a predilection for fancy embroidered waistcoats and hand-sewn silk shirts high in the collar and long in the cuffs. Narrow-faced with a thin patrician nose, he wore his yellow hair a shade too long for his senior's approval. He had the daunting blue eyes, reputed to be ambition's best asset, of a man destined by his professional capabilities to one day be seated in Rogers's cooling chair.

'Sorry about your golf, David,' Rogers said, seating himself at his desk. 'We've a problem, so read this first.' He passed him Inspector Orriss's report.

'I've read it,' Lingard replied, handing it back and seating himself in the visitor's chair. 'It's required reading for people kept waiting in unoccupied offices. Since when have we concerned ourselves with idiots killing themselves on rail crossings?' He took a small ivory box from a waistcoat pocket and pinched out snuff, inhaling it with an eighteenth-century elegance and scenting the air around him with attar of roses.

'Only since this morning. And after I'd been closeted in the mortuary with friend Twite.' Rogers told him in detail of the pathologist's finding. 'I'm forced to accept it,' he finished, 'even although he can't begin to suggest how it happened. Nor, if it comes to that, can I.' He frowned as if that were something different altogether.

'You've considered the possibility of somebody putting the boot in?' Lingard suggested. 'The belly's always a favourite target for some of our less kindly brothers.'

'Yes,' Rogers said, although he hadn't. 'But it'd have to be a hell of a big boot, and the injuries don't seem to fit it anyway.'

'Your check on the name index hasn't delivered anything useful either,' Lingard said. 'It's in your tray and I've read that too.'

Rogers retrieved the unnoticed piece of flimsy paper and read it. *Records Name Check. 11.32 a.m. JOHNSON, Dhugal Gordon, (27), 103 Balmulloch Road, Cambuslang, Glasgow. Road Traffic Accident M6 Wigbeck Junction, 1 February. Died Abbotsburn Hospital 2 February. RTA Report 234/PC807 Callaghan.*

He made a sound like 'Um' and thought about it. 'He'd have to be an old-looking twenty-seven,' he said finally, 'as well as having to be resurrected alive and kicking from the cemetery eight months later to do it all over again. I've probably a hyper-suspicious mind, David, but I don't accept coincidences all that easily. How many Johnsons called Dhugal Gordon – and Dhugal can't be all that common a name – can get themselves killed and finish up in the same hospital before we begin to think there's something odd about it?' He put the paper back into the tray. 'I'll be digging into that,' he promised.

'I stand abashed,' Lingard murmured, not being remotely

so. 'You're going on leave on Saturday. Aren't you going to hand the digging over to me?'

'I've started it, so I'll stay with it.' He made it definite, knowing that a compromise wouldn't work with a detective who thought enough of his own abilities not to like being second man in any investigation. But then Rogers exaggerated to mollify, suspecting that he had been sharper over coincidences than he had intended. 'Naturally, I shall need you at hand to do all the clever bits, David.' He stood from the desk. 'First thing,' he said, 'is that we see what's exactly what at the cottage. And we'd better go in your car.'

Belted in the passenger seat of Lingard's vintage Bentley, Rogers accepted that being allowed to ride in her was equated by Lingard with being permitted access to the Queen's Garden Party; he also accepted his well-known prohibitions against slamming the doors too hard or knocking out pipe ash on the bodywork. His 'true and only love' – as Lingard insisted on calling her – was immaculate in Brooklands racing green with a long strapped-down bonnet, yards-long stainless steel exhaust pipes, wire-spoked wheels and a canvas hood now folded back to expose them to the afternoon's sun and to the coolish airstream's uninhibited battering over the two tiny wind-screens.

The village of Alwick lay in a turn-off from the main road, its visible substance appearing to consist of about thirty houses and cottages, the White Lion Inn standing in the shadow of a towered church and its graveyard, a telephone kiosk and a combined grocery shop and sub-post office. Gorres Lane, concealed between hedges thick with Old Man's Beard and almost unfindable, was a cul-de-sac. At the fag-end of it, surrounded on three sides by trees, was the appropriately named Hidden Cottage.

Rogers banged the black knocker on the Dutch door, painted a revolting maroon, and took in the exterior of the cottage as he waited. Its thatch was black and ragged, pitted with what looked like mouseholes and blotched with moss. Limewashed a now fading pink, the bulging plastered wall had a blackish-green mould climbing its footings from the small flowerless and weed-covered garden at its front. Curtains had been drawn inside the small wooden-framed windows, giving it a secretive blank look. A clapboard porch enclosed the door on which he had knocked. It was empty of anything indicating occupancy, the cement step showing no signs of milk bottles having been left there. A second check on the narrow garden where he thought he had seen something odd, decided him that the two shallow furrows in it had been made by a car turning around in the lane.

'I'm going round the back,' Rogers told Lingard. 'You wait here on the off-chance that God-knows-who may open the door.'

An earth drive, sprinkled sparsely with gravel and rutted from a car's wheels, led him to a cement hardstanding and an unkempt garden with an ancient greenhouse, the whole enclosed by trees golden in the sun of an autumn's dying. Patches of leaked engine oil showed clearly where a car had been standing on the cement. The back of the cottage had nothing to it but another maroon door, close-curtained windows and the skeletal remains of a creeper that had climbed the wall and died. Rogers lifted the latch of the door and pulled – it was bolted, for he could see no keyhole – then knocked on it with his knuckles, refusing to wait for the answering silence he expected and returned to Lingard.

'Somehow, I seem to have brought this with me,' he said to him, holding up the key found on Johnson's body. 'If it fits, I'm going in. If I'm found committing an unlawful entry there's no point in both of us being complained about. You trot around and chat up some villagers. Find out what they know about Johnson; what he does, how long he's been here and so on.' He smiled genially. 'It's telling my grandmother how to suck eggs, but preferably women who can loosen their corsets and get down to a bit of serious gossiping with a nosy detective.'

With Lingard gone, Rogers unlocked the cottage door and opened it, finding himself in a twilit low-ceilinged sitting-room lit only by the glowing bars of a canopied electric fire. Switching on a light, he passed between the furniture over the islands of heavy rugs on the unpolished wooden floor to the doorless entry to a rising staircase. It was steep, narrow enough to cause his shoulders to brush against the side walls, and led to a small landing giving access to three white-painted doors. One led to a bathroom overlooking the rear of the cottage, the other two to bedrooms with sloping ceilings, only one of which was furnished. Satisfied that the cottage was unoccupied, he returned to the sitting-room and, after pulling back the curtains from window recesses as deep as cupboards and switching off the fire, began a methodical search.

The furniture, fat chairs and a sofa upholstered in dusk-pink, small single-legged leather-topped wine tables and an oak sideboard, was near to new and, he could see, definitely up-market. In a cupboard of the sideboard were bottles of cognac, a pricey whisky and imported vodka, mixers and crystal drinking glasses. A copy of *The Times*, dated the previous day and opened at the foreign news page, rested on the arm of a chair close to the fire. A *Guardian* of the same date, disarranged as though it had been dropped in haste, lay at the side of a chair opposite to the other. Two books stood on an otherwise unoccupied mantel-shelf. One contained a collection of Betjeman poems, the other titled *Is Evolution Proved?*. From each, the first page had been cut. On the floorboards, inappropriately near the foot of the stairs, was a large portable stereo radio tuned in to the Radio 3 wavelength. On one of the windowsills was a glass vase of white chrysanthemums, fresh enough not to have made the water in which they stood smell. A tweed hat with a turned-down brim rested on an ornament shelf and, by its side, was what appeared to be a scrap of brown fur. It was, when he examined it, a detachable moustache of artificial hair. Propped against the wall near the door was a heavy blackthorn walking stick with a knobbed handle.

On the negative side, there was no television set and no telephone, nor were there any pictures on the lumpy papered walls, or ashtrays. Nor, when he had finished with the room, had he found any kind of a document.

The larder in the kitchen contained a drum of Bath Oliver biscuits, opened packets of breakfast cereals, instant coffee, cartons of long-life milk, two cups and saucers and two small plates; the cutlery drawer, four lonely looking silver-plated spoons. There was a new electric kettle, but neither cooker nor refrigerator.

In the bedroom, Rogers found the double bed and its continental quilt almost unused and of expensive make. A pair of navy-blue pyjamas was beneath one of the pillows, a filmy white nightdress folded on the quilt. He could smell no scent on the nightdress and that he considered a minus, having a sensitive nose for identifying scents to those wearing them. Inside the single wardrobe hung a green tweed jacket and cavalry twill trousers, the pockets empty, two each of nondescript shirts and ties, a pair of stout size ten half-boots and two blue dressing gowns, one larger than the other. Apart from a small bedside table, floor rugs and another electric fire, there was nothing else.

The bathroom, equipped with an ancient geyser, had towels, three packeted toothbrushes and pastes, a box of bath soaps, two nailbrushes, a used toothbrush and paste in a plastic beaker, a tortoiseshell hair comb, a battery shaver and a large stand-up magnifying mirror. A towelling robe hung on a hook and the tray on the bath held sea sponges and a bottle of body oil. What there was not – and what he thought he should have found in the bedroom – was a woman's cosmetics.

'I am,' Rogers told himself with heavy irony as he descended the stairs, 'beginning to believe that Johnson isn't quite what he seems to be, that he doesn't live here and that when he visits there might be a female someone else with him who could have a penchant for wearing stick-on moustaches.'

Leaving the cottage and relocking the door, he sat in the Bentley to await Lingard's return. He filled his pipe from his rubber pouch, lit it, leaned back and did some thinking. In the period before his death, Johnson was as much an enigma as had been the cause of it. As with the old rusting car which hadn't gone with his clothing and personal goldware, neither did the near-decrepit cottage go with his choice of furnishings, drinks and reading matter. The deliberate concealment of his identity, the use of the address of the cottage on his driving and vehicle documents, negated, he was certain, the place as a weekend retreat for a married couple. A further perplexity that thickened

24

the fog of his near-incomprehension lay in the absence of the woman. If he could believe the evidence of the two newspapers, she had almost certainly been there yesterday. It was no comfort to him in his present state of ignorance that, unless she were found to be dead also, the answer to it might be ludicrously and embarrassingly simple.

Lingard, entering the lane, appeared to suffer none of his senior's frettings. Climbing into the car, he said, 'I found out this much, George. Shock horror revelations; the village seems to play about par for the course on drinking after licensing hours, glue-sniffing and a not uncommon addiction to husband-swapping.' He pushed in the ignition key. 'We're going?'

'Hold your horses,' Rogers growled. 'Give me what you've been told first.'

'For what it's worth I got it from three disapproving females and one apparently unswappable husband, and it needs sorting.' He took out his ivory box and pinched snuff into his nostrils, flapping loose grains away with a green silk handkerchief. 'Johnson,' he said. 'Somewhere between 45 and 55, average height and lightweight to medium build. Brown hair – believed – and moustache, and a cultured voice when he said "Good-morning" which was seldom. Toffee-nosed, one of the women said. Carried a walking-stick and most often seen wearing suits, colour uncertain but brownish, and a fisherman-style hat pulled well down over his eyes. Once or twice a fawn raglan raincoat. He always had . . .'

'No spectacles?' Rogers interrupted him.

'Nobody mentioned them, so I assume not. As I was about to say, he always had a woman with him. A "Mrs Johnson" they said, with a fair amount of insinuation that she wasn't likely to be. Aged variously between 20 and 35, slim or thin, tallish or medium height depending on whether seen walking or sitting in the car, black hair worn shoulder length or nearly so, sometimes hidden under a head scarf, and two of them agreeing on a generous amount of face-painting. She most often wore those saucer-sized sun-glasses and clothing which they called "towny", by which I imagine they meant fashionable. Tarty, according to a couple of the women, and "a gorgeous bit of homework" from the man whose wife then happened to be out of earshot.'

With Rogers unspeaking and manifestly unsurprised at what he had said, Lingard continued. 'Generalities,' he said, 'unless that's something else you already know. They rent the cottage from a Mr Oliver Barrington who no longer lives here, and have done so for the past five or six months. Furniture delivered in a van which none of the four I spoke to saw. The Johnsons were called weekenders, although they'd normally only stay a night and part of the following day, and then not necessarily at weekends. None of those I spoke to knew of their arrival this week or, of course, of their leaving. They rarely left the house and, when they did, only out into the rural footpaths away from the village. When they were met, they made it obvious that there would be no social matiness by not stopping. They never visited the shop, post office or pub and certainly never invited anyone to visit them. When seen, they always arrived and left in an old car – plum-coloured, apparently – make and number unknown, the man driving. When he wasn't, the car was believed to have been tucked discreetly out of sight at the rear of the house.' Lingard beamed self-mockingly. 'Logical conclusion. Disgustingly priapic man having it off in territory not his usual habitat with a lady not his lawfully wedded wife.'

'Stout fella!' Rogers was cheerfully sardonic. 'I said I'd need you for the clever bits. Incidentally, his moustache was a fake. I found it in the cottage.' He told Lingard the results of his search, then added, 'Whatever happened that took him away from reading his newspaper, happened when it was dark and unexpectedly enough for him to leave the electric fire burning. And, whatever it was, might not have happened to him only. I want the wood behind the cottage searched before dark in case our lady with the black hair is unlucky enough to be buried there. You never know,' he said, seeing Lingard's look of surprise. 'If Johnson was killed here and she was about – as I believe she was – it could be.'

'Unless she did it,' Lingard suggested.

'In which case she won't be buried there and we've acquired ourselves a possible suspect.' He pulled a face. 'Though just for

26

what, unless it's the unlawful disposal of a dead body, I can't think at the moment. Still, we'd be idiots not to check. And talking of checking, I want Sergeant Magnus to sort the house out for fingerprints, hairs, fibres and any bits and pieces I may have missed. Today.'

Lingard shook his head. 'He's away until tomorrow. I'll get one of the other chaps.'

'No.' Rogers preferred Magnus who, he considered, was that rarity possessing an instinct for finding the almost unfindable. 'It'll do if he comes first thing in the morning. For you, I've a special job I want done as soon as we get back. There are a pair of Johnson's spectacles in my office in a Goldthorpes' case. Now that we seem to have some slight doubts about who he might be,' he said with heavy irony, 'take them there, get them examined and the prescription measured and checked against their records for a name. For me,' he added, clipping on his safety belt, 'I need to have words with somebody or other at the hospital about a man who seems to make a habit of killing himself in accidents.'

5

Before leaving his office for the hospital Rogers sent for, and read, PC Callaghan's report on the fatal road accident of eight months earlier. In essence, it said that the Johnson from Glasgow, driving a Ford saloon north to south on the motorway at 10.15 p.m., had inexplicably, no other vehicle being involved, driven into the concrete buttress of a flyover bridge. Seriously injured, he was taken to the nearest hospital, which happened to be Abbotsburn, by ambulance and placed in the intensive care unit where he died at 4.40 the following morning. The Glasgow police had been informed and had reported back that Johnson, an unemployed waiter, was not on record at their CRO, was a transient lodger at the address given and no relatives were known or had been traced.

Far from being happy with what it told him, Rogers instructed the Information Room inspector to contact the Driving and Vehicle Licensing Centre and request details of the replacement of his own problem Johnson's driving licence.

When he parked his car on the forecourt of the hospital it was late afternoon, the sun was hidden by grey cloud and there was a chill in the air. Inside, the labyrinth of corridors he had to negotiate to the administration block were suffocatingly hot with the all too familiar smell of floor polish and disinfectant. He was told in the general office that the Chief Administrative Officer was not available – he didn't believe that – but that his deputy, Miss Kelf, might be. Rogers said that he thought she might be able to help him and, after she had been told over a telephone who he was and answered that she was available, he was shown into her office.

Miss Kelf, whatever her attributes in administering to the needs of the hospital might be, appeared not to be a woman given to smiling at or shaking hands with a visiting policeman. The small name plate on her desk said *Marian Kelf* where Rogers would have more easily accepted *Medusa*, particularly as it had standing by its side a card showing a coffin with a cigarette lying in it and a printed *Thank you for not smoking* on it. Hair tied back tightly, grey eyes in what could have been attractively neat features that had a few freckles, an equally neat blue-suited figure from what he could see of it behind the desk, provoked an initial measuring up of her as a woman who spoke to men only through clenched teeth. And, with that off-putting disposition, probably still virgo intacta in her possibly wasted thirties.

He smiled amiably at her, for one never knew and, in the absence of being invited, said 'May I?' and sat in the chair near her desk. 'I'm sorry to bother you, Miss Kelf,' he said. 'I've a small problem about a man called Johnson who died here earlier this year. Not about the circumstances of his death, but about the disposal of his personal effects. I assume you'll still have the record of it?'

She frowned. 'We would, but how does it concern the police?' Her voice was schoolmistressy, downgrading his enquiry to being a tiresome nuisance.

28

He smiled, less amiably, for she was sounding distinctly unco-operative. 'I can assure you that it does. May I see it, please?'

'Shouldn't I have some sort of an authorization from your Chief Constable?'

'No, you shouldn't.' He was patient with her, having met too many of these hedging bureaucratic defenders of bits of paper. 'I am authorization enough for the release of the details of a dead man's property of which you are only the bailee. And in the absence of the Chief Administrative Officer, I know that you have the authority to show it to me.'

She thought that over for a few moments and if she was surrendering, she didn't show it. Then she picked up her telephone, dialled a two-figure number and tapped a ball-pen impatiently on the desk top as she waited for it to be answered.

'Bring me the current patients' property register,' she said to somebody apparently as much an object of her distaste as was Rogers. They both waited in an unspeaking silence until a girl entered after knocking, laid a book on the desk and left without uttering a word. Miss Kelf patently showed clenched teeth to her female underlings as well.

She opened the book, flipped a couple of pages, then pushed it across the desk to the detective. 'I shall expect you to treat the information as confidential,' she said.

'I'll certainly promise not to pass it on to the KGB,' he assured her gravely. He didn't look to see what her reaction was to that, but the pen was being tapped again.

Against Johnson's name and address, his date of entry to the hospital, the date of his departure – discharge or death – was a list of the unextraordinary bits and pieces a handbagless man carries necessarily in his pockets. The list included the driving documents which, Rogers presumed, had been retrieved from the wrecked Ford. In the final column, marked Disposal, was a red ink notation; £17.28p to Patients' Amenities Fund. NHI card to DHSS. Remaining items destroyed 2nd April.

'Do I take it that "remaining items" means just what it says?' he asked. 'Driving documents as well?'

'It does,' she said tersely, reaching out to retrieve the book.

He put his hand on it. 'I haven't finished with it,' he told her. 'I'm about to question its accuracy.' He showed his teeth at her again. Female frigidity could sometimes be thawed by warm smiles. 'I'm concerned about the driving documents. How were they supposed to have been destroyed?'

He was wrong about the possibility of a thaw, the Rogers charisma failing badly, and he was now placing a modest bet with himself that she had to be wearing tin knickers. She said frostily, 'While I don't keep the records myself, you'll have to accept that they are correct. I don't appreciate your quite offensive suggestion that they are not.'

'Apart from the fact that the registration certificate should have been returned to the Licensing Centre, how were the documents supposed to have been destroyed, Miss Kelf?' he asked, his swarthy face imperturbable.

'Other than valuables, the property of a patient dying in the hospital remaining unclaimed by a relative is burned in the incinerator after three months by a porter.'

An establishment shift of responsibility, he guessed, should she prove to be wrong. 'Any porter?'

'Not any porter. One of the night porters who happens to be on duty and knows what is to be done.' It seemed from her grey eyes that she was talking to an invisible somebody behind his left shoulder and he assumed that she didn't much care for his looks.

'On whose authority?' he asked.

'In effect, the Chief Administrative Officer's,' she said, impatient of his continued questioning, 'but in practice not by any particular person. The disposal is arranged as routine in the general office, the property bagged and put in the appropriate store for disposal. That store is cleared periodically by a porter.'

'And we'd know which porters were on duty whenever it was burned?' Or not burned, he qualified to himself. He decided that she had a rather luscious mouth if it only turned up a little.

'There is a duty roster, although I don't have it. There should be a copy in the general office.'

30

'Should the driving documents still be in existence and being used, would that surprise you, Miss Kelf?'

'It most certainly would.' She was bristling, her administrative sensibilities offended. 'It's not possible, so why should you think it is?'

'A hypothesis,' he answered blandly. 'And something I'm trying to confirm.' He stood from his chair, putting affability in his expression. 'I'm grateful for your generous help,' he said, the lying words not sticking in his throat as they should have done. 'I hope I don't need to trouble you again.'

Even before he reached the door she had dismissed him from her attention and was pulling open a drawer of her desk to show it. He hoped that he wasn't being too masculinely chauvinistic, but he did believe that a romp or two in bed with a forceful male body other than his own might bring an occasional smile from behind her clenched teeth.

6

Before leaving the hospital, Rogers had visited the general office and had been shown the porters' duty roster for April, isolating the names of the two porters on night duty during the week when Johnson's property had been ordered to be burned. That one had since died, the other having emigrated to Australia, was, as Lingard had put it earlier, about par for the course.

Back at his office he found, left on his blotting pad, a message form and a print-out from the computer in Information Room. The message form stated briefly that Detective Inspector Coltart, having used eleven men and a sniffer dog in the search, had discovered no signs of a burial either in the wood at the back of Hidden Cottage, or in its garden.

The print-out gave him an unworthy feeling of *schadenfreude* at the bossy and unhelpful Miss Kelf's coming discomfiture. It told him that a replacement driving licence had been issued to Dhugal Gordon Johnson on the 28th April on a change of address from 103 Balmulloch Road, Cambuslang, Glasgow, to Hidden Cottage, Gorres Lane, Alwick.

Just like that, he thought, leaning back in his chair and preparing to worry at it. A change made by somebody who knew that the dead man had no relations to bugger things up by claiming a return of his property or wanting to bury him. Johnson the unemployed waiter entering the hospital, and Johnson the financially well-off womanizer resurrected to leave it. A man coy enough to wish to conduct his sexual liaisons in a rented cottage under an assumed name; a man, without doubt, having more money than morals. Secrecy and an adopted name made him either a duplicitous married man or somebody in the hierarchy of a profession or establishment – such as Rogers's own – given to frowning on a man's treading too publicly the primrose path.

Too, he must be a man who was either of the hospital, or having a larcenous contact working in it. Which contact could mean either the porter who was dead and incapable of saying 'I did it', or the porter not immediately available from the other side of the world who could prove, should he have any urge to survive, to be as equally uncommunicative. Manifestly, the spurious Johnson in the mortuary could not now be regarded as having been so enviously fortunate in his secret affair, perhaps even less so in his choice of the woman with whom he had been having it. While it didn't make the manner of his death explicable, it could make the reason for the disposal of his body understandable.

Or, he theorized, had there been more than one woman taken there at different times? Had the black-haired woman been but one of them? There had been a disparity in the descriptive details given of her, few though Lingard had obtained. The absence in the cottage of women's clothing, of cosmetics, the small store of new toothbrushes and soaps could, using a fairly flexible imagination, point to different women attending there; logically, each kept unaware of her predecessors. That the pyjamas were kept under a pillow, suggesting repeated visits by the man, and the nightdress, presumably dropped on to the bed on arrival, suggested one or infrequent visits. Although Rogers could convince himself that he would never indulge in that kind of methodically organized profligacy, the thought 'Lucky devil!' came into his mind.

When Lingard entered the office, he did so with an air of successful accomplishment restrained by modesty. He sat, fed his nostrils with attar of roses while Rogers waited, then drawled, 'Were I you, George, I wouldn't have any failing eyesight tested at Goldthorpes. I used your name freely and told them what a miserably bastard you could be if frustrated when they objected to searching through several hundred patients' cards for those spectacles, and you're now not too popular. Luckily the prescription and the frame type were unusual enough together to limit it to two patients. How would one Laurence Huke, solicitor, fit the bill?' His expression said that he knew it would not and that he was being flippant.

'Skinny? Yellow hair? A notorious tightwad?' Rogers snorted. 'He doesn't *like* women, let alone spend money on them. And I'd have recognized the miserable stinker in the mortuary anyway.' Huke was not one of Rogers's friends.

Lingard said, 'So you would. He'd hardly go for our man in the fisherman's hat, would he?' He looked smug. 'Errors and omissions excepted, the other man does. Simon Scrope Ungrish, consultant in obstetrics and gynaecology, whose description, other than for the hat and false moustache, fits. How does that grab you, George?'

'Like a vice, and more than you know,' Rogers said. 'Even so – a medical consultant! I'd have said hardly believable as our Johnson if I didn't know there had to be a connection with the hospital.' He told Lingard what he had learned of the use of the driving licence and its theft from the dead Johnson's property. 'The first thing is his identification. So far as I know, I've never set eyes on him and wouldn't be able to. But friend Twite must have . . .' He pulled at his lower lip, then shook his head. 'Obviously not or he would have said something. His face is badly cut about and distorted, and you do tend to look different when you're dead. I don't suppose it'd have occurred to Wilfred in a thousand years that he was chopping up a medical colleague who'd been dumped in the mortuary under an assumed name.'

33

'But potentially embarrassing for him?' Lingard suggested.

'Yes, it'll be more than awkward if it is Ungrish. He'll be made to feel an incompetent idiot at the least, so I'll have to do something to dig him out of his hole.' He looked through the window at his side. The sun had gone down behind the moor whose shadow now darkened the town and signalled the switching on of street lamps. It invited the putting up of feet in front of a coal fire, which he now knew wouldn't be for him.

'It's a sad truth, David,' he said reflectively, 'that the mysterious death of a consultant in obstetrics and gynaecology could mean a lot more flak coming our way than it would have for an unknown and unemployed Johnson. We'll be expected to strain every sinew, explore every avenue, et cetera; so, of course, we'll do it and carry on as we've always done. Two things for you.' He stuffed tobacco in his pipe as he thought them out. 'First, call yourself Jones or somesuch and cook up a reason for wanting to contact Ungrish on a medical matter for the wife you don't happen to have. Then telephone the hospital, his private consulting rooms if he has any, his home . . . Where does he live, by the way?'

'Capstone House at High Moor,' Lingard replied promptly. 'Apart from usually contacting a consultant through your doctor, God knows what I'll say if we're wrong and I find myself speaking to him.'

Rogers grinned at him. 'You're a pessimist, David. I'm sure you won't. Just find out that he hasn't been seen or spoken to since last evening, and where he's now supposed to be. Second thing. Try the *Post and Globe* for a photograph. It might come in useful for an identification. Third, take a couple of bodies with you to Alwick tomorrow morning and have every available villager questioned about the goings-on at the cottage. The place must be buzzing with interesting gossip by now. I,' he said, reaching for the telephone, 'am about to put poor old Wilfred into a paranoiac depression or similar.'

7

The body store, adjacent to the mortuary and racked with refrigerated drawers, was, for Rogers meeting Twite there, more chilly than had been the darkness outside. Too, it took something from the joy of living.

Twite had been worried by Rogers's insistence on not discussing details over the telephone, the detective only warning him pointedly that he was about to share the problem arising from the death of Johnson which he had so blithely loaded on to him. This was, as Rogers had remarked earlier to Lingard, a now different matter from investigating the unknown Johnson; for Ungrish, should it now prove to be him, was a man who would be judged to be of superior flesh and intellect and, even though dead, an overdog still capable of swinging a lot of hierarchical weight. Rogers doubted that Twite, had he known, would ever have made that personal remark about what he had called a whacker.

The pathologist pulled the labelled drawer open and lifted the blue plastic covering from the head and upper part of the body, managing an uncertain smile. 'I've looked again at my notes,' he said, 'and I still can't see what problem I can have.'

Looking at the mangled flesh, its appearance unimproved by the dim yellow lighting and thankful that he hadn't to see all of it, Rogers made a silent and provisional vow to curb any future ambitions he might have to indiscriminate fornication if this were the end to which it might come. 'It's a question of identity, Wilfred,' he said. 'Tidy up the face and I think you might recognize him.'

Without putting on rubber gloves, Twite pushed his fingers at the stiff flesh, manipulating it to a more natural configuration and pressing back into position the flaps of torn skin. 'Why all the secrecy? Why not tell me who, old chum?' he asked.

'No.' Rogers was definite. 'That wouldn't be an unassisted identification. But if I'm right, he's a colleague of yours.'

Twite, manifestly worried, stared at the features of the dead man, still far from what they must have looked like in life, then crouched to see them in profile. In doing so, his own features had lost completely any trace of his normal bonhomie. Straightening himself, he muttered, 'Judas bloody Iscariot! It can't be!'

'No, it can't. Not him.' Rogers had seen dawning recognition in his eyes. 'Say his name, Wilfred.'

'Mr Ungrish. Simon Ungrish.' For a moment he was angry with the detective. 'Why didn't you tell me before?'

'Because I've only just found out and, unlike you, I never knew him. I presume he *was* well known in these parts?'

Twite groaned and banged the heel of his palm against his forehead, a fat and amiable man achieving the impossible by managing to look haggard. 'Senior consultant in gynaecology, member of the House Committee . . . I didn't know him all that well, but I should have recognized him. What the hell am I going to say?'

Rogers was sorry for him. His colleagues – sure to be holier-than-thou in their hindsight – would never believe that anyone other than a medical cretin could spend a couple of hours dissecting a corpse and not recognize it as being that of a fellow medico. Even his normally waggish approach to his gruesome surgery, his smoking of proscribed cigarettes – especially scented ones – could be used adversely against him. Rogers said, 'In the first place, not to panic. I'm not filling you in about how I found out, so you can have an innocence of mind. Go straight from here and tell whoever it is who orders your destiny that you've discovered the man the police mistakenly call Johnson isn't who he's supposed to be; that although terribly disfigured in his features there was something about them that nagged at your thinking afterwards. You came back here, did a necessary repair job on the face and realized to your horror and distress that this so-called Johnson was the revered and absolutely well-known Ungrish that you'd been chopping up. First things being first, you notified the uncomprehending

Rogers who said that it was, indeed, a strong possibility, although he'd never believe that the body could ever be visually identified, even by its own mother. My back's broad and I think I can survive being slandered.' He put a sympathetic arm around a not too reassured Twite's shoulders. 'You might then, Wilfred, get off with not being unfrocked or whatever it is you're worried about.'

He had intended telling Twite that he, in turn, now owed him a dinner, but thought that that would be heartlessly piling Mount Ossa on to Mount whatever-it-was.

8

Where women were concerned, Rogers would admit readily to being a rank coward in being death's dark messenger, never having understood how to cope with feminine grief and easily unmanned by its weeping.

Having been told by Twite that Ungrish had a wife, he was now on his way through the saffron-lit streets of the town to see her, driven in a patrol car by the uniformed Woman Sergeant Jarvis. She, he had determined, having had her own husband shot dead in attempting to arrest a mentally deranged pig farmer and showing none of the bitterness of widowhood, would be better fitted for the unenviable task of breaking the bad news. Rogers liked her enough with her schoolgirl's ingenuous features overlooking an incongruously matronly body, to feel guilty about unloading one of his hang-ups on to her. But not nearly enough for him to consider changing his mind.

'Go no further than her husband being involved in an accident on the rail crossing,' he had briefed her. 'Nothing about his dying under the name of Johnson and, if she questions it, nothing about the delay in notifying her. You just don't know. And when she's over the worst of it, tell her that I'm waiting to speak to her.'

High Moor, a thickly foliaged suburb above the town, was, for Rogers, synonymous with money in freely flowing quantities and with no early morning blanching at receiving large bills in the mail. When Sergeant Jarvis braked the car to a halt on the forecourt of Capstone House, it was apparent to him that, unless Ungrish had married money, there had to be lots of it in the practice of gynaecology. Screened from the road by a high wall, it was a large turn-of-the-century building, its frontage over-elaborate with secondary gables silhouetted as twin peaks against a starlit sky, its windows lightless. A small lamp illuminated the inside of the church-like porch and its panelled door.

Sergeant Jarvis tugged at the iron bell-pull at its side, waited, then tugged again. In the night's quiet, Rogers had heard from the car the loud sounding of its interior buzzer. He climbed out, the last place in which a man with a phobia against weeping women needed to be found. 'You'd better wait here, sergeant,' he said with a put-on air of reluctance, 'while I look around the back for signs of life.'

Walking around the corner of the house, he saw that the grounds extended some distance to the rear, a stretch of white paddock fencing showing dimly against rising ground and a straggle of trees. A pool of yellow light thrown on to the ground near the fencing gave shape to a large outbuilding. Approaching it, he could see that it came from the open door of a barn. Entering, he found himself in a storage room partitioned off from the main structure. A youth in a leather floppy-brimmed hat, crouched down at the engine of a red and silver motorcycle, looked up at him in surprise and then stood. Not more than a well-muscled eighteen years, he had coarse black hair sticking out from under the hat, black eyes, a sharp nose and olive skin. There was an undisciplined and uncouth gypsy look about him as if his pockets could be stuffed with snared rabbits. He wore dirty over-tight jeans, a tee-shirt that looked slept in and a gold-coloured ring in the lobe of one ear.

Rogers said 'Good-evening,' deciding as he did so that the youth could not possibly be one of any Ungrish family brood. 'I'm looking for Mrs Ungrish,' he explained.

'Was it your motor I 'eard come in?' His voice was rough and very male, his eyes showing insolence.

'Yes.' Rogers didn't believe that he was going to like him.

The youth shrugged. 'Then she ain't in,' he said, dismissing him from his attention and turning to crouch at his motorcycle. That close to Rogers, he smelled strongly of body sweat and engine oil.

'Do you know when she might be?' When he received no reply, Rogers took out his warrant card and dug a hard finger between his shoulder-blades. 'Up,' he said sternly, 'and on your feet.' He held the warrant card in front of the startled face. 'Look at it.'

The youth straightened, screwing his eyes at it. 'I don't understand what it means,' he said sullenly, obviously not able to read, but equally obviously knowing what it was.

'It says that I'm a police officer, on duty and asking you politely where Mrs Ungrish might be.' He had seen the glint of hostility in the black eyes, a reaction familiar to the detective. An all-policemen-should-be-crucified reaction, enemies to be avoided or, if possible and unlikely to be detected doing it, hit with a thrown bottle. 'What's your name?' Rogers asked before his other question could be answered.

'Mr Gillard.'

'And you work here?'

'Yes.' He wasn't liking the questioning and showed it.

Rogers looked at his watch. It was eight-fifteen. 'It's late, isn't it? Don't you have a home to go to?'

'I sleep 'ere.' He looked across the room at an inner door. 'Mrs Ungrish lets me sleep in the tack room. It's better'n lodgings an' I look after things while they're out.'

'Such as a horse?' Rogers had heard the occasional sound of a muffled stamping from the other side of the partition.

''Orses,' Gillard corrected him. 'Two of them.'

'So now tell me when Mrs Ungrish might be back.'

'I don' know. She must 'ave gone out when I was gettin' the 'orses in.'

'And Mr Ungrish? Where is he?'

'Don' know,' he mumbled.

It might have been Rogers's misreading of it, but he thought he had seen dislike in Gillard's eyes at his naming of Ungrish. 'When did you last see him?'

Gillard thought about that. 'I 'eard 'is car go out yesterday morning, but I didn' see 'im.' His black-nailed fingers were pulling at the oily rag he held.

'That's the Alfa Romeo?' Rogers said, fishing into Gillard's grudging replies.

'No.' He was scornful, not thinking much of Rogers as a knowledgeable detective. 'It's a Merc.'

Rogers smiled. 'Of course. How stupid of me; a Mercedes. Perhaps Mrs Ungrish was using it?'

The scorn was there again. 'No. She's got 'er own.'

Rogers didn't ask him what it was, but was certain that it wouldn't be a rusty old Cambridge registered in the name of Johnson. Not yet having heard a car entering the drive, and now certain that Gillard was one hundred per cent gypsy and unlikely to tell him anything he wanted to know, he said, 'While I'm waiting for Mrs Ungrish, I'd like to see your horses.' He smiled again and lied, 'I do some riding myself.'

'These ain't riding 'orses, they're Shires. Rufen'am Shires,' he said as though it explained everything.

Rogers made himself look interested. 'Lead on, laddie. I'd still like to see them.'

Gillard's attitude towards the detective had altered at his mention of horses; not much and not a changing into anything approaching friendliness, but a lessening of his hostility. Tossing his rag in the direction of the motorcycle, he opened a door in the partition and Rogers followed him through it into the pleasantly pungent smell of a stable.

With lights switched on, he saw that what had been a barn had been converted to accommodate four stalls, flanked by a recently sluiced cement passage. The horse's hindquarters showing over the half-door of the first stall surprised Rogers with their massiveness; almost level, he judged, with his own height. Gillard said, ''Er's my favourite,' then unbolted the half-door, touched a restraining hand to the horse's flank and stood beneath her huge head to fondle it. 'Don' stand be'ind 'er,' he warned the detective. ''Er's in foal an' a kicker.'

Rogers had had no intention of doing so, amiable although she appeared to be. Ponderously immense, jet black and barrel bellied, a white blaze down her long nose and shaggy white hair over the fetlocks, her hooves crushing the straw on the floor were like iron-shod mallets. She had been recently groomed to an immaculate glossiness, her mane and tail smooth from combing. Gillard, whatever else he might be, seemed to be good with horses.

Rogers was impressed. 'Mr Ungrish breeds them?' The most unnecessary question of the day, he thought.

'They're 'ers, not 'is. The other'n, too.' Gillard nodded his head in the direction of a further stall from which Rogers had heard soft whickering noises.

He had also heard a car's engine at the front of the house, and its stopping. Give Sergeant Jarvis something like twenty minutes to break the news, he decided; to do whatever comforting and philosophizing it needed to have the unfortunate Mrs Ungrish in some sort of interviewable condition, when he would be able to get on with what he was supposed to be doing about her husband's death.

'I'd like to see the other one too,' he said to Gillard with a show of renewed interest, 'and have you tell me what you do with horses you don't ride.'

9

Rogers pulled at the door bell, feeling that were he ever called upon to investigate the improbable theft of a couple of Shire brood mares weighing a ton apiece, he might now know what he would be looking for. He had also learned by implication that the dead Ungrish had not been one of Gillard's favourite people; primarily, it seemed, because he hadn't cared much for the horses, and, in return, they hadn't cared that much for him.

Sergeant Jarvis opened the door to him, nodding and whispering 'She's gone to tidy up.' Asked how she had taken the news, she pulled a face. 'Not too badly, but I think it'll hit her later,' she said. 'I told her that you were waiting to see her.'

Rogers followed her through the hall and a door into a sitting-room where Jarvis sat while he remained standing, taking in whatever information the room had to offer. The stuff he had seen in the cottage certainly hadn't been taken from here. Not that he thought it would have been, but odder things had happened between husbands and wives. A five-cushions-long sofa and three well-padded wing chairs were orientated towards the vast pink-brick fireplace in which two people could sit warm and comfortable should they not mind the smoke from the beech logs burning on its fire-dogs. A glass-fronted cabinet contained enough delicate porcelain and crystal for Rogers to decide to keep his sometimes clumsy bulk away from it. A shiny black baby grand piano, with a Spanish shawl draped on it and used as a stand for a few framed photographs, stood in the corner near the fireplace. Pictures and paintings – he thought one of a horse and groom had, even for this house, to be a copied Stubbs – all but concealed the crawling-with-faded-flowers wallpaper. The oriental carpets he could only guess about, but they were thin enough, looked old enough, to worry him about standing on them. Only one of the lamps had been switched on, its lighting shaded to such a discreetness for him not to be concerned about his late evening chin stubble.

He heard her descending stairs before the door was pushed further open and she stood there, looking at him and appearing to be undecided whether to enter the room. He saw her as a woman in her early forties, tall and thin with an angular uncertainty in the way she stood. Not unattractive and with a nun-like gentleness, her features were sharp planed and clear of make-up, her pale mouth sad where, he thought, it would normally be shyly pleasant. Her dark brown hair, worn short and straight, was arranged as if it didn't matter very much. The herring-bone tweed skirt she wore with a tight-fitting moss-green sweater over a thick white linen shirt emphasized her thinness, the excess of silver throat chains and bracelets bedecking her suggestive of something in her personality that escaped the detective.

He said, 'I'm sorry to impose on you, Mrs Ungrish,' and walked towards her, stopping when she decided to enter, visibly holding herself under control.

'Please,' she said. 'It's quite all right.' Her voice sounded strained, pitched so low that he had difficulty in hearing the words. Seating herself in one of the wing chairs with the lamp behind her, only the flames of the burning logs illuminating her face, she folded her hands on her lap. 'Do sit down. Mrs Jarvis says you wish to speak to me.' Her eyes, a shadowed green and preternaturally large in her pale face, glistened from an earlier weeping.

'Only in so far as I may perhaps explain anything about which you are in doubt. And to ask one or two necessary questions,' he said gently, accepting that this was going to be a treading-on-eggshells interview. 'You may, of course, wish to postpone it until later when you've a relative or friend with you.'

'I'm perfectly all right, and there isn't anybody I want with me.' A spasm twisted her face. 'I can't believe it,' she whispered. 'May I see him? Tonight?'

Bloody hell! he swore to himself. He knew it had to come, but not this early, not when she was so vulnerable. 'Sergeant Jarvis has told you that he'd been in a collision with a train last night?'

Her mouth formed a soundless 'Yes.'

It was probably unfair to judge her in her grief, but he thought that he could detect in her a twitching neuroticism. He fumbled with his words, seeing in his mind Ungrish's terrible mutilations and his almost unrecognizable face, wondering why she hadn't already understood. 'It wouldn't be the best thing,' he said. 'You're probably puzzled why you've only just been told . . . there is a reason . . . having been hit by a train it was . . . there were difficulties about his identification.' Please God, he prayed irritably, *you* make her understand and don't let her cry.

She was silent for moments long enough to allow Rogers to appreciate the well-bred and civilized outside quietness of a

43

High Moor evening. Then she said softly, 'I see, and I'm sorry. I'm being rather stupid, aren't I?'

'Perhaps it might be arranged later,' he suggested, knowing that it never could be. When she made no answer to that, he said, 'When did you last see him, Mrs Ungrish?'

She lifted a hand to her mouth – it was shaking and he noticed how thin her wrist was with its oddments of bracelets – in a gesture of anguish, reminding him that he, and not the silent Jarvis, was now concerned with the human equivalent of a ticking bomb. 'Yesterday,' she whispered. 'Yesterday morning when he left for the hospital.' Her face almost crumpled. 'I didn't even manage to say good-bye . . .'

'Well, we don't always know, do we?' he said with a self-acknowledged banality. 'Were you worried that he hadn't returned home last night?' It was, he felt, the most diplomatic way of asking her why, if she had been, she hadn't reported his being missing.

She shook her head. 'He often has to stay overnight at St Barnabas Place. He has sleeping accommodation over his consulting room.'

Under the circumstances that sounded feeble to him, St Barnabas Place being virtually next door to the Minster and no more than three miles from High Moor. But, he thought cynically, the cottage could have been necessary were there a medical ethic prohibiting casual fornication over consulting rooms, or within genuflecting distance of a bishop's church.

'An odd question, Mrs Ungrish,' he said carefully. 'He *did* leave in the Mercedes, did he?'

Her eyes were bright with brimming tears, her bottom lip shaking. 'Of course. Is it . . . is it still there?' There was no real interest in her voice.

'No,' he said ambiguously. Any moment now, if he didn't call it a day, she was going to ask him what her husband was doing on a remote godforsaken rail crossing, late at night and a good seven miles from his consulting room. She was going to have to know. That, and most of the other squalid details. But not now; not while she was still raw and bleeding.

He saw Jarvis, seated behind Mrs Ungrish, shaking her head

warningly at him, her schoolgirl's face frowning. He stood, turning to go. 'I think I've troubled you enough, Mrs Ungrish,' he said, 'and I'm terribly sorry to have inflicted my questions on you.'

Her voice was almost inaudible when she looked up at him, misery in her expression. 'He wouldn't do it on purpose, would he?'

'That,' he told her firmly, 'is definitely not so, and you mustn't begin to think it might be.'

He left her, feeling troubled that his visit hadn't done her much good, walking just short of hastening out of the room with Sergeant Jarvis putting a brief comforting arm around her before following him.

Outside, parked alongside the police car, was a tomato-red Rover 2-litre saloon fitted extravagantly with accessories and gadgets. It didn't quite go with the image he had formed of Mrs Ungrish's persona; but, he assured himself, there was no law prohibiting it and it might be a woman's manner of compensating for having a philandering husband.

10

Dropped at his office by, Rogers thought, an incomprehensibly disapproving Sergeant Jarvis, he had sent a waiting Lingard home after listening to the results of what were now the largely unnecessary checks on Ungrish.

There had been no answers to his telephoning Ungrish's private consulting rooms or his home. The gynaecologist had last attended at the hospital during the morning of the previous day, but had missed without explanation his attendance on the morning just passed. None of those to whom Lingard had spoken had had any contact with the living Ungrish since the day before, or apparently knew that he was now dead, that information deciding him against calling his home number again.

Lingard had also produced a photograph of Ungrish which he had borrowed from the *Post and Messenger*'s office, Rogers having felt a need, apart from identifying him visually as Johnson, to see what his latest obligation to villainy unpunished looked like in life. He saw in glossy black and white the head and shoulders of a man whom the camera had caught in a looking-down-the-length-of-an-arrogant-nose attitude. Maturely good looking, there was intolerance in his pale eyes and a hardness in the unsmiling mouth. Rogers knew that he would hate to have been a junior to him in his profession, and summed him up as having been the antithesis of his gentle and twitching wife. Putting the photograph in the so-far meagre file on Ungrish's death, he sent for Detective Inspector Hagbourne.

Congenitally morose, Hagbourne's features suffered pouched hangdog eyes that bulged with any rise in his blood pressure – the result, his colleagues alleged, of having been married too long – a suitably down-turned moustache, and more creases than his age warranted. Being numerately intelligent, he was normally given the department's crime load of embezzlements, company frauds and any villainy committed on paper. With it, possibly quite adventitiously, went a remarkable nose for sniffing out the whereabouts of stolen or otherwise missing cars, and a mistaken Rogers believed that he was doing him a favour in sending him away from his figures and out into fresh air.

'We're looking for a Mercedes, Thomas,' he said. 'I don't have its registration number, I don't know its colour. It belonged to Ungrish, whose death you must by now be intimately acquainted with.' That meant that if he were not, he had better get on and be so. 'On and off he parked it in the hospital forecourt. Somebody there will have the details if you want them. He's left it somewhere I also don't know, but most likely where he garaged the Cambridge.' He dangled a tagged key from his fingers. 'This was in his pocket and it's labelled number three, undoubtedly for a lock-up garage, probably for one here in Abbotsburn.' He flipped the key to Hagbourne and smiled encouragingly. 'Find it, Thomas. There can't be more than . . .' He thought, wanting to keep his guess within

46

acceptable bounds. 'Should we say well this side of a hundred? And they'd be mostly in groups, as this one obviously is.'

Hagbourne's expression, apparently set in its mould, never changed as he picked up the key. 'You'll expect it to be in the name of Johnson, of course?'

'Of course,' Rogers said. 'It'd have to be that, wouldn't it?'

Following Hagbourne's departure and a subsequent conversation with a Chief Constable understandably tetchy about not having been told earlier, he had telephoned Katherine. She had been far from pleased at the prospect of his possible withdrawal from their arranged visit, indicating clearly and firmly that she would be going on her own should he not find it possible, given his authority and need for her company, to delegate his investigation to a subordinate. That was fair enough and what he expected, but it rankled. It left him even more worried about the suppositional pernod-drinking, *pissoir*-haunting roué he was already detesting, and who was, he convinced himself, even now prowling the Montparnasse cafés in search of solitary and seducible women.

Anaesthetizing his fretting about Katherine with a large malt whisky from the bottle he kept in his desk drawer for unspecifiable emergencies, he reapplied his mind to his job. The late evening emptying of the Headquarters building of its staff was doing nothing for his low in investigational achievement. He hadn't got far in his digging out of useful information about a death that, as yet, he was unable to classify as murder, manslaughter or an Act-of-God accident which, if the latter, would be none of his responsibility. It appeared to his necessarily convoluted thinking that he was, and would be until the following morning, bogged down in inactivity, yet finding it difficult to convince himself that he could conscientiously lay down his handcuffs and go home to bed. And that, he remembered glumly, being still unmade. Dissatisfied with the few facts he had, frustrated at not having been able to ask Mrs Ungrish any significant questions, he knew that he wouldn't sleep until he had more information about the promiscuous gynaecologist.

With the discomfited Twite now almost certain to have made

his confession to higher authority, and with a professional belief in the gabbiness of his fellow citizens, Rogers could accept that the identity of the body in the mortuary was now common knowledge throughout the hospital. Using the telephone again he dialled its number, asking to be put through to the Dame Janet Woodbridge ward. Sister Anderson, he was informed by the nurse answering his enquiry, had gone off duty an hour earlier.

Ward Sister Morag Anderson had in the past – between other more attractive engagements, Rogers suspected – shared some not too intense emotions and an occasional bed with him until deciding that he wasn't wholly what she wanted from a man. He had thought that it might have been his addictive attachment to his pipe that had decided her, for she was rabidly anti-smoking. But the casual affection generated between them had remained and Rogers, a mite ruthless when he had to be, intended capitalizing on it. There being no number listed for her in the telephone directory, and having a need for air not made stifling by stale tobacco smoke and unread crime files, he decided to walk through the darkened streets for an unannounced visit to her apartment at the rear of the hospital.

He knocked on her door after climbing the three leg-aching flights of stairs to it, having cautiously concealed his pipe in a pocket. Opening it to him she looked surprised and, although he searched for it, with no somebody's-already-here dismay in her pleasantly handsome face. Wearing a cotton robe decorated with flaring red poppies and a hand-towel turban over her wet black hair, she was damply warm and pink from a bath, her healthy buxomness smelling headily of sandalwood-scented soap and a woman's skin.

Unsettling for him as her appearance was, he kept his expression neutral as though seeing her still wearing her royal-blue uniform, starched linen cap and upside-down fob watch. 'Rogers on duty, Morag,' he said to avoid a misunderstanding, and smiling with it. 'I'm sorry to call at an inconvenient moment, but could I have a few minutes when you're dressed?'

She smiled back at him, an assurance that he was still in acceptable good odour. 'Come in,' she said. 'You can have your few minutes, but I'm not getting dressed. I was going to bed.'

He stepped through the door, following in the wake of the smell of sandalwood. She sat him in a chair near the gas fire and said, 'I'm drying my hair, so shout out what you have to say.' She stared at him with the forthrightness that nursing sisters used on their ward patients, her eyes capable of deciding on the condition of his liver, the colour of his tongue and whether his bowels had moved that day. 'It has to be about Mr Ungrish, hasn't it?' Her voice still retained the lilt of her Welshness.

'You've heard then?' He had assumed that she and everyone from the nursing manager down to the kitchen washer-up would.

'Of course I've heard,' she said brusquely. 'He's there in the mortuary, isn't he? Poor sod,' she added as she vanished into her bedroom, leaving the door open. Then, 'What happened?' she called out from inside.

Rogers mumbled something unintelligible and waited, not at present in the business of giving out information.

'I heard that he'd been found on the railway,' she said. 'In some sort of mysterious circumstances nobody seems to know anything about. Give, George, before I show you the door.'

'That's what I'm trying to find out. The nobody not knowing anything includes me,' he exaggerated, although not all that much. 'Which is why I'm here. If I can get some background to him, to his social activities, his friends, it might help.' That was safe enough, for she was one who would soon know whatever details Twite had given in his apologia.

She was silent for a moment or two and he could hear her vigorously rubbing her hair. Then she said, 'You already know a thing or two about him, don't you?'

'A thing or two,' he was forced to admit. 'I understand he was something of a ladies' man.'

'In confidence, George? I wouldn't want any come-back.'

'Scout's honour,' he promised. He wasn't much liking this room-to-room digging for information, preferring to be in a position where he could read any evasions or hesitancies in her face. 'Tell me what you know about him.'

'No. You ask me and I'll tell you what *I* know and what I

49

think *you* should.' She must have been telepathic for, before he could make his start, she said, 'Come on in, George, for God's sake. I don't want to go on shouting, and I never noticed you were very backward about it the last time you were here.'

'Same place, different time,' he murmured to himself, 'and women never let you forget.' He rose from the chair which had been cramping his buttocks anyway and went in. She was seated at a dressing-table, combing her still-damp hair. He thought it nice hair; a little long for a nurse, but knowing that she arranged it in a chignon for duty in her ward.

She didn't turn her head but looked at his reflection in the mirror. 'I want to see when you're being devious,' she said, 'so sit on the bed behind me.'

That made the two of them a good match, and he sat obediently. 'For the moment, just between you and me, Morag,' he said carefully. 'Our friend seems to have been carrying on with another woman. I don't know who, but I need to find out.'

She smiled and raised her eyebrows at him. 'If you're going to ask me if I'm her, I'm not. I didn't like him. He did once do a fumble with his zip – metaphorically speaking, of course – and try to climb aboard, but I wasn't having any. I don't need to be *that* popular.'

Morag could, Rogers knew, be bawdy when she wished to be. 'I never thought it for a moment,' he said, smiling back at her.

'Liar,' she said cheerfully. 'It's probably why you came barging in tonight.'

'So who else?' he asked.

She shrugged. 'You know what it's like in a hospital. Consultants, surgeons, anaesthetists and housemen – quite a few of them on the make for our young nurses. They wouldn't be men if they weren't. Even the occasional visiting GP and the odd busybodying copper.' She had given him a quick grin at that. 'Nobody advertises it, of course, and nobody names names if he has anything to lose. But it's an activity that's known about and accepted, if not actually approved.' She poked the end of her pink tongue out at his reflection. 'Like you and me, George.

50

Nobody knows anything unless you've been boasting about it in the police canteen.'

'I did put a notice about it in the personal column of the *Daily Telegraph*,' he said, feeling just a little uncomfortable about her reference to him. 'And it's all to do with man and the nature of the beast. Official question, Morag. Can you put names to any of the female hospital staff who might have hopped into bed with our friend? For me?' he coaxed her.

'Not even for you, George,' she said firmly, 'and if it's official, I can't remember. Perhaps later a name might come when I know more about what's going on.' She picked up a plugged-in hair drier and, switching it on, turned its nozzle on to her hair.

'But there were some from the hospital?' he asked, recognizing obduracy when he heard it.

She nodded, intent on fluffing her hair under the drier. The movement of her arm tautened the thin fabric of her robe and showed the paleness of her breasts beneath it, reminding Rogers of basic earthy matters.

'And outside?' He kept his eyes away from her body, his thoughts concentrated on his questioning.

'I wouldn't know,' she said, 'but I'd imagine so. I'll say this for him. I believe he suffered from a form of satyriasis and couldn't control it.'

It was, Rogers knew, as with nymphomania, easy to condemn it, to be censorious of it, but it was, after all, a malfunctioning of the body like haemorrhoids or duodenal ulcers. As an afterthought, he conceded that it must be easier to bear, for its alleviation was invariably more pleasant. He said, 'So there could be a flock of them?'

'I'm not so sure about lately,' she said, 'but if he'd chosen to make a list of them some time back, he'd probably have qualified for an entry in the Guinness Book of Records.'

Rogers was reflective. 'I'd have thought,' he suggested, 'that considering what he was obliged to see professionally most of the day, he wouldn't have been particularly enthusiastic about renewing an acquaintance with it as a social activity.' Seeing the smiling derision on her face, he said, 'All right, so I don't know

51

what I'm talking about. I don't suppose either that those activities would extend to his patients?'

'No,' she said positively, frowning her displeasure at even the possibility. 'That would be unthinkable, highly unprofessional, extremely dangerous for him and definitely not on.'

'Of course,' he said hastily, 'but I had to ask. Do you know Mrs Ungrish? I have seen her, by the way.'

'Poor Isabel. She took it hard, did she? I know her, of course I do. She's on the library book rota and goes round the wards once a week handing them out.'

'I thought a very nice woman.' He was fishing, already believing she was.

'Too nice for *him*,' she said with a touch of contempt.

'Do you think she'd know what he was doing? Or suspect?'

'Gawd!' she scoffed, as though doubting his common sense. 'You're not serious? She'd be stupid if she didn't, and she's not that. There would be a hundred different ways she'd know.'

'And not do anything about it?' Rogers thought that if she hadn't, she would be a woman in a million.

'Possibly not. Probably not if he hadn't been too obvious, or flung it in her face.' Morag was slightly amused at his question. 'But if she did, she'd certainly be more subtle about keeping it dark than he could ever be. You don't have to abandon a plushy life style just because your husband is having it off on the side with someone he's not likely to leave home for anyway. You just close the gate to him and, if it's the way you feel, open it to somebody else.'

'That's one way of putting it,' Rogers said drily; then, casually and watching her expression, 'Does Alwick ring a bell with you?'

Her forehead creased. 'The village? Should it?'

'Probably no more than, say, an old mauve-coloured Cambridge car. Or the name Johnson.' He watched her for that, too, but there was no revealed recognition.

'You're looking hawkish, George,' she said tartly, 'and you're wasting your time.' With her hair now dry, she was combing its glossiness; slowly, almost languorously, her thoughtful eyes fixed on his reflected image.

He stood, deciding that there would be no more unless he turned a friendly interview into an interrogation. 'I'm grateful, Morag,' he said as he moved to leave the bedroom, 'and sorry if I've been a nuisance. Perhaps we can have another chat when I know more.'

She turned her head, her eyes humorous, then swung her body around on the stool to face him. 'You've disappointed me, George,' she said lightly. 'Don't you wish to trifle with my affections?'

Not continually seeking a woman with whom to go to bed, he was, nevertheless, as weak and flawed as the next man when opportunity offered. He turned back to her, thinking about an all alone Katherine and then of the lecherous and literary roué loading her glass with the cognac that usually made her so appreciative of his own attentions. A firm believer in insuring against potential losses, he said gravely, 'It's an outrageous suggestion, and I was just about to get round to making it.'

'But not too seriously, I hope,' she told him calmly. 'There is a someone else.'

'Then God rot him, whoever he is,' he answered gallantly. When she threw off her robe and slid naked into the bed, he said with a mocking solemnity, 'Just in case we happen to be caught in flagrante delicto, please note that I'm now officially off duty. Otherwise I don't think that it would be approved.'

When he had switched off the light and was undressing, taking off his shirt with more haste than dignity, she said dreamily, 'I don't know what it is about me that attracts middle-aged men bent on seduction but, whatever it is, don't let your enthusiasm keep you here a second after midnight. I do have to get some sleep in.'

It was, he considered when he later let himself out into the darkness of a deserted and chilly street, one of the more interesting endings – although one brought to it at an almost breathless speed to make the midnight deadline – to a reasonably useful interview he had had for some time.

11

Oversleeping by half an hour gave Rogers an unaccustomed malevolence towards a depressing autumn morning. Scowling through the bathroom window as he dried himself from his shower, he saw heavy grey clouds nearer to the ground than they should have been and sweeping veils of rain laying waste his already neglected garden.

Having assured his conscience that getting his head on the pillow of an affectionate nursing sister's bed had been unpremeditated and therefore should be accounted no more than a minor misdemeanour by Whoever-it-was up there, he was on the verge of convincing himself – not with the same assurance – that he might, with no loss of official face, pass the investigation into Ungrish's death over to Lingard. If he could, then all that stood between him and the Paris flight with Katherine in twenty-four hours' time would be that damned stack of unread crime files waiting in his office.

He was still undecided when the telephone bell rang. Swearing and wrapping the towel around his waist he went downstairs; not joyously because, as with the green telephone in his office, he was usually only called so early at his home number with bad news, or about something having gone wrong.

It was Detective Sergeant Magnus calling from the kiosk at Alwick village. 'Sir,' he said, sounding a little out of breath. 'I've just arrived at the cottage and there's a dead body hanging out of the window at the back.'

'What!' Rogers wasn't at his most brilliantly conversational first thing in the morning. 'Goddammit, sergeant, that's not possible!' he almost shouted, knowing that it was going to be, immediately convinced that the Whoever-it-was up there intended to make him pay for his minor misdemeanour with Morag.

'No, sir,' Magnus replied, deferring to his senior's irascibility, 'but I'm afraid it's there just the same. A youngish chap, and he's obviously broken into the place during the night with the screwdriver he's got sticking out of his pocket. The stuff he'd stolen is in the kitchen and he must have died just as he was getting out through the window he'd forced to get in.'

'All right, sergeant,' Rogers said equably, having quietened himself down. 'It's sunk in. What killed him?'

'Nothing that I can see, sir.' Magnus sounded puzzled. 'No visible marks on him, no bleeding, no anything. He just seems to have died.'

'I take it you don't know who he is?' His brain was working hard to find any similarity with the cause of Ungrish's death – and failing; Magnus's 'no anything' having suggested the possibility.

'No, but I should think he's a local layabout.'

'He needn't have been on his own. You've searched the house?' Rogers had removed the towel from his waist, and, standing naked and damp, was drying himself with it. It was, he thought, an undignified way of conducting a question and answer situation.

'Naturally, sir. There's nobody there and he's been dead some time.' Rogers had trodden not too delicately on Magnus's professional pride and he heard it in his voice.

'I knew you would,' he said to make amends. 'I wasn't thinking. You'd better get back to it and wait for me. I'm already on my way and . . .'

'Sir!' Magnus interrupted him, surprised. 'Mr Lingard's just gone by in his car.'

'Get hold of him then. He's there for something else, but he's to go to the cottage. Tell him I'm arranging for Dr Twite to attend.'

Disconnecting and then dialling the Pathology Department of the hospital, he left a message for a Twite not yet arrived to meet him at the cottage, prepared to certify a man dead and to tell an anxious Rogers how and when. Discarding reluctantly any idea of breakfast and the coffee his waking-up metabolism needed, the daily confirmation of his own durability he got from the obituary columns of the *Daily Telegraph*, he returned upstairs to dress, pondering wholly now on the inconvenient bizarreness of a dead man being found hanging out of the window of another dead man's cottage, and not making any sense of it at all.

It was still raining when he turned his car from the main road into Alwick, passing the department's dark-blue utility van parked on the forecourt of the village hall. The detectives it had carried were, he hoped, even now having their ears battered with malicious gossip about the goings-on of the man the villagers knew as Johnson.

As he had anticipated, Lingard's Bentley, its canvas hood up, was parked outside the cottage and he pulled in behind her. With the pink walls dark with rain, its thatch a sodden blackness, the cottage appeared even more decrepit and neglected and Rogers, putting on the raincoat he had brought with him, walked the puddled earth drive to its rear. The surrounding trees that had, the day before, been a sunlit leafiness were now a dripping dankness with the smell of decay in them, a fitting background for the dead man awaiting him.

Lingard and Magnus were standing outside by the open maroon door, both aware that sheltering from a mere rainfall when on duty might be considered a feebleness of investigationary spirit. They were brooding on the upper trunk of a body that protruded at an angle from the kitchen window, and which had been covered with a rain-soaked yellow blanket that reached down to the wet cement below.

Rogers nodded his arrival as he joined them. 'You know, David,' he said extravagantly to the damply elegant Lingard, 'I've a shrewd suspicion there's something very odd going on around here.' He indicated the blanket. 'Not like this?' he asked Magnus.

Magnus, the ginger-haired sergeant with the flair for finding the microscopic scrapings and smears of villainy done, said, 'No, sir. He was already wet, but I covered him in case anybody happened around here while I was gone.'

Rogers lifted the soggy blanket from the body, wrinkling his nose at the released smell of dead flesh. Clearly that of a youth, he was supported on the window sill by his waist, both arms hanging stiffly towards the ground. He wore a scruffy black jerkin spangled with silver-coloured studs, his hair dyed a harsh yellow and fashioned into a freakish Mohican crest. The thin neck had drooped in death and Rogers had to crouch to examine his features. They were immature and unprepossessing with a few acne scars, a light juvenile fluff on the chin and jowls, and in them what he read as a terror of approaching death. There were no visible signs of his having met it by an exterior physical violence.

'Poor devil,' Rogers said, letting the blanket fall back on the body, the repugnancy of its deadness muting his pity for it. 'At least we can be certain he isn't another gynaecologist. He's probably the local probationary housebreaker.'

'And possibly not so local,' Lingard disagreed, 'if that's his bike propped against the side of the greenhouse.'

Rogers hadn't noticed it, but he managed amiability. 'Don't make it more difficult for me, David. I could have done without any of this.' He said to Magnus, 'I'll have the details, sergeant, and in the house where we won't get soaked.'

Inside the kitchen, Rogers saw that the dead youth's black-trousered legs were in a kneeling position on a draining slab of the sink. Apart from being as scruffy as the jerkin, the trousers and shoes were dry. On a working top away from the window stood the radio he had seen on the sitting-room floor the day before, five bottles of brandy and whisky, a small torch and a blue-cloth bank bag.

'That's exactly as I found him,' Magnus explained when he had Rogers's attention. 'I came in from the front and started to plug in my lights, heard a door bumping against its latch from the back and came to see what was happening. It was the inner kitchen door and when I came in I thought I'd disturbed chummy doing a bolt for it through the window.' He grimaced. I'd dived in and grabbed him by the ankles to pull him back before I realized he was dead. He was cold, but I searched the house in case he had a mate hiding away somewhere. Then I covered him with a blanket from the bedroom and phoned you.'

Rogers thought about that. He could understand an unoccupied cottage being broken into – he had seen the screw-driver and the marks of its blade on the wooden frame of the forced kitchen window – and the theft of the radio and desirable liquor from it. What he could not yet understand was why the youth died an apparently non-violent death in the act of climbing through the window without his torch or the proceeds of his theft. And why not the easier exit from a door which had only been bolted on the inside? He could have been disturbed and fleeing in panic, but that would hardly account for his dying in doing so.

'You were here before me,' he said to Lingard. 'What does this do to you? However he died, and I imagine we'll know by the time Wilfred's finished with him, I can't see any connection with friend Ungrish.'

'There obviously isn't,' Lingard murmured, looking pensively at the body while he pushed snuff absent-mindedly into his nose. 'A strictly non-professional housebreaker, I'd say – you've noticed no gloves – probably unemployed and, from his reprehensible hair and clothing, no doubt unemployable. There's nothing in his pockets to show who he is and, for the moment, I believe he's come from somewhere other than this village. Yes?'

Rogers nodded, Lingard's opinion being beyond effective disagreement. 'And how did he die?' he asked.

'Ah! I can't guess any more than you can, but I'd say he's a bit on the young side for a heart attack, and to die of excitement in having got himself some loot seems a bit far-fetched. Perhaps,' he suggested flippantly, 'there's a resident ghost of terrifying aspect that frightened him to death.'

Magnus, a man not over-endowed with humour and obviously thinking that he had listened enough to an inconsequential discussion, said to Rogers, 'I forgot to mention it, but it looks as though chummy served himself a whisky in the other room. Might that have some bearing?'

'I'll check,' Rogers said. 'In the meantime, you'd better take his fingerprints and photograph him before Dr Twite arrives. You'll have a job to afterwards. Then, perhaps, you'll get on with your looking for whorls and ulnar loops or whatever.' He added amiably, 'And don't let Mr Lingard's ghost frighten you into not going upstairs on your own.'

The sitting-room was much as Rogers had seen it last and had not been reduced to the familiar unmanageable chaos in a search for stealable property, only the doors of the sideboard being left open. On its top was a part-filled bottle of whisky and a one-third-empty bottle of ginger ale. A tumbler, obviously having been used, rested on the arm of one of the fireside chairs.

'If he put back what whisky there's missing from the bottle,' Rogers said to Lingard, 'he could have been drunk. Regurgitation of vomit?' He shook his head at his own suggestion. 'No. We would have seen it.'

'Simple alcoholic poisoning? Inhibition of his breathing?' Lingard shook his head also. 'Perhaps not. That'd probably take more whisky than what's gone, and we would have smelt it.'

Rogers felt the frustration of not knowing. 'For God's sake, let's leave it, David,' he growled. 'It's what we have post-mortems for. You go on back to digging out dirt from the village worthies and, possibly, finding out who our dead villain happens to be. I imagine he has a very worried mother and father somewhere. Ah!' he said as an afterthought, 'something I keep forgetting. There're usually two keys held by a tenant. I've only one. It might be interesting to know where the other happens to be. Have the landlord found and check that there were two. We'll then go on from there.'

With Lingard gone and because he was having second thoughts about it, Rogers told Magnus – busy at photographing the body from inside and outside the kitchen – that he wanted the bottles and tumbler that the youth had used examined for fingerprints, then packed for the analysis of their contents at the Forensic Science Laboratory. He expected nothing from it, but knew from his experience of Murphy's Law that the nothing he expected would never be discovered beneath a stone left unturned.

He returned to the sitting-room and went to a window overlooking the lane, staring out as he filled and lit his pipe. In the damp oppressiveness of the shadowed interior, while

59

accepting that the filthy weather could be influencing him, he felt as if he was growing a mould on his skin, wondering how a man like Ungrish could choose to leave the felicities of Capstone House for the gloomy decrepitude of Hidden Cottage and the transient pleasures of tomcatting. And also thinking that Twite was taking a bloody long time doing the miserable few miles from Abbotsburn to a waiting detective superintendent impatient to get on with something else.

12

Rogers accepted that Twite was never a man to forego feeding an enormous breakfast of eggs, bacon and toast into his face in order to rush himself into examining a body he would know to be physically incapable of going anywhere, and it was another twenty minutes before he pulled his cream shark-snouted Citroën Safari in behind Rogers's more modest car. That particular marque of Citroën, together with Lingard's silk shirts and thick bundles of currency owned by other people, were probably the only things capable of creating in him something like the sin of envy.

Twite, wearing a new white macintosh with epaulettes and leather buttons and carrying his bag of tools, clambered from the car, a reluctance to get wet showing in his expression. 'I had a job to find you, old chum,' he said to Rogers who had come out to meet him. 'It's Hidden Cottage right enough.'

'But not hidden enough for Ungrish,' Rogers told him. 'This is the place he used as Dhugal Johnson for mating with his female friends.'

Twite stared at the cottage, disbelief in his fat face and the rain forgotten. 'You're having me on, of course,' he said. 'The message was that you had a body for me.'

'So I have, Wilfred. It's waiting for you in the kitchen,' Rogers assured him. 'And we'll deal with it after I've filled you in with things about your respected colleague.'

In the sittingroom, he gave Twite as much detail about Ungrish's adoption of Johnson's name and his use of the cottage as he thought necessary for his appreciation of what was being investigated, conditioning him by apparently generous information to his intended demands for some in return.

Unusually serious, Twite listened in silence, only saying when Rogers had finished, 'That's something I'd rather not have known, George. You've put me in a position where I'll feel obliged to pass it on to the Chairman of the Medical Committee.'

'Why not? It won't be any news to him,' Rogers said. 'He was told enough of it last night, and I'm sure much of it's been bounced around the hospital by now.' He raised his eyebrows at the pathologist. 'Does it surprise you that much? That he was doing his extra-marital thing out here? And almost certainly with some of the hospital staff? You knew about that, didn't you?'

Caution was written clear in Twite's features as he picked at his moustache. 'That's all a bit off-limits for me, old chum,' he muttered. 'A fellow medico and all that nonsense. I'd really prefer not to natter about it.'

'For God's sake, Wilfred!' Rogers said, more sharply than he had intended. 'Don't *you* be coy with me. Do you want me to sniff around every doctor and nurse in the hospital until I do find out? Probably creating more scandal than it warrants? In confidence,' he urged him. 'Cross my heart and hope to die.'

Twite's eyes, an obviously well-nourished dark-brown, stared at the detective, appraising him. 'I heard noises upstairs. Is there someone else here?'

'Sergeant Magnus. He's too busy dusting for fingerprints to worry about us.'

Twite, moving his bulk as far as he could from the bottom of the stairs, said, 'It'd be unethical of me to chinwag about the private affairs of a particular member of the medical staff, nor . . .' When Rogers opened his mouth to interrupt, he held up a pudgy hand. 'Hear me out, old chum. I was about to say that nor would I. However, if you *are* twisting my arm, I can mention one or two things which might help about a hypo-thetical character usually called A Most Superior Banger.'

That, to Rogers, was almost certainly how Ungrish was referred to in the underground gossip of the hospital and he accepted the equivocation. 'Your arm *is* being twisted,' he said genially.

Fumbling beneath the skirts of his macintosh and bringing out an old-fashioned silver case, Twite took a cigarette from it, lighting it as he considered. 'First of all,' he said, keeping his voice low, 'our hypothetical Most Superior Banger is, to his patients, a highly respected medical man. Otherwise, and to those who work with him, he is excrement of the first order. He isn't liked and inside opinion has it that the women who apparently do like him must be either over-awed by his eminence or of the same kidney.'

'Or professionally ambitious?' Rogers suggested.

'Possibly, although I don't believe he can do much about that. Allow me a little spite, but don't some secretaries sleep with their office bosses for similar reasons?' Twite showed his teeth. 'Perhaps some policewomen do likewise, old chum.'

'God forbid such an impropriety,' Rogers said with mock sanctimony. 'We don't get the time, anyway. Are you going to give me names?'

'I don't know any, and I wouldn't pass them on if I did. But don't think that his beddings were . . . are confined to the nursing staff.'

'Come off it, Wilfred.' Rogers wasn't believing the not knowing part. 'You're not up in front of the General Medical Council. Gossip has to name names to be worth the telling.'

Twite shook his head decisively. 'There's suspicion, but that isn't enough.'

'No,' the detective agreed, although with inner reservations, 'but it can be helpful.' Recognizing a brick wall when his nose flattened against one, he said, 'Can you imagine your Most Superior Banger demanding of an office clerk or a porter his access to a property disposal store? Or asking either to hand over the unclaimed driving documents of a man who'd died in a road accident?'

62

'Of course not.' Twite had been astounded at the suggestion. 'He'd be mad to attempt it. It'd be all over the hospital in no time.'

'So I thought. But if he had an association with one of the women in the general administration office to do his dirty work for him, it'd be possible, wouldn't it?'

'Possible, yes, but I'd think unlikely,' Twite said dubiously.

'Unlikely or not, Wilfred, it happened with the help of someone.' Rogers would never accept a limit to the stupidities of a man with an itch for women. 'Would hospital gossip be saying anything about his relations with his wife?'

'You mean, should he have one?' Twite pursed his lips, obviously working out how far he could go with his equivocating. 'If he had, and I'm not saying that he has, there could be a whisper that he's seen his solicitor about a divorce. Grounds for it unknown, if you need any these days, but I'd have thought the shoe should be on the other foot.'

'Might she be reciprocating in kind his screwing around?' Rogers tried to imagine Isabel Ungrish doing it, improbably with the local curate or horse doctor, and discarding it immediately.

Twite shook his head vigorously, his jowls wobbling and ash from the cigarette in his mouth falling on his macintosh. 'Not the type, old chum, and never the vestige of any scandal. I think she'd be more interested in her horses. If she had any, of course,' he added hastily.

'That doesn't sound too unlikely,' Rogers said drily, 'considering who she's married to. Where would he garage his car if he attended at your hospital?'

'He wouldn't, because there aren't any. He'd use the forecourt like everyone else.' Twite was beginning to show signs of wanting to get out from under.

'In addition to, say, a Mercedes, would he be likely to own an old mauve Cambridge?' Another of the more routine questions, but Rogers occasionally provoked a recollection with them.

'If he did, I haven't seen . . . that is, I don't think he would.' Twite looked around for an ashtray and, finding none, dropped his cigarette end on the floor and screwed his shoe on it. 'The body, old chum,' he said firmly. 'I've enough paperwork piling up on my desk to choke two donkeys, and you're being no help.'

Rogers had winced about the cigarette end, making a mental note to tell Magnus. Should he not, the sergeant would find it, packet it and give it an exhibit number for somebody's future confusion. 'You can't see him quickly enough for me,' he growled. 'I happen to want him cleared from my plate too. He's a housebreaker, I'm sure not connected with Ungrish other than wanting to steal his property, and he's hanging out of the kitchen window waiting for you to tell me how he died.'

Outside, now holding back his impatience to be relieved of the apparent anomaly disrupting his primary investigation, he stood hunched against the rain while Twite, having fitted on parchment-coloured rubber gloves – to Rogers they resembled peeled skin from dead hands – began his examination of the body. Looking happier, a witness leaving the stand without having committed himself, he moved one of the hanging arms against its stiffness. 'Ah, rigor well set in,' he said. 'With rain and a chilly night air considered, I'd say he died between eight and twelve hours ago. Does that fit?'

'God knows,' Rogers replied. 'As long as it happened during the night, it doesn't matter all that much.'

Stooping to get below the drooping head, Twite thumbed back the eyelids, made a face and then forced further open the mouth to depress the tongue and peer into the throat. Unzipping the jerkin, he felt around at the upper part of the trunk with his fingers, withdrawing them and looking at their tips. 'He doesn't appear to have been shot, stabbed, bludgeoned or strangled,' he said, straightening himself and grunting in doing it. 'There're signs of asphyxiation, a significant cyanosis which could be brought on by a lack of oxygen in the blood and which would mean he had breathing difficulties before a complete failure of the respiratory centre. That's a provisional diagnosis,' he added cheerfully, stripping off his gloves and tucking them inside the youth's jerkin before reaching in his macintosh pocket for his cigarette case. 'It could, of course, be that the poor bugger feels as cold as I do.'

'I'd even be happy with that if you could be definite about it.'

64

Rogers thought that Twite had been a little too casual and hurried in his examination. 'Could it have been caused by a retention of vomit in the windpipe? He'd been drinking whisky on the premises.'

'It could. And by half-a-dozen other means as well.' Twite did the careful stately walk of a fat man towards the door. 'I think we have a death from natural causes here,' he said, 'and I'm damned if I'm going to get any more wet than I am already. I'll have him stripped in the comfort of the mortuary and sort out the rest there.'

'I can have Magnus hoist him back in the kitchen for you,' Rogers offered, needing a more positive result. Although pitying the unfortunate youth, he could not help feeling an unworthy resentment that in dying his death he held the potential for being a bloody nuisance.

Twite, already through the door and lighting his cigarette, wagged his head, something Rogers considered he was doing too often. 'Not for me,' he said briskly. 'I've seen enough, but I'll put myself out for you by doing the full examination immediately after lunch.'

'You're a miserable sod, Wilfred.' A mildly irritated Rogers showed only friendly amiability as he followed him in. 'I hope you get indigestion.'

'You too, old chum,' Twite retorted with an equal amiability. 'And should you breathe a word of what I've been daft enough to mention, and should I ever get you on one of my tables, I promise I'll do my stuff on you with a rusty knife.'

Opening the door to let a hurrying Twite out, Rogers surprised a man standing before it. Holding an umbrella over his head with one hand, his other was clenched and raised as if about to knock. He was a heavy stoutness in an ancient tweed jacket, grey flannel trousers, a black dickey and a clerical collar.

But for the collar, Rogers's reaction would have been to swear, for his prospect of an early return to his office and a revivifying cup of coffee was patently about to vanish.

65

13

'My name is Dodson,' the man said. 'Vicar of St Edmund's.'
Balding, with features vaguely reminiscent of a friendly moose,
his wide-gapped square teeth were exposed in good fellowship.
He held out his hand to the detective who shook it, saying
'Detective Superintendent Rogers. Can I help you?'

'I'm sorry if I'm intruding,' he apologized, 'but it's possible
that I may be of assistance to you.'

'In which case I'd be grateful,' Rogers said as Twite squeezed
past them both in his anxiety not to become involved.

Following Rogers into the sitting-room, Dodson closed his
umbrella and twirled it, spraying water drops on to the floor and
wall. 'I've just been interviewed by one of your officers and he
suggested that I spoke to you personally.' The stem of a pipe
protruded from the breast pocket of his tweed jacket that itself
gave off the strong odour of years of exposure to tobacco smoke,
allowing Rogers something of a pipe smoker's fellow-feeling
towards him.

'I'm glad you have, Mr Dodson,' Rogers felt forced to lie, and
he smiled. 'I can't ask you to sit, I'm afraid. The house is being
examined for fingerprints and suchlike and I wouldn't care to
have my sergeant think the worst should he find contact traces
pointing to the local vicar.'

'Oh dear, that wouldn't do at all, would it?' he replied,
beaming his toothy smile, then changing it to a proper gravity.
'Do I understand that you are here enquiring after the death of a
young man? So soon after Mr Johnson's tragic accident?'

Rogers ignored the Johnson bit. 'I am. Do you know him?'

'I think I may have met him. I might have seen him looking
into this very room.' He pointed his umbrella at one of the front
windows. 'Through there.'

'You did?' Rogers felt less than excited about this. 'Last
night?'

'Oh, no. Certainly not. It was on Friday the thirteenth of August. If he is still here, should I not see him to confirm it was he?'

'I'd like you to,' Rogers said, his interest reactivated, 'but could you tell me about it first? And why you appear so certain of the date?'

'I *am* certain, Mr Rogers. Friday the thirteenth sticks in my mind because superstition makes it an unlucky day, and it also coincided with the feast-day of Saint Botolph. I suppose one could say that it was my ill-luck to have aroused his anger.' He was dabbing at the rug on which he stood with the ferrule of his umbrella and frowning.

Rogers made an encouraging noise in his throat, but said nothing.

'I could see clearly because it was a full moon that night. A beautiful night and I was walking my dog, Daniel, to do his customary business.' He gave an apologetic smile at having to mention this canine addiction to using a public highway. 'He's rather an elderly spaniel, by the way, and I have to walk him quite slowly. I came into the lane, as I do most nights, intending to go to its end and then return. When I was approaching here, I saw this man standing in the garden with his back to me and quite obviously looking through a crack in the window curtains. Aren't those sort of people called peeping Toms? To be truthful, even though he was in the moonlight and I was only about twenty yards away, I thought at first glance that he was a woman because of his long hair. You know, so many of them wear trousers now and one doesn't . . .'

'I'm sorry to interrupt,' Rogers said, and doing so, 'but long hair? You're quite certain?'

'*Quite* certain.' Probably taking advantage of the interruption, he had filled his pipe – it looked old and charred enough for him to have acquired it second-hand at his theological college – fired it with a match and then continued speaking with it between his teeth. 'I rather believe it was Daniel who saw him first but, anyway, I was wearing my crêpe-soled shoes and I fancy that he hadn't heard me until I was nearly upon him, so to speak. I had stopped, wondering what he was doing, and he came towards me because, to get out of the lane, he had to. When he was closer to me I could see that he was a man and I asked him if I could be of any help.' His face reflected the perplexity of something having gone wrong. 'He stopped then, although I don't believe that he had intended to. It so surprised me, Mr Rogers; he was furious, in such a dreadful rage. Although he must have seen that I was a churchman, he literally hissed at me and said why didn't I mind my own something business. I told him that I was sorry to have upset him, that I only wanted to help, but that seemed to make him worse. He didn't raise his voice – I imagine he didn't wish to be heard by anybody – but he called me some quite unrepeatable names that he must surely regret, and said that were it not for my some-thing collar he would smash my face in. I thought, I really thought, that he was about to strike me, Mr Rogers, although I hadn't said anything to provoke him. Truly I hadn't.' The recollection of it was obviously worrying him, the disconcerting fact that a clerical collar need no longer be a certain protection against offered violence.

'But he didn't?' Rogers felt sorry for him. His belief in a loving brotherhood of men must have been badly shaken.

'No. He suddenly left me and almost ran down the lane. Then I heard a car being started and driven away.'

'You hadn't seen it when you came into the lane?'

Dodson took his pipe from his mouth, stuffed fresh tobacco on top of whatever hot ash remained in the bowl and lit it. The smoke that reached Rogers's nostrils smelled of burning coffee grounds. 'No,' he said. 'At least, I don't remember doing so. It's quite common, you see, for cars to be parked in the road.'

'I'm assuming that you didn't know him, Mr Dodson, and that he wasn't a local, or you would have. Would you describe him, please?' Never, Rogers decided, could he have been the freakishly-haired youth lying dead in the kitchen, and his snooping around the cottage must have a significance.

'Well, a young man; I'd assume to be about twenty-five.' Dodson touched his hand to his shoulder. 'Long straight hair down to here. A sort of blond colour, but it could have looked that pale in the moonlight. He was a small man but quite well

built, and I'm so grateful that he didn't try to hit me. His face
. . .' He looked as though he was searching for words that were
not uncharitable. 'I don't really think I can describe it now, but
it struck me as being brutal . . . not nice at all. Perhaps I'm
being unfair because he was angry all the time I saw him . . . I
have the impression that he had been drinking . . .' He trailed
into silence, suddenly miles away and apparently back to his
unpleasant encounter.

'His clothing, Mr Dodson?' Rogers prompted him.

'Of course, I'm sorry. Denim trousers, very narrow and
faded in patches. Artificially done, I'm told, although I don't
understand why. Then, just a shirt; not dark, a lightish colour.
It was a warm night and he wouldn't need more. I don't believe
I saw his shoes.'

'And the time?'

'About eleven o'clock. Just before I normally go to bed.'

'And Mr Johnson was here at the time?' Rogers didn't feel it
necessary to identify him as Ungrish.

'Somebody was. I could see a light shining through the
curtains.'

'You knew him, of course?'

'Regrettably not. I called here on three occasions to introduce
myself, but he was in on only one of them. And then,' he said
with an expression of cordiality rejected, 'I must accept that he
refused to answer the door to me.'

It seemed to Rogers that Dodson's parishioners had chosen
not to tell him that there was an outbreak of professional-class
fornication within a stone's throw of his vicarage, and he
decided not to further complicate his present disillusionment
by informing him of what he would inevitably learn in due
course. 'He could have been in the bathroom or some place
where he couldn't hear you,' Rogers suggested. He didn't like
to see a nice old man's feathers ruffled.

'Yes, that could have been so. I mustn't judge too hastily.' He
hesitated, tapping the stem of his pipe against his big teeth. 'Mr
Johnson *was* found on the railway, wasn't he?'

Rogers nodded. 'He was.' He would have called that answer
devious in anybody else.

69

The vicar looked relieved. 'I couldn't think it would be connected, but it did concern me at the time.'

'What wouldn't, Mr Dodson?' Rogers asked him. 'And when?'

'On Wednesday. I heard a fox screaming – a vixen, I think – and I wasn't sure then that it was. You've heard one, I imagine?' He smiled his goodwill through the smoke he was puffing out, apparently approving of policemen.

'Yes,' Rogers said. He had, several times, and each time finding it difficult to accept that it hadn't been made by a man or woman being agonizingly strangled. 'And a pretty bloodcurdling sound it is too. How did it cause you concern?'

'Well, just hearing it, I suppose. I was in my garden when it happened. If you take a straight line from it to here, it's only a matter of a hundred yards or less, and I can see the roof of this cottage from over my hedge. I couldn't see it that night, naturally, because it was dark and, anyway, I was only out there to light the heater in my greenhouse. I breed exotic fuchsias in there and they do need heat, even in October. That was when I heard that dreadful screaming. A quite unearthly sound, isn't it?'

'It is,' Rogers agreed. 'You weren't certain though, were you? You wouldn't be mentioning it to me had you been.'

'No, I confess I was not. There's only one vixen I know of around here and she has never come into the village. The dog foxes do, but not vixens. At least, not to my knowledge. One hears her in the distance, and that very seldom. Only when she wishes to mate, I understand.'

'But now you think it might not have been her you heard?' Rogers asked patiently. 'Or do you still think it was?'

Dodson worried at the pipe stem with his teeth. 'I don't suppose I would have given it another thought had I not heard the car. I'd been in the greenhouse for about ten minutes – perhaps a little longer – and was closing the door when I heard a car's engine being accelerated. Quite unreasonably loud, too. It must have been at the far end of the lane, although I couldn't see any lights. Then I could see them reflected on the undersides of the trees and the car came out of the lane much too fast with the wheels making that screeching noise, coming past the vicarage towards the main road.'

'Did you see it?'

'No. The hedge, you know. Only its roof.'

'Did you connect the screaming with the car, Mr Dodson?' Rogers would accept that he had, but hadn't wanted to.

'I didn't know what to think,' he said. 'Until I heard that Mr Johnson had been killed in his car and thought it to be somewhere around here, I had no reason to connect them, other than praying that the car hadn't hurt the vixen. Now that I know the poor man was killed on the railway, I see that I was right and that they weren't.'

'Still, I would like to know what time it was that you heard the car leaving the lane.' Rogers side-stepped the screaming, for he could guess that it might, just might, have been Ungrish dying.

'It was a quarter past eight exactly. I do know because my church has a tower clock and I heard it strike once as I came out of the greenhouse. I was due at a parochial parish meeting at eight-thirty, so the time was important to me then.' He looked shrewdly at the detective. 'You are not so certain that it was a fox, are you?'

'I've an open mind on it, Mr Dodson,' Rogers said, he thought not very convincingly. 'Perhaps you would now look at the body and see if he's recognizable as your peeping Tom. I've a feeling that he may not be, but I shall still remain extremely grateful for your help.'

When Rogers ushered him out into the still-falling rain, he knew that the dead youth was unquestionably not the angry long-haired man of Dodson's encounter; nor was he recognizable as being one of the villagers. With the vicar out of hearing, he said a hitherto bottled-up 'Bloody damn!' and hurried with all the urgency of a deprived drug addict to his car before anyone else came between him and his need for coffee.

71

14

Sitting at his desk with the damp trouser legs and shoes he had decided to let dry on him, Rogers was jotting down the notes he would need for his future report on the investigation. Although with a sufficiency of caffeine surging through his veins, there were only bloater paste sandwiches in his stomach; a cross-grained canteen manageress, disdainful of famished detective superintendents, having refused him a late-cooked breakfast. And it was still raining.

He had put the stack of crime files out of his sight in a cupboard because they not only appeared to be reproaching him in a paperish way, but were also a depressing reminder of Katherine and the Montparnasse *auberge* he now accepted he was irretrievably fated to miss. His skull seemed thronged with anonymous dead bodies, unfindable live ones, missing cars and vignettes of mouths flapping away in denying that their owners knew anything about anybody.

He had sent for a Missing Persons printout, finding no entry for the reported loss of a youth with yellow hair and acne. However much he had put his mind to it, he was unable to fathom how, in dropping dead during the course of a felonious housebreaking, the unknown youth could logically have any connection with Ungrish, or with his death. But his persisting anonymity left the detective in a mood to wish that the tattooing of names on the buttocks of newly-born *Homo sapiens* was mandatory, if only to relieve harassed policemen of incipient stomach ulcers.

And then there was the not unimportant cause of Ungrish's death. He now had a folder of photographs of a dead Ungrish taken before he had been removed from Twite's necropsy table. Examining the injuries to the lower part of the body that had apparently bled did no more to help him in deciding by what means, or how, Ungrish had been killed than had his earlier examination of them in the flesh. That it would eventually be made plain to him was of no immediate comfort to him. He had a perhaps old-fashioned belief that, if murder it had to be, then it would have been better done in a manner explicable to both the medical profession and the police alike. That Twite and Morag had been less than forthcoming about the gynaecologist's lovers was, although understandable, an obstruction. How otherwise he would discover the identity of the woman with him at the cottage on the evening of his death promised hours of blind-alley enquiries. Short of breaking the legs of either, he had to find a way of overcoming the vow of silence they appeared to have taken.

He had thought around the angry long-haired man's encounter with the unoffending vicar. Even for the shorter type male – a species notoriously prone to spitting aggression in proving that they were as physically able as any bigger man – being surprised peering into a window seemed not to be an adequate reason for the show of fury at the man disturbing him. More likely, in Rogers's experience, discovery usually caused a rapid retreat into sheltering obscurity. Nor was it normally within a peeping Tom's *modus operandi* to practise his heavy-breathing voyeurism away from his own familiar patch, and rarely through ground-floor windows where there would be a minimal expectation of viewing the room's occupants engaging in sexual galumphing. So it need not be too wild an assumption that, already simmering with a jealous rage, he had been checking on his wife or his girlfriend being entertained by Ungrish, venting his frustrated endeavour on the innocent Dodson. That made him very interesting indeed, for men in an anger of jealousy could so easily let it loose in murderous violence at a later date. And that later date could have been Wednesday, the car racing away being his, the scream coming from the man he had just killed.

There had been the recollection of a solitary incongruity, a too-ready referral that had come to nudge his mind at the cottage while his attention was on something quite different. That promised, he thought with some probably unwarranted optimism, at least a reason for a few pointed questions. Questions that were not about to be asked while he sat at his desk sucking at the pipe that, in his introspection, he had let grow cold. Staring out through the windows at the rain, he wondered idly what the hell Sherlock Holmes would have done about it all. With no tetchy Chief Constable or paperwork to worry about, he would undoubtedly have smoked a couple of pipes of his Afghanistan shag, played a sonata on his fiddle, then, calling for a hansom cab and crying out 'The game's afoot, Watson!', have vanished stuffed to the ears with cerebral brilliance into a pea-souper fog. He, Rogers, had only persisting rain but, undeniably uncomfortable as it could be, doing something active in it was preferable to writing notes on a dry desk.

He lifted the receiver of his telephone and dialled the number of the hospital. Asking to be put through to the Dame Janet Woodbridge ward and then to Sister Anderson, he spoke to her. 'Rogers here, Morag,' he said, 'and about to ask a favour.'

'I thought you'd already had one,' she replied. 'What now?' There was nothing in her voice to suggest that she was euphoric about the previous night.

She hadn't sounded very encouraging either, and Rogers thought that she might have somebody with her. 'Your opinion and advice,' he said, as if he really needed it. 'Do you think that the hospital's top brass would be happy about a team from my department going around the wards searching out one of the nursing staff who has a husband or boyfriend with shoulder-length blond hair?' His intention to do that was minimal.

'Hold on a moment.' He heard the rustling of a hand placed over the mouthpiece and muffled words telling someone to excuse her for a few minutes before returning to him. 'You know damned well they wouldn't,' she said with a distinctly unfriendly crispness, 'and neither would I. Why are you asking *me*?'

'I wanted to scout the ground out first.' Subtlety was what he had intended. 'It's information I do have to have, but I'm anxious that I shouldn't upset your people in getting it.'

'Is he the one who did it? At that place you asked me about?'

Although it was apparent that she had since heard something of the details of Ungrish's death, he wasn't prepared to add

74

anything to hospital gossip. 'I don't know yet that anybody's done anything,' he said, being ambiguous and bland at the same time. 'That's why I'm searching around for witnesses . . .' He paused as if he were hit suddenly by an idea. 'Would you prefer to find out yourself who he might be?' he suggested. 'I think I could leave it with you without getting myself into official hot water; and all hush-hush, naturally. I would only do this with somebody who's absolutely responsible and who I can trust, and I know it's something within your undoubted capabilities,' he added with what he suspected to be overloaded soapiness.

'She wouldn't be in any trouble, would she?' Morag appeared to be softening.

'I can think of no reason why she should; it's *him* I'm looking for,' he assured her, pushing it while she was still malleable. 'He's about twenty-five, the hair's blond or near enough and shoulder-length. He wears tight denim trousers, seems to be something of a lout with a nasty temper and drives a car. It isn't much, but I imagine it'll do. Could you sniff around in a quiet sort of way and pass whatever you get to me as a matter of urgency?'

'You do know that you're a scheming bastard, Rogers, don't you?' She said it flatly, but without rancour.

'Not altogether,' he replied cheerfully, having got his own way. 'There's a little corner of me that's extremely soft on the most attractive of ward sisters.' When he closed down he knew that it wasn't wholly flattery, regretting without being too unhappy about it that she hadn't suggested he should call at her apartment to collect whatever information she might have obtained.

As he reached for his pipe to relight it, the telephone bell rang, the switchboard operator telling him that a Mrs Isabel Ungrish had been trying to contact him. Leaving her number, she had asked that he should call her as soon as possible.

When she answered, her voice was composed with no under-tones of grief in it or any indication that she might weep. Rogers, in a manner he had always associated with on-the-job undertakers, said, 'You wished to speak to me, Mrs Ungrish?'

'Yes.' She sounded hesitant. 'Did you come to call again last night? After you had left?'

'No.' That puzzled him. 'I hadn't intended to. That is, not until later today. Or tomorrow, depending on . . . well, how you were.'

'I see.' She was silent for a second or two. 'A car stopped outside the gates and then went away. I'd gone to bed and all the lights were off. I thought . . .' She trailed off into silence.

'It wasn't me, Mrs Ungrish,' he said gently, 'but I think I should come up and discuss it with you. Now?'

'Please, if you would. I'll be waiting for you.' Her voice was strong again and she disconnected from him abruptly.

He replaced the receiver thoughtfully, determined that he would conduct this interview without the inexplicably disapproving presence of Sergeant Jarvis who had managed to make him feel brutal and uncaring in dealing with a woman's bereavement.

15

Driving his car between the open wrought-iron gates in the high brick wall, the tyres crunching on wet gravel, Rogers estimated their distance from Capstone House to be no more than sixty yards, visibility being only minimally obstructed by a copse of slender silver birch trees now largely denuded of their leaves and bare-boned. The house, a couple of hundred years' solid in greenstone blocks with its lichen-covered roof tiles just visible behind the twin gables, looked smaller in daylight than it had in darkness. The porch and its arched door were architectural anachronisms, giving Rogers the impression that church organ music, the smell of incense and stained-glass windows lay behind them.

Mrs Ungrish had either seen him arrive, or had heard his car, for the door opened before he could reach for the bell-pull. She looked dreadful and, at that moment, could have been dressed in see-through underwear for all that Rogers noticed her body, his attention riveted on a face that it would have been kinder not to look at too closely. She had put on carelessly a hard scarlet lipstick that robbed her mouth of its gentleness, painted woad-blue shadow on her eyelids and rubbed pink blush patches over her angular cheekbones. Unless the underlying nun's innocence of her face was discerned through the paint by recollection she looked a tart; a neophyte tart entering the profession in middle age. The scent with which she had doused herself smelled extravagantly, coming from her in overpowering waves.

'It's good of you to see me,' Rogers said, thanking God he had been able to hide his astonishment, 'and I won't keep you long.'

She gave him a smile which was more of a grimace and stood aside for him to enter. Walking behind her, he saw that she was still hung around with her silver chains and bracelets, and wearing a tight-fitting dark grey jersey suit that fitted tightly her body's breastless gawkiness.

In the sitting-room with its curtains partly drawn and twilit with no lamps switched on, she sat him in one of the wing chairs near a fireplace dead with cold ashes, taking its twin opposite for herself and waiting for Rogers to speak.

He felt that there was a febrility about her, an inner distraction that made him nervous of her stability; resembling, as it had struck him before, a female ticking bomb. Knowing that his usual amiability would be out of place, he kept his expression and voice grave. 'I understand that you thought I'd called here a second time last night, Mrs Ungrish; that a car stopped outside your gates. Would you tell me exactly what happened and why you thought it was me?'

Her green eyes, so large for the thin and garish face, were intent on him, and she waited a few moments before replying. 'I had a visitor after you'd gone,' she said, 'who offered to stay with me for the night. I didn't wish that and when she left I went to bed. There seemed nothing else I could do. I was still awake when I heard a car at the entrance. It had a very quiet engine, but I heard it. And I heard it stop. I knew the gates were open and I waited to hear somebody coming, the car door opening and closing. When there was nothing, I got out of bed and looked. I couldn't see it properly in the dark, but it was there on the road outside and parked across the entrance. I couldn't see any lights on it and while I was watching I heard the engine started and it moved away.' With her hands on her lap, she was twining her fingers. 'I thought it must be you, or that you had arranged to keep the house under guard.'

'No, it was neither,' Rogers answered her. 'What sort of a car was it?' It was an odd experience to hear a cultured voice coming from the red tawdriness of her mouth. And, while she had been speaking, he had wondered at her extraordinary reaction to becoming a widow. He knew that they could have a tendency to splash out on expensive clothes or a new hair style as though their late husbands had been oppressive penny-pinchers, but he had never encountered one so apparently unostentatious whose choice it had been to paint and scent herself in such bad taste. To Rogers, it made her grief all the deeper. As was his own pity for her now that it was necessary that she be told more about her husband's death.

'I don't know,' she said. 'It was a dark colour, and large. Which was why I thought it might be a police car.' She seemed reluctant to accept his denial.

'I'm not saying it wasn't, Mrs Ungrish,' he said patiently. 'It could have been. Sometimes our traffic patrols park for a few minutes to check on something, or to call up headquarters. All I can say is that I had no occasion to put a guard on your house or to have a visit made. What was the time, by the way?'

'I'm afraid I didn't look, but certainly after eleven and probably nearer midnight.' She looked away from him then, a tic visible in the corner of her mouth as she wiped her palms with a tiny handkerchief. 'You weren't honest with me last night, Mr Rogers, were you? I mean, what you said about my husband.' It was an accusation and not a question; not aggressive, but more of a reproach.

Rogers, leaning relaxed against the leather of his chair, stiffened. 'No,' he admitted. 'Perhaps not wholly. I was intending to tell you today.' Let her say it, he warned himself, in case

78

he chose the wrong dishonest thing he was supposed to have said.

'My friend told me last night,' she continued as if he had not spoken. 'She said that as I appeared to know nothing, to have been told nothing, it was kinder that she should tell me. He was killed, wasn't he? Not on the railway at all . . . and in someone else's car. Why?' She started tearing at the handkerchief she held, and cried out, 'For God's sake, *why!* Tell me what happened!'

Rogers wondered why she had bottled that up while they had waffled on about the probably quite unconnected incident of the car. 'I didn't tell you before, Mrs Ungrish,' he said gently, 'because it seemed to me that breaking the news of the death of her husband to a woman is as much initially as she should be asked to bear.' When she made no comment on that he went ahead, choosing his words carefully. 'As you were told last night, your husband was in a car that had been in collision with a goods train. That much was so. What was not is that the car was registered in the name of Johnson and was not his Mercedes. There is evidence that he was already dead when the collision occurred. Which means that he was put into the car, driven to the level crossing and left there on the line to be hit by the next train that came along. We don't know how he died, only that the injuries which killed him were internal.' He stopped, uncertain how much more she knew.

'Why should that be done?' she asked, back to the controlled tautness that appeared to be her present norm. 'And who killed him? Why would they? He hadn't done anything to anybody . . .'

'I don't know the answer to either yet, and there's no evidence yet that he was killed by anybody.' He thought that the questions must now be asked, hoping that she wasn't of the breed of women who canonized their newly-dead husbands just because they were dead, and irrespective of what they had actually been in the erring living flesh. 'Would *you* know why he should be found in a car registered in another man's name?'

'Certainly not. He left here in the Mercedes and he would have had no occasion to. Have you asked the other man? Have

79

you . . .' She cut herself short and looked down at her restless fingers. When she lifted her head to his waiting silence, she said, 'I'm sorry, Mr Rogers. I am unfortunately unable to pretend . . . at least, not for long. And I hope that you won't either.' She hesitated, biting at her lower lip and leaving lipstick on her teeth. 'He was with a woman, wasn't he? Was it her car? Had she been with him?'

'You believe that there was another woman?' he equivocated.

'I know there was. Is this something you don't wish to tell me?' She sounded agitated, pulling at the handkerchief again.

'I can only tell you what I know for certain,' he said. 'Do you know who the woman is?' With the windows closed and the air motionless, her scent was pervasively strong and even Rogers's nose, itself a connoisseur of women's scents, felt satiated with it.

'Of course I do.' There was a brief showing of spite in her expression. 'He used to come into my room after he'd been out with her and give me her name and address.'

That had been sarcasm and the detective winced. 'I had to ask,' he murmured. 'You've no idea at all?'

She was jerking her head with, Rogers guessed, an inner disquiet. 'Silly women do get crushes on their gynaecologists . . . he loved that, you know.'

'You think she might have been a patient?'

'That's something else he wouldn't be likely to tell me, isn't it?'

He thought that because she had chosen to mention it she knew, or suspected, the woman to be so. For a man who was widely known to have had his extra-marital intrigues, the women concerned seemed to be blessed with a well-protected anonymity.

'I know that questions may be hurtful,' he said softly, 'but they are necessary. Would you bear with me if I ask more?'

'Yes. Just so long as you too don't treat me as a complete idiot.' There was bitterness there and her features appeared sharper, the gentleness fugitive beneath the make-up. 'I have pride, Mr Rogers. The thought of that woman knowing I was being deceived . . . and now everyone will. I shall have to leave here . . . go away to where nobody knows.'

'I'm sorry,' Rogers said again, deciding not to pile on the anguish by letting her know that most of the hospital staff knew already, and must have known for some time. And also wishing that he could have left this interview with somebody else. 'If that's what you want, I'll tell you what I know about your husband. He was using the name Johnson and owned the car in which he was found dead. He also rented a cottage at Alwick in the same name, using it to meet the woman with whom he was associating.'

Rogers waited for something from her, for she had clenched her hands at that, the tendons prominent in the thin wrists, but she said nothing, only shaking her head dumbly.

'I don't know,' he went on, 'whether he met his death by accident or otherwise, but it could possibly be otherwise. That being so, I have to find out who the woman is. I think that you could help me, even though indirectly.' He cocked his head, making it a query and continuing when she remained silent. 'Going back to Wednesday morning when your husband left you, did he say that he wouldn't be back that night?'

'He rarely did, and he didn't then. It was a situation I had to accept.'

'But when he didn't come back, you accepted that he would be with this woman?'

'Not necessarily. There obviously were occasions – had been – when he would be unable to return home for proper reasons.' She looked away from him, an expression on her face as though she had just realized something and was making a decision that required frowning and curling strands of her hair around her fingers. Rogers remained silent, that being an almost certain prompter of further speech; and, waiting, noticed on the baby grand a framed studio photograph of a younger and very attractive Isabel Ungrish. Not emaciated as she now was, her face appeared pleasantly smooth-fleshed, her good-humoured eyes looking into the camera's lens with no suggestion of haggard neuroticism. When she had finished thinking it out, she turned her head back to him, her blue-lidded eyes asking understanding. 'I think that you should know,' she said, 'because the police usually find out, don't they? And I wouldn't wish you to . . . not everything. I told you a little lie about my visitor last night. It was a man, a friend of mine. And he didn't actually visit me – he couldn't do that, of course – but he telephoned.' She wasn't finding it easy to tell the detective this, and some of her attention was on scratching inelegantly at her ankle. 'I wouldn't have known whether my husband came home on Wednesday evening, and he might have done. I was out with my friend until very late . . . until about one o'clock. I can't really say whether my husband had been in the house or not. He could have been and gone out again – he sleeps at the back where I wouldn't need to go to get to my own room. You do understand, do you? It's quite an innocent friendship, but it could be misinterpreted.'

'Yes, they usually are,' he said, recalling the bawdy Morag's comment about opening the gate to somebody else. 'Might it not be better to tell me who . . .'

She interrupted him. 'Oh, no!' she wailed. 'Please don't ask me. You aren't being fair. He's a professional man of very high standing . . . gossip would ruin his career. *Please.*' Her eyes were pleading with him, her fingers now plucking at the fabric of her skirt.

'I won't press it,' he promised her, adding *for the moment* under his breath, 'and I appreciate your telling me.' She could have been honest about it, and if she had been it had obviously taken some moral courage for her to be so. But he was cynical and partly disbelieving about it, for he knew that no investigating detective could afford to be otherwise.

She was chewing at her lip again and, possibly, already regretting her confiding in him. Then, surprising him, she said, 'My husband murdered Abigail, you know.' Her eyes brimmed and a trickle of tears ran down into the pink patches on her cheekbones. 'He said she smelled . . . was unhygienic. That she was old anyway.'

Rogers nodded gravely as if he understood, the tears filling him with a foreboding of uncontrollable weeping and a wish to be somewhere else. 'And Abigail was . . . ?' he asked.

'My darling little tortoiseshell puss,' she said. 'I loved her so much, and she loved me. She couldn't help being incont . . . he didn't like her at all and objected to my kissing her. Do you kiss cats, Mr Rogers?' That was obviously going to be a yardstick by which, in her eyes, he would stand or fall as a caring human being. And she certainly seemed more sorrowful about the loss of Abigail than about that of her husband who, he had noticed, had never once been referred to by his given name.

'When I have the opportunity and they allow me to,' he assured her with some truth. 'He had her put to sleep?'

'No. He did it himself when I was out. Forgive me,' she said, the tears ended and dabbing at her eyes with the shred of handkerchief. 'I don't know why I mentioned that.'

Rogers didn't either, still not knowing in his ignorance of a woman's thinking processes whether she would be sad or grateful for her husband's dying. 'Don't read more into this than I intend,' he said, 'but had he any enemies known to you? Anybody else who could have had a grudge against him?'

'Other than me, do you mean?' She was staring at him, a wounded deer look in her eyes. 'About what he did to Abigail? Is that what you mean?'

'I obviously didn't, Mrs Ungrish.' He cursed his ill-judged question, feeling that she was wilfully misunderstanding him, reproaching him, and he tried to conceal his irritation at this manifestly neurotic woman with her distracting mannerisms. 'I meant somebody like a cuckolded husband. Even, perhaps, the woman herself.'

She shook her head, the chains around her throat clinking. 'No, I know of no one,' she said, her distress threatening to return. 'How could I?' She paused for a moment, biting at her lip again and looking away from him. 'I'm sorry . . . there was somebody. I listened when I should not have and it was despicable of me.'

'I'd be grateful if you'd tell me,' he said gently. 'It could be important.'

'Yes,' she said, 'I do understand that. I came in from the garden one evening and heard the telephone bell ringing. I must have picked it up at the same time as my husband did on the extension in his study. When I heard him speaking I should have put it back. I know I should, but I didn't. There was a man speaking to him; saying that if he didn't keep away from his fiancée he would be sorry. My husband was angry and said, "Damn you, who are you?" or something like that. The man said "Never you mind, just leave her alone or you'll be sorry". And then he said that he would make him pay for it anyway. My husband never said anything more but put the telephone back.' Her mouth shook. 'He must have heard me listening because he came straight out and said how contemptible I was to listen in to his calls. He didn't say what it was about and I didn't ask.'

'You didn't have to, did you?' His irritation with her had gone and he felt sorry for her. 'When was this?'

'I'm not certain . . . about two months ago I think.'

'And this man? What sort of a voice did he speak in? Educated? Rough? With a particular accent?'

'A rather coarse one. A common one.' She didn't appear too certain. 'I can't remember that there was any accent.' She came back to what was obviously nagging at her. 'Do you think he was the Mr Johnson whose name you said he was using?'

'It'd be unlikely, wouldn't it? In fact, I'm certain not.' She seemed not to have understood what he had told her.

'But you do really think he was killed? In Mr Johnson's car?'

She was confused and he decided it better to leave her with the misunderstandings unresolved. 'No more than I did, or did not, before,' he said. 'We have to consider the remotest of possibilities when we don't know the circumstances leading to a death.' He stood from his chair, foreseeing more awkward questions. Already he had given her more detail than he had intended, getting little in return; done too much talking for a man convinced that one could not do that and think at the same time. Too, he thought that she had had enough; damned certain that he had. 'I'm sorry if I've upset you,' he apologized. 'I'll keep in touch and let you know if I find anything out about the car you saw.' He left her sitting, he thought somewhat taken aback by his hurried departure from the room and feeling that he was deserting her in her unhappiness.

It had stopped raining while he had been suffering the over-scented sitting-room and there was a fresh dampness outside to clear his nostrils of it. Turning his car from the forecourt, he could see that the two shire horses had been let in to the paddock. Beautiful in their glossy massiveness, they were cantering as if just released from a prison cell, their manes streaming and their hooves kicking glistening sprays from the wet grass.

And seeing them, Rogers recalled that Twite had mentioned horses as being Mrs Ungrish's particular interest, had also known last night only just what the professional man in good standing had told her by telephone, and was as a consequence forced into the detective's unwilling consideration as being possibly the anonymous friend and informant. If he were – and Rogers, who carried suspicion about with him in the same pocket as his warrant card, saw no particular wrong in it – it would explain his rather extreme reaction in the mortuary when he had identified Ungrish. And, in his consideration of it, it touched his sense of the incongruous to imagine the overhanging fatness of the gourmand pathologist in conjunction with the attenuated and gentle gawkiness of the woman who might be claiming him in innocent friendship.

16

With his breakfast too recent a memory for a larger meal, Rogers was prepared to lunch at his desk on two cheese sandwiches and coffee, theorizing that his metabolism would need a little more support than it got from tobacco smoke. With the sun shining through his windows he was feeling edgy with the need for significant action, his restlessness in his black executive-style chair making it squeak like an irritated mouse, this being one of the promptings for him to get out and do something useful.

Lingard came into his office as he was about to eat, sitting in the visitor's chair and smiling with what Rogers regarded as satisfaction about something achieved. 'Tell me the hilariously good news while I feed myself,' he said. 'You do have some?'

'Something,' Lingard agreed. 'But nothing we hadn't expected. Our sulphur-haired villain's been identified. He's one Neville Pring, aged eighteen years and unemployed since leaving school, unless you can regard petty thieving and minor housebreakings as being an employment. He's on record for it and has done community service and youth custody for his discovered sins. Reported to us as missing an hour ago by his mother, who lives at Blackfell. Last seen at eleven o'clock last night when he was supposed to be going to bed. Came the morning and no Neville down for breakfast, bed not slept in and no bicycle in the shed. I think we can assume that his mother was frightened that he'd been arrested on a job and delayed reporting him missing until she was sure that she wasn't going to be told.'

'Poor woman. It's always the mothers who suffer the sins of their families,' Rogers observed. 'She knows he's dead?' It was as he expected and, with nothing about it connecting the dead youth with Ungrish, forgiving himself for a lack of interest in his dying.

'By now, yes. I've sent a policewoman out to tell her.' Lingard took an ivory box from his waistcoat pocket and pinched snuff into his nostrils, the air filling with the scent of attar of roses. 'We can scrub him from the book, can we?'

'Definitely,' Rogers agreed. 'We've enough problems without his coming into them, although I'd still be interested in why he should die suddenly at his age. Is there a record of previous health problems?'

'Not with us. But no doubt his mother will mention it if there were.' He changed the subject. 'The house keys,' he said. 'Barrington the owner's been traced and he doesn't know anything about Johnson being Ungrish. It's all straightforward and he says he handed over the only two keys he had to him.'

'So somebody seems to have the second. Probably the woman, eh?' He frowned. 'Don't you think it odd that Ungrish should be carrying his key around with him? Shouldn't it have been where he'd leave it, in the inside lock of the door?'

'An idiosyncrasy of his?' Lingard didn't see it in the same light as Rogers.

'It could be,' Rogers said, although he wasn't believing it so. 'Is there anything more from Alwick?' He had eaten his doughy sandwiches, wished from the heavy feeling in his stomach that he hadn't and was filling his pipe to smoke with his coffee.

'Nothing more useful than what I got at first visit,' Lingard said. 'Apart, that is, from what the reverend vicar told you. Occasional comings and goings of the Cambridge, variously described as a Ford or a Vauxhall and coloured light blue, purple or black depending on whether it was light or dark when seen. Nor was our friend a man to keep to a rigid timetable, or to advertise his visits. The White Lion attracts a lot of outsiders for its bar food, so a fair number of cars are bobbing about the village street and some of his visits must have gone unnoticed. Most of the villagers knew of him, but only a few knew about him. From the reports I've had – they're not down on paper yet, George – there were at least two females he brought to the cottage. One was younger than the other we were told about, and seemingly plumper. But she was seen only in the car, and then way back in the summer when the evenings were light. There's nothing about either likely to help in identifying them, and certainly nothing about them to suggest that they might be bought and paid-for trollops. Incidentally, the news hasn't got around yet, so to the village he's still the mysterious Mr Johnson, more or less accepted to be a townee womanizer and more envied – at least by the men I spoke to – than condemned.' Lingard showed his teeth and added, 'Shacking up with different women doesn't appear to have attracted as much lubricious interest as we more saintly characters might imagine.'

Rogers worked that over in his mind as he finished his coffee. 'Nothing much there, is there?' he grunted. 'If that'd been me, they'd have had my name, address and date of birth, together with that of the woman I'd have improbably taken there.' He shook his head at the thought. 'I've overlooked something, David. Ungrish's consulting rooms at St Barnabas Place.'

He knew that he should not have for, as a detective inspector, he had been called mysteriously and in great haste to them by the then consultant's receptionist. The consultant, known to Rogers as an alcoholic, was dead. He had gone to bed naked, slicing his wrists and ankles with a scalpel and bleeding to death. What had remained vividly in Rogers's memory was that he had sterilized the scalpel before doing it, replacing it when done into the tumbler of fluid at the side of the bed. Medical consultancy was now appearing to him to be a profession vulnerable to an early death.

He said, 'There's sure to be a receptionist or nurse employed there, even if it's out of business at the moment.' He grinned encouragingly at Lingard. 'See whoever she might be and use your exquisite tact on her – fairly urgently, David. God save me from misplacing my suspicions, but she could be our unknown female from the cottage.'

Lingard looked pointedly at Rogers's empty plate. 'I'll take a minute or two off in the canteen before I do. I can never interrogate females successfully on an empty stomach.' He stood and moved to the door. 'Hagbourne's lurking out in the corridor. He's found Ungrish's car and bursting to tell you how.'

Hagbourne, the pouches prominent under his eyes, wore his customary and misleading world-weary look as he placed a car-servicing folder, a plastic wallet of driving documents and a mixture of keys on Rogers's desk. 'I was lucky, sir,' he said, never a man to admit that it might be good detective work. 'I did have a couple of spare bodies helping me. The Mercedes is with G. H. Crapper, motor engineer of Canal Street, repairs done expeditiously and lock-up garages for renting. And, you'll remember, a shifty bugger lucky not to be inside for handling a couple of stolen cars. Five lock-ups in an open yard at the back and number three rented to a Mrs D. Johnson, Gorres Lane, Alwick, who paid six months in advance with a cheque signed D. G. Johnson for the garaging of a Cambridge saloon. She filled in Crapper's name and the amount only, by the way, then explaining that her husband would be using it more often than she would, and occasionally for another car in its place. Believe him or not, Crapper swears that he never actually saw her husband, or the Mercedes, shutting up shop as he does at six every day except Saturdays and Sundays when he closes for the weekend.'

'As he needn't, of course,' Rogers said. 'Ungrish would be careful that he didn't. But sticking his neck out, for all that. You have her description?'

Hagbourne snorted his derision. 'For what it's worth, which is nothing. He said his memory wasn't too good and he'd only seen her the once.' Life had obviously lived down to his opinion of it, Rogers guessing that it hadn't been helped by his habit of poking a disgruntled finger into the chests of close-mouthed and unliked suspects. 'She could have been about twenty-five, or thirty-five, or even more – depending, although he couldn't say on what. Medium brown hair – he thought; dress, well, ordinary; speech, no particular accent but just like any other woman's. She'd been carrying a handbag – ordinary again – because at least he could remember her taking the cheque from it. He did agree though that she had two eyes, a nose and a mouth, like normal. And he thought that she walked there because he couldn't remember seeing a car. And,' he added with an immense disgust, 'he didn't think that he'd recognize her again even if the bleedin' fuzz used thumb-screws on him.'

'No matter, Thomas,' Rogers consoled him. 'I'm not about to detail you to find her.' He prodded a finger at the keys; the No. 3 garage key he had passed to Hagbourne, ignition and lock keys with the Mercedes logo on them, and an old mortice lock key. 'That door key looks as if it's from the cottage. Where was it?'

'Under the driver's seat,' Hagbourne told him. 'An odd place to keep it.'

'Not if it's got a married man's guilt tag tied to it.' Rogers was disappointed at its finding, having hoped that the unknown woman would have been in possession of it when he eventually found her. 'Check it with the key Magnus'll have. It's probably the spare.' He poked his finger at the car servicing folder. 'Why do I want this?'

'There's an interesting repairs and replacement invoice in it from the Kirkallen Garage,' Hagbourne said. 'It's dated the sixteenth of September, but the Mercedes was collected from

89

the Arts Theatre car park by the breakdown truck on the fifth. It seems that while Ungrish was swanning it in the theatre all four tyres were slashed, the wheel trims hammered into lumps, the windscreen and rear window glass smashed, the radio aerial and windscreen wipers tied into knots, and the side panels given the works with white paint from an aerosol. There could be more . . . yes, there is. The petrol filler cap was forced and thrown away, and gravel and earth put into the tank. Somebody'd used up a hell of a lot of venom on it and the bill amounted to £964.' Although it hadn't happened to Hagbourne's car, his expression appeared to suggest that it had.

'I'd murder the bastard who did that to mine,' Rogers growled. 'There's more to it than that, though?'

'Yes, there is. It seemed interesting enough for me to speak to the manager at Kirkallens. Not that it mattered to him, but he told me that he understood Ungrish wasn't intending claiming on his insurance for the damage. Which surprised him; particularly as he'd already been told that it was going to cost a bomb to put the car back into shape. He got matey enough after a while to tell me a bit more. Apart from the squiggles made with the aerosol, *Leave Her Alone* had been sprayed in large letters on two of the door panels. He said that Ungrish had told him that whoever had done it had obviously mistaken his car for one belonging to somebody else, but he thought he was uncomfortable about it just the same. You can guess why he wasn't intending to claim on the insurance?'

'Yes. They'd want confirmation that he had reported it to us. He hadn't?'

'No, quite definitely not. I checked it when I got back.'

Rogers grimaced, his brown eyes thoughtful. 'It's all a bit off-putting for a married man working off his thingy outside the home, isn't it? I can almost feel sorry for him. I mean, nearly a thousand pounds . . .'

The bell of his green telephone rang and, lifting the receiver, he flapped his free hand to dismiss Hagbourne. 'Rogers,' he said into it, anticipating problems that rarely failed to materialize from a call to its unlisted number.

His caller was Twite. 'It's me, old chum,' he said. 'I did the examination early to stop you worrying.'

'Good for you.' Rogers was relieved. 'I hope we can now forget him.'

'I don't think you'll want to when you've heard me out. Have you got your pencil and paper handy?'

'God almighty, but I hope you're joking, Wilfred,' Rogers growled, his relief short-lived and about to die. 'Tell me.'

'Our body died by asphyxiation,' he said, 'posing the question, which came first? Just that, or his heart causing it by dying on him? That, my old unhappy chum, is something you can forget because it was beautifully sound and healthy. So far as the asphyxiation is concerned, there's no obstruction of the air passage by food or other oddments; no signs, as I told you this morning, of strangulation, throttling or smothering. There're also no signs of pressure or compression of the chest; in fact, no real evidence of why he died at all. His blood shows a condition of anoxaemia; for your undeveloped physiology, a gross shortage in it of carbon dioxide which usually results from a paralysis of the respiratory centre. So what caused it, old chum, eh?'

'You know I'd be guessing and you're not asking me, Wilfred.' Rogers could guess, however, that he wasn't going to be happy about whatever it was. 'So you tell me what did.'

'I'll try.' Twite sounded abnormally cheerful, which meant that he was near enough to being certain in his diagnosis. 'The most obvious conclusion is that the paralysis was caused by a poison of some kind.'

'Some kind?' Rogers echoed him, surprised but not prepared to show it. 'Can't you say what?'

'Of course I can't. Not right here and now. But I can tell you that it was neither a corrosive nor an irritant and, because it attacked the respiratory centre, almost certainly not a metallic poison. It leaves me believing that he's had an overdose of one of the vegetable poisons.'

'You mean something like deadly nightshade?' Rogers's mind was struggling to grasp the implications. Two years previously he had investigated a case of fatal poisoning by a witch's brew of deadly nightshade and now wasn't happy that it could fit the circumstances of this particular death.

'No, I don't.' Twite was obviously drawing it out. 'Something like the barbiturates? Heroin? Or cocaine? Most of them may cause an asphyxial death, and they're very much on the streets at the moment.'

'That I do know,' Rogers said, 'but he didn't have any drugs on him, and that's for sure. Can't you narrow it down?' He saw with his mind's eye the opened bottle of whisky at the cottage, realizing with a totality of pessimism – and almost groaning with it – that the answer he didn't want was going to be found in its remaining contents.

'Not even for you,' Twite assured him. 'I'd be guessing. It's a laboratory job as well you know. I've taken what stomach contents there are, some blood and brain samples, and they're ready for you to collect with my best wishes for a happy delivery.'

'And that'll take days,' Rogers said, wanting to throw the telephone through the glass of the nearest window.

After disconnecting from him, Rogers sent for Sergeant Magnus who had now returned, instructing him to forget for the moment the classification of any finger impressions he might have found at the cottage – he had found some, Magnus said – and to collect the samples from the mortuary. Together with the whisky and ginger ale exhibits, he was to deliver them personally and without delay to the Forensic Science Laboratory. Then he put through a call to the laboratory's director, doing what he called his grovelling act in making it seem that his professional future depended on it, quoting the pathologist's opinion as Holy Writ and asking for a most immediate analysis of whatever it was that had apparently caused the death of the unfortunate housebreaker.

Twite's finding and diagnosis had somehow made a mockery of the sun flooding into the office, which he was now prepared to leave before anything further came in to confuse the direction of what had hitherto appeared to be a relatively straightforward investigation.

17

Having to negotiate the hospital's corridors again to reach the administrative offices was, for Rogers, a depressing suffering of over-familiar smells of past meals, wax floor polish and the pungencies of antiseptics that he would carry in his nose long after he had left. He tried to ignore as much as he could the sickly green paint on the walls, the floor-level pipes giving off blasting heat that could only weaken a patient's morale, and the men and women in white coats who always looked horrendously brisk in their anxiety to pour nauseous fluids down unwilling throats or to stick needles into shrinking flesh. Although considering himself a man necessarily hardened to viewing dead bodies, he averted his eyes when passing an open door to a ward in case he happened to see those things being done. Also being a man who, not too long ago, had suffered detention in one of the wards as the result of a battered skull, he was willing enough to admit to anybody interested that hospitals frightened him. He was fully determined not to allow his body into their care again; to die, if one day he had to, in his own bed.

Giving his name only to a girl through the glass louvres of an enquiry window in the general office, he asked if Miss Kelf was available. While he waited she used the telephone, looked uncomfortable at what she was listening to and returned to him. 'I'm dreadfully sorry,' she said. 'Miss Kelf is in conference and won't be able to see you.'

'Is that all?' he asked, recognizing prevarication when he heard it.

'I'm afraid so,' the girl said, giving him the grace of an apologetic smile.

In no frame of mind to be put off by bureaucratic obstructiveness, if that was what it was, he walked the few yards to her office and stood outside the door. Hearing no sounds of voices he opened the door without knocking, prepared to apologize effusively should he be mistaken. She was sitting at her desk alone, doing nothing more than showing surprise at his entry. 'I knew she'd misunderstood you, Miss Kelf,' he said genially. 'You aren't in conference at all, are you?'

She was not, he admitted to himself, remembering him with any affection, the surprise she had shown being followed by an icy glare. 'I am under no obligation to explain my reasons or movements,' she said, very much in her clenched-teeth mood, 'but I was about to go.' Complementary to her features, her plain grey dress with its immaculately white collar and her strained-back hair gave her the appearance of a stiff and bloodless severity.

He closed the door and moved to her desk, wondering whether anybody had ever seen a warm smile on the neat freckled face that could promise so much if there were. 'I'll speak either with you or your chief, Miss Kelf,' he said, mildly enough. 'I rather think you'd prefer it to be with you.'

She stared at him, her grey eyes still chilly. 'I shall overlook your rudeness,' she snapped, the executive rebuking a subordinate, 'but be brief and please come to the point.'

Rogers held on to his geniality, knowing it would irritate her further and, knowing that he wouldn't be asked, sat uninvited opposite her. Glancing around him, needing to evaluate this woman who, looking as though she would refuse to allow herself to sweat, he now suspected of having passions running in her blood. It was a sparsely furnished room, almost painfully neat. There were no feminine niceties in it such as flowers and potted plants, photographs or pictures. Other than the desk on which was a blotting pad, two trays – one with two or three papers and a magazine *Hospital Update* in it – a telephone and a china jar containing three ball-pens, there was a green filing cabinet, a glass-fronted case with a handful of books in it, a white enamelled radiator that gave off an enervating heat and the two chairs on which they were sitting. Concluding that this particular Deputy Chief Administrator was not exactly overworked, he compared her meagre amount of paperwork ruefully with his own stack of unread crime files.

He said, 'I assume that you now know the details of Mr

94

Ungrish's death, and that the circumstances of it are being investigated?'

At his mention of Ungrish her face had tightened and she nodded briefly. 'Mr Ungrish had no connection with this department, if that is what you are looking for.'

'Was there not?' He tried to look astonished. 'Haven't you heard that he seems to have had some connection with the man Johnson I spoke to you about?'

'No I have not.' There was an only just definable wariness in her voice, brusque though it remained.

'Is the register you referred to yesterday kept in the general office?'

'Yes. Can that be of any possible interest to you?' she moved impatiently in her chair. 'Please come to the point.'

'But under your supervision?' he asked, ignoring her demand.

'I have access to it when necessary, which is not often.'

'I see.' He was now about to chance an uncertain arm on a quite frail supposition. 'Would you know how many patients called Johnson are entered in it during the course of ten months? I mean, it's a reasonably common name.'

She looked at him as though she thought him stupid. 'I would not.'

'I thought not,' he said equably. Then, casually, 'You know, it did strike me as being rather strange that when I asked you about a man called Johnson who had died here earlier this year, you could look him up in the right month without any hesitation. The *right* Dhugal Gordon Johnson, too; forenames I happened not to have given you. In fact, you didn't question whether he was the Johnson I was interested in or not.'

In the silence that followed he could hear from another room the clacking of a typewriter and a male voice saying unintelligible words. More immediately, the radiator behind him was making liquid gasping noises. Although her features remained expressionless, her hands resting on the desk's top were being kneaded restlessly. 'I don't know what you are implying,' she said at last.

95

'I'm not implying anything.' Rogers had withdrawn his geniality, his swarthy face stern. 'I'm making a statement, an accusation if you like. Johnson's driving papers – recorded in your register as having been destroyed – were found on Ungrish's body. Which means that they had been stolen. By him? By somebody in this department with access to the property and who could steal them for him? Somebody like you, Miss Kelf?'

For a woman who could be visualizing her arrest, or a charge of theft, the ruination of what must be a fairly top-brass job, she held herself well against his accusation. She stood from her desk, a flush of red rising on her throat and hating him. Something, he thought, he could bear lightly even from a woman whose body, seen for the first time on its feet, was certainly something to overheat the blood of any man. 'I don't know what you are talking about,' she said, her words brittle, 'but I want you to repeat that to the Chief Administrative Officer.'

'You are so right,' Rogers answered her, standing and wondering whether he had shot his bolt at the wrong bird, or that she was calling his bluff. 'I should have spoken to him in the first place. He would want to listen to Crapper the garage chap at first hand anyway. And, of course, there *is* the question of fingerprints at the cottage . . .'

There was again a fraught silence during which she seemed transformed into a vulnerable girl, all self-assertion fled and the indecision of fear in its place. She sat as if her body had suddenly softened into bonelessness, staring in her anguish at him while he, despite the hatred for him he knew would still remain, felt pity for her.

He lowered himself back into his chair and said, 'Now that you've decided to be sensible, perhaps you'll tell me about your association with Ungrish and the theft of the documents.' Admitting to an earlier misjudgment about her wearing tin knickers, he also had to readjust his thinking that a romp or two in bed with a man would do things for her temperament. Apparently it had not; at least, not where Ungrish had been concerned. He decided against cautioning her, sure of nothing yet.

'I didn't take them,' she said in a low voice. 'I don't know who did.'

'But Ungrish did get the information about Johnson from you?'

'I believe I mentioned it to him. He asked me one day if I could tell him . . . he had heard about his death, I suppose.'

'That didn't surprise you? A gynaecologist asking about the property of a man killed in a road accident?' Rogers wasn't believing her evasions, or believing her a luckless innocent caught up in the guilt of another's crime.

'I wondered at the time, but was hardly in a position to refuse him.'

'Or to refuse renting a lock-up garage for him from Crapper? A man, incidentally, who we've interviewed and who's given us a description.' Mentioning the close-mouthed Crapper had been a shot in the dark, but it had hit home and he was now certain in his questioning.

'You've brought him with you?' she asked; then, in a whisper, 'Please don't. Not in here.'

Rogers saw no reason to deny what she had mistakenly assumed. He said, 'Then it isn't necessary for him to identify you?'

'No. Mr Ungrish asked me to do it for him.'

'In a dead man's name? Knowing that it was dishonest, that he was in possession of stolen documents?' He sharpened his voice. 'You must have asked him why.'

'No, no.' She was breathing as though with an obstruction in her chest, her expression one of looking into unrelieved darkness. 'Could we talk about it at some other time? Somewhere else?'

'We can go to the police station,' he suggested. 'Now, if that's what you prefer.' He wasn't about to allow her off the hook on which she had snagged herself. 'No?' he said when she dumbly shook her head. 'As you wish, of course. What was your relationship with Ungrish that made you a party to his theft and deception? Were you lovers?'

'*No!*' Her denial was vehement, spat out. 'We were friends. Just that.'

97

'But friendly enough for you to stay with him at the cottage? You do know the cottage I'm talking about, don't you?'

'Not to stay, no. Only the once.'

'And that on Wednesday,' he said with all the appearance of knowing. 'The night he was killed.'

She bowed her head, putting her hands over her face, her fingertips pressing into her forehead with only her trembling mouth left visible. 'I didn't know, I just did not,' she moaned, shaking her head as if in pain.

Rogers swore to himself. She was about to weep on him, to soften with her femaleness the implacability he was bringing to bear on what was now an interrogation. Although he hated having to lean hard on a woman, he wasn't going to allow it; not when she was now revealed as the missing woman and, possibly, responsible in some way for Ungrish's death. Remembering her yesterday's lack of any emotion but resentment, her coldness and bossiness, when she must have known about Ungrish having died, he could not believe that he would be doing her an injustice. He spoke to her in a fractionally less stern tone of voice. 'Miss Kelf. That isn't going to help you at all. I want you to realize the seriousness of your position. Ungrish was killed, possibly murdered at the cottage, and you were there. In the absence of an acceptable explanation of your involvement you are not too far from being arrested and charged.' With something or other, he qualified to himself, having so far nothing that could be called admissible evidence. '*Look at me,*' he said with emphasis.

After a short wait she lowered her hands and, with no glistening in her eyes, he saw with relief that she hadn't been weeping. Although her face was strained with emotion, he could see that if she still considered him an unloved enemy, she was concealing it. And that, he knew, could be a deliberate falling back on her female defences.

'So far,' he said to her, 'I have been getting answers from you only sufficient to indicate your complicity in Ungrish's misdemeanours, but doing yourself no justice should you happen to be innocently involved. It's a matter for you to decide, but if

98

you have no unlawful connection with his killing you may think it better to tell me now.'

'And then you'll arrest me?' she asked tremulously.

'I might,' he conceded. 'It'll depend on what you tell me – or don't tell me – and what truth I believe there might be in it.' He was beginning to sweat, though gently, in the excessive heat, the radiator being not too far from his back.

'May I think about it for a few moments? Please? On my own?' Her eyes were no less grey than they were before, but they now held in them a look he took to be cajolery.

'I'm afraid not,' he replied, unsure of her intent. 'Do whatever thinking you feel necessary while I wait.'

Knowing that she wished to avoid his gaze on her, he rose from his chair and lodged his buttocks on the uncomfortably narrow window sill with his back to her, looking out into the afternoon's pale sunshine. At ground level, much of what it fell on was blocked by the rear of the hospital's brickwork, the cramped intervening space being used for the parking of cars and the storage of wooden crates; the latter, he convinced himself, having been used to deliver vast quantities of hypodermic syringes and needles. It was not wholly uninspiring, for what he saw provoked an image in his mind of what should have arisen before. It hadn't an all-encompassing certainty and when he heard Kelf say 'Will you come, please,' it interrupted his attempt to relate what he had learned of her with the image that had been invoked.

Returning to his chair, he said, 'You wish to tell me now?'

'Yes, as much as I am able.' She was calm, appearing to be in control of her emotions.

And calm women, able to control their emotions, could make capable liars, Rogers reminded himself. About to give her the legal imperative which amounted to saying 'Never be idiotic enough to admit to a policeman whatever offence you happened to have committed', he said, 'First, I have to tell you that you are not obliged to say anything unless you wish to do so, but that anything you do say will be taken down in writing and may be given in evidence.' He withdrew his pocket book and pen from an inside pocket.

99

'Please . . .' she said, almost pleadingly, and for a brief moment he thought she was set to use the softer side of her femininity on him, '. . . not in writing. I really don't wish to sign anything.'

Rogers shrugged, repocketing the notebook and pen. 'As you wish, but it would be primarily in your interest if you've nothing to hide.'

'I do wish.' It was with a made-up mind that she spoke. 'Mr Ungrish and I first met at the last hospital staff Christmas party. We then discovered that we both belonged to the High Moor golf club, although we had never seen each other there. That wasn't unusual, for the ladies' section has a separate club room they may use. We played a few rounds together because it was convenient to arrange a match here at the hospital. Later, because he insisted on betting a meal on the result, we occasionally dined together. That, until Wednesday, was the extent of our friendship.'

She stopped there, looking down at her blotting-pad, then back to Rogers. When he said nothing, only nodding his acceptance of what she had told him, she continued. 'I don't wish to tell lies, I can't. He did ask me about Mr Johnson's property and I did tell him. It was foolish of me to do it, but I honestly didn't question why he wanted to know and he didn't tell me. So far as I knew then, he could have had a perfectly legitimate reason for doing so.' She pulled nervously with her fingers at the collar of her dress. 'Later, he told me that his wife wished to divorce him and he intended to invest some of his money in a different name so that he wouldn't be robbed of half of his capital, as well as half of his home, by her solicitors. That meant he had to have a separate address too. He said that he had rented a little cottage at Alwick and had bought another car so that he needn't use his own to get there, possibly being recognized as he was well known in the district. I didn't see anything unreasonable or unlawful in any of that. When he asked me to rent a garage for him I felt that I couldn't refuse, for by then I realized that in giving him the information about Mr Johnson I could be held to be at fault.'

'So you felt forced to call yourself Mrs Johnson, to pay with a cheque made out in a dead man's name?' Rogers was straight-faced. Like a priest in the confessional, he had spent a police-man's life being comprehensively lied to and he had, to spend it successfully, to know when it was being done. He expected to be lied to and had no justification for objecting to it, but he did resent the implication in the lying that he would be gullible enough to swallow it.

'I had to, don't you see? I was frightened that I would lose my job if it was found out.' She was, Rogers could see, also frightened of it now.

'You drove the car there?'

She shook her head. 'No, I went there in my own.'

'I'm sorry to have interrupted you,' he said. 'You were about to tell me what happened on Wednesday.' He gave her an encouraging smile as though to assure her that he was with her every inch of her lying way. She couldn't know that Rogers, as an interrogator, was at his most dangerous when polite and apparently understanding.

'Yes, I was,' she agreed and Rogers fancied that he could hear the clicking and whirring of the brain behind her smooth forehead as it sorted out that which he was about to receive. 'Mr Ungrish invited me out to dinner that evening, to the Hart's Head Hotel at Moorfield. On the way he said that he would like to drop in at the cottage to collect something he needed for the following day. He suggested that I might be interested in seeing it while we were there. I wasn't actually, but I could hardly say so.' She hunched her shoulders, crossing her arms over her breasts, hurt tightening her face. 'It wasn't that at all. When we were in there he lit the fire and asked me if I would like a drink. I said no, because we would be having wine with our meal and I don't really care for anything beforehand. Then he said, was it worth while going all the way to Moorfield on a wet night as he had food in the larder. It seemed so silly. It wouldn't have been a proper meal and I . . . I began to be a little frightened.'

Because she had so obviously paused for Rogers to ask why, he did so.

'It was his attitude . . . it had changed. He came over to me – I was standing near the door because I was nervous – and he held my arms with his hands. He said, why did we go on pretending? Then the filthy beast touched my . . . my breast . . .' Her breathing quickened and she managed a spinster's expression of indignant embarrassment, the impassive-faced Rogers wondering with an inner derision how much more of this schoolgirlish innocence she was intending to contrive.

'Go on,' he said, his irony concealed. 'There must be more, and it won't offend me.'

'There isn't really. He tried to kiss me and I told him to stop it, that I wanted to leave immediately and go home. He called me a bitch and said things to me that I couldn't repeat; horrible things about leading him on and why did I think he had taken so much trouble with me. And did I think that I was too . . . well, you know the kind of thing. When I insisted on leaving he became furious and shouted at me, told me to go – only he didn't use those words – and to find my own way back. I was so relieved, so happy I could get away from him that I didn't care. I ran most of the way through the village until I saw the telephone kiosk near the post office. I rang the taxi rank here in Abbotsburn and a taxi came out and took me back. And that's all I know about Wednesday . . . truly . . .' she said, trailing off to a hesitant silence.

'An upsetting experience,' Rogers said gravely. 'And that was the last you saw of Ungrish?'

'Yes. I was dreadfully shocked when I heard that he had been found dead in his car. I thought that he had done it . . . perhaps because of me.'

'But you now know he hadn't, that he was killed elsewhere. Possibly at the cottage, yes?'

She was meeting his stare with the earnestness and frankness that lying can summon to its aid. And, oddly, with her few freckles more pronounced. 'Yes, and I don't understand it. I swear I don't. He was perfectly all right when I left him.'

It had not escaped him that what she had told him would need any questioned truth in it to be supported or contradicted by a man who was now speechless in a mortuary refrigerator. It decided him not to question the absurdity of her account of what had happened, but to tie her down to a few facts for his later demolition of it. He asked, 'What time did you arrive at the cottage?'

'I don't know. But I did meet him here in Abbotsburn at six-thirty.'

'Which would mean you arrived some fifteen minutes later. How long do you estimate you were in the cottage with him?' He wanted to add with more irony, 'when you were defending your virtue', but thought that he had better not.

'I don't honestly know. It seemed like hours, but it couldn't have been very long. I was back in Abbotsburn ages before eight o'clock.'

'Of course.' He accepted it understandingly. 'Where did Ungrish park the car when you arrived? At the rear of the cottage?'

She hesitated before answering. 'Yes. But we had to go to the front entrance to get in.'

That had been, he considered, an unnecessary explanation. As if by way of a casual observation, he said, 'I found a nightdress – an expensive-looking white one, I should add – folded on one of the beds upstairs. Sort of ready for use, you know? I mean, it wouldn't have been there unless somebody had gone there with the intention of staying the night, would it?'

The sudden widening of her eyes showed that it had been an item she had forgotten, and that something frantic was happening inside her head. 'It wasn't mine, and I don't know anything about it.' That had been difficult for her to get out and there had been a hunted look in her face.

'Of course not,' he agreed benignly. 'It couldn't be, could it, and it doesn't matter. We can always check with the shops that stock that brand and find out who bought it. And then there's the question of the two newspapers somebody had been reading from two chairs that evening. You wouldn't have had time, of course?'

That had been something else she had forgotten and she made a strangled noise that could have been a 'No'.

He waited a few moments, then said, 'Do you have a more

regular male friend than Ungrish was? Or even, perhaps, a husband or ex-husband?'

'No, I don't.' For probably the first time, that sounded like the truth. 'Why do you ask that?'

'It's nothing.' He brushed it aside as if it were. 'I'd like your address, Miss Kelf. I shall probably want to see you later and I know you won't want me to embarrass you further by calling here again.'

'No,' she said, her anguish plain at its implications. 'I live with my mother and you mustn't. *Please.*' He felt for her in what she must see as a catastrophically black and inescapable situation.

He took out his wallet, extracted one of his visiting cards from it and handed it to her. 'Write it on the back of this for me, will you? And your telephone number. I'll give my name only if I call and your mother answers.'

Writing on it obediently, she returned the card to him and, holding it by the edges, he put it back in his wallet. Then he stood and moved to leave. 'There *is* something that does puzzle me about Ungrish,' he said. 'I can't understand why he should have made an enemy of you – which he had, hadn't he? – when it was so obvious that you had it in your hands to ruin him socially and professionally.' He shook his head with an assumed air of bewilderment, opening the door and closing it on a woman who had stared at him with nothing to say that would not have made matters worse.

18

Rogers's plasterboard and polystyrene office with its *trompe-l'oeil* wood veneers and impersonal metal and plastic furniture was a permanent affront to his sensibilities, lessened only by the hope that, in time, his pipe-smoking would mellow the glaring whiteness of the walls, ceiling and paintwork to an interesting tobacco-yellow. It was an office in which he had to spend far too much time and from which he was always seeking an escape; an office to which he was forced to return at intervals in order to record on official paper what he had done, or had failed to do, and to further the activities of his investigations.

He had returned to it now with necessary things to do about the discomposed Marian Kelf, but another matter was intervening. A uniformed PC Knowler stood in front of Rogers's desk, waiting as he read the form brought to him. Knowler's divisional superintendent had telephoned Rogers, telling him that one of his PCs on car patrol had, in early September, been directed to what appeared to have been a disturbance at the home of Mr Simon Ungrish. At the time it had rated no more than an Occurrence Book entry but, having read the report of Ungrish's death on the daily crime bulletin, Knowler had recalled the incident and had brought it to his superintendent's notice.

What Rogers was reading was a copy taken of the Occurrence Book entry. *Sunday, 11th September. Domestic disturbance – Simon Ungrish, Isabel Ungrish and Obadiah Gillard, Capstone House, High Moor. Emergency 999 call received by Station Sergeant Duffield 11.20 am. Woman, hysterical, reporting 'terrible fight' between husband and employee at Capstone House, High Moor. Rang off without giving name. PC 1013 Knowler contacted 11.24 am and ordered to scene, arriving at 11.35 am. Woman, identified as Mrs Ungrish and as emergency caller, informed PC all now quiet and police not needed. PC asked to see husband who admitted minor disagreement with Gillard, a groom employed at premises, but that his wife not well and had exaggerated altercation and panicked. Wife present and confirmed this. Mr Ungrish uninjured but with red mark on left cheek. PC interviewed Gillard in stables. Stated that there had been no fight, refused to discuss what had happened. No signs of injury. S/Sgt Duffield informed and instructed no further action.*

'Very interesting and succinct,' Rogers said when he had read it. 'But I'm sure you've more to tell me about their attitudes and what was said.'

Knowler, a university graduate entry to the force and doing his two years' practical beat work to fill out his uniform with an experience of criminous and bloody-minded humanity, was, to Rogers, a slim and pale youngster much as he himself had been as a probationary constable. Despite his callowness, he looked capable and self-confident.

'Yes, sir,' he replied, very much as though he were giving evidence from a witness box. 'I did not believe any of them, and I was certain that Mrs Ungrish was under duress. When she answered the door I could she that she had been crying. She told me that there was no need for any action by me as she had wrongly assumed what had happened. I insisted that to satisfy myself and my superiors I must see both her husband and the employee with whom he had allegedly been fighting. She led me into a room – most unwillingly I should say, sir – and I saw Mr Ungrish sitting on a sofa with one hand holding his stomach and the other holding a glass of what appeared to be whisky. He removed the hand from his stomach when he saw me and said 'What the hell do *you* want?' I saw that he had a narrow red mark on his cheek beneath the left eye and about two inches long. It could have been the beginning of a bruise, although I am not certain about that. I also saw that he had dirt smears and dust on his trousers, which were otherwise immaculate. I said to him, 'Sir, we have received an emergency call from Mrs Ungrish saying that you were engaged in what she said was a terrible fight with an employee.' Mr Ungrish replied, 'You are mistaken, as you can see perfectly well for yourself. And so was my wife. She isn't well and her condition caused her to mis-understand and exaggerate a minor altercation which is my private concern only. This is my house and you are trespassing, so you may now leave. I have nothing to say to you or to anybody else.' Or words to that effect, sir,' Knowler added carefully. He had sounded a shade stuffed-shirt, having probably added formality to the passage of words.

'And Mrs Ungrish?' Rogers asked.

'She was standing at my side, sir. Mr Ungrish was most arrogant and authoritative in his attitude towards both of us, and it seemed to me that she was frightened . . . no, not quite that, but very nervous of him. And I am quite sure that she had been crying before I arrived.'

'Did she have make-up on? You know, fairly heavily?'

Knowler looked surprised. 'No, sir. None at all.'

'Carry on then.' Rogers was becoming impressed with Knowler, no longer wondering why he had been allowed out without a senior constable to nanny him.

'Sir, I told Mr Ungrish that I would go but that I must insist on seeing the employee concerned before I did. He said, "See who you damned well like, just so long as it is out of my house." I asked him where he was and what was his name and he said that as far as he knew or cared he should be in the stables with the horses and that his name was Gillard. When Mrs Ungrish suggested that she should show me where the stables were, he said, "I don't think so, Isabel. He should be quite capable of finding something so large as a stable." He said that in a sarcastic tone of voice, sir.' Knowler didn't sound as if it had discomposed him at all; not a man, Rogers judged, to be overawed by Ungrish's arrogance. 'Mrs Ungrish showed me out then and as I left she whispered that she was sorry that she had caused me so much bother. I went to the back of the house where I knew the stabling had to be and found Gillard in a store room sitting astride a motorcycle. He refused to get off, would not look at me and appeared to be in a temper. When I did get him to speak he denied that he had been in a fight or in disagreement with Mr Ungrish, or with anyone else. I could not see any signs of an injury on him or of his having been in a scuffle, although he was untidy and his clothing was dirty. This, I admit, could have resulted from his working in the stables, but at the time I didn't think so. He was insolent and continued to refuse to say anything other than to repeat his denial that he had been fighting. I have to say, sir, that I am certain he was lying.'

'That's the gypsy in him,' Rogers said. 'And the sight of your uniform.'

'Yes, sir, so I understood. Obdurateness is the word I should have used.'

'And, of course, there's Ungrish. Is it your opinion that Gillard was shut up by threat or coercion?'

'I'm certain of it, sir.'

'So am I, for all the good it does us,' Rogers agreed. 'Where did the supposed fight take place?'

'It wasn't said, sir, but I gathered in the stables.'

'I know your meeting with Ungrish was brief, but give me your assessment of his personality. I've only ever met him dead and it wasn't with him then.'

Knowler was dubious. 'That's difficult, sir. I saw him only when he was angry, but it seemed to fit him. Domineering? Used to having his own way? Overbearing to Mrs Ungrish? He seemed all those things, but he could have had a more likeable side to him which the circumstances of my visit would hardly bring out.'

'I suppose not, but I've yet to hear anyone suggest that he was less than disliked by his fellow men.' Rogers wondered if that was the corollary to being liked by women. 'Is that the lot?' he asked.

'Yes, sir. I reported the full facts to Sergeant Duffield, who instructed me to endorse the Occurrence Book "No further action" as neither party would substantiate the complaint.'

'Quite right, too,' Rogers said cynically. 'One of the benefits of living in a free country is that we possess an inalienable right to a punch-up with somebody we don't like.'

With Knowler dismissed and sent off to prepare a report on what he had recounted, Rogers used his internal telephone and asked for Woman Detective Sergeant Millier to be sent to him. Millier was an elegant and striking blonde with dark-blue eyes and a beautifully sensual mouth that Rogers considered an unsettling disruption to the men in his department. Were he ever to permit himself to lust after a woman, he might – police disciplinary regulations notwithstanding – lust after her. As it was, he had managed to convince himself that in choosing her from the four women detectives at his disposal for an enquiry, it was for her intelligence and investigational talents alone.

'A chore you'll enjoy, sergeant,' he said to her when she arrived, noting that she wore a suit in a charcoal-grey similar to his own, but enlivened by a sky-blue silk scarf around her throat. 'Collect a nightdress from Sergeant Magnus's office and find out from which shop or store it was bought. This afternoon, before they close. It seems to be a newish and expensive one with a maker's name on it, so it shouldn't mean too many visits if it was bought locally. If whatever shop sells them hasn't the names of the customers buying them, it'll probably have a record of their cheques or credit cards. You're looking for a customer called Marian Kelf – address, 41A Cumberland Crescent – who, I'm certain, left the nightdress in Ungrish's cottage. You know what's happened there?'

She nodded, not a woman given to garrulity, but the beautiful mouth curved in a smile for him.

'Good,' he said affably, wishing to God that she was anybody but a policewoman, that he could equate the way in which she looked at him with a burning wish that he weren't her departmental head. 'One other thing that'll wait until you've sorted out the nightdress business. A woman's wig which I don't have. Probably shoulder length, and brown or black. If I'm right, Miss Kelf will have bought one of those too. And there can't be many salons here that'd stock them.' He thought he might be piling it on her a bit, so added, 'If the situation fits, take somebody with you to help. I must know this afternoon.'

Having sent for Detective Inspector Hagbourne, he began filling his pipe as he waited, this relief for his nervous system being delayed by the telephone bell ringing.

'It's me,' his female caller said with an exaggerated Welsh accent, 'so don't say my name over the phone. I've some information for you.'

'I'm sure I'll love you for it,' he said, putting down his pipe and reaching for a pen. 'Fire away.'

Her voice, discarding her native lilt, was back to a ward sister's crispness. 'Fire away, bloody nonsense,' she retorted. 'It isn't that simple and I'm three hours late for my lunch. If you want it, you'll listen while I'm eating it at the De Reszke Cavendish in fifteen minutes' time.'

'Yes, but . . .' he protested before she cut in with 'Don't forget to bring your wallet with you,' and hanging up on him abruptly.

'That,' he thought as he lit his pipe, was typically Morag; peremptory and bossy, speaking to him as she might to a drunken and verminous patient brought into her ward and, like Twite, expecting him to fork out smilingly for a meal. But, he conceded, for all that, a woman he was fool enough to feel affection for and to admire. When he shaved next, he would search his reflected face for the signs of the emotional softness that must now be creeping up on him.

A morose Hagbourne, having been only on the odd-job side of the investigation and visibly wilting under the pressures of his own work load of paper crime, showed an edge of non-enthusiasm for what Rogers proposed to add to it. He had the ability to make his senior feel a ruthless slave-driver.

'Another not too difficult job, Thomas,' Rogers said cheerfully, making it sound a triviality, 'which I'm sure won't take you long – and it's urgent. You wouldn't know because I've only just left her, but we have in our sights a Miss Marian Kelf, who is a hospital brass hat, one of Ungrish's mistresses and the woman your friend Crapper described so vividly. She was at the cottage as near as dammit at the time Ungrish could have been killed. She's told me, not too truthfully I suspect, that she quarrelled with him over a little matter of virtue defended, ran out leaving him there upright and breathing, and telephoned the rank from a kiosk for a taxi to take her back to Abbotsburn. She says she arrived somewhere here before eight, which unsurprisingly doesn't fit in with the local vicar hearing a scream from near the cottage shortly after that time. It could have been Ungrish dying, although the vicar did think it might have been made by a fox. What doesn't tie in with the fox is that he also heard an unidentified car leaving the lane in a hurry about ten minutes later. You've got the picture?'

'You want me to find the taxi-driver – if he happens to exist.' At least Hagbourne appeared anxious to get on with it and to get it over.

'Oh, he might, Thomas, but the time he picked her up might not be as she says. There can't have been more than one fare needing collection from a place like Alwick even on a wet Wednesday evening, and I want a taxi-driver with a good memory for her description. Not another Crapper.' Rogers passed him the visiting card, now in protective plastic, on which

Kelf had written her address. 'I've to go out, so see that Magnus gets this when he returns from the laboratory. With luck it's got her finger impressions on it and it'll make his day.'

Putting his coat on to go out, Rogers thought glumly of the inroads made on his income by his ex-wife's maintenance, leading always to an end-of-the-month thinning of his wallet and thanked God that the De Reszke Cavendish was unlikely to have on its afternoon's menu anything more hideously expensive than tea and Danish pastries for an apparently starving Morag.

19

Rogers, a man who accepted that food was only a fuel to keep his blood pumping strongly and his body in prime breeding condition, did not consider dining out one of the joys of life and had, consequently, never visited the De Reszke Cavendish. When he entered it, he knew that he was destined to pay dearly for having a uniformed commissionaire open the door for him, for walking on the lush carpeting and for the laundering of the old-fashioned linen tablecloths and napkins. The walls, papered in purple and gold, were heavy with ornate gilt-framed mirrors reflecting the discreet glittering of a huge central chandelier and the few tea drinkers and pastry eaters in there. Troughs of flowers between the tables gave a hothouse fragrance to the air.

Morag was already eating at a two-seater table, her coat folded over the back of her chair. The fawn jacket and skirt she wore with a chocolate-coloured shirt, her loosely arranged black hair, camouflaged her ward sister's severity and her unwomanly penchant for poking hypodermic needles into people. The small pink-shaded lamp on the table gave a softer femininity to her face. It also gave light to what she was eating; to Rogers's disbelieving eyes, a large crab, its split shell garnished with strips of anchovy, masses of cream-sauce-covered fish pieces with bowls of salads and cut French bread on either side.

'I'm sorry I'm late, Morag,' he apologized, taking the chair opposite her. 'Car parking problems again.'

'Yes,' she said, 'and you needn't look at my plate like that. You can't have it because it's not on the menu. It's a regular order the manager has done for me. He was one of my patients.' As if that explained everything.

'A fortunate man,' he offered diplomatically. God, he was certain, was no longer on his side, only on hers. 'I'm not hungry anyway. If I have to have anything, it'll be a coffee.' Against her newly-scrubbed freshness he was conscious of his own staleness, the emerging stubble on his chin and jowls, and the crumpled legs of his once soaked trousers now mercifully hidden beneath the table.

As if he had been heard, a black-frocked waitress came to the table, took his miserable order with slightly raised eyebrows and left. He smiled at Morag digging her fork into the crab's shell. 'I'm here,' he prompted her, 'with ears agog.'

'I shouldn't be doing it for you, George,' she said, 'but you'd have found it out for yourself if I hadn't. Your long-haired man's been noticed waiting around outside the hospital on several occasions. At least, I think it must be him. He's blond, in his twenties, unhandsome, said to be scruffy and what the person who told me called short-assed. Whether he's got a car . . .' She shrugged her unknowingness, putting crab into her mouth without taking the gaze of her clear brown eyes from him.

When he was about to put a question to her, she said, 'Shut up, George, and listen or you'll put me off. One of the trainee nurses from Outpatients has been seen with him a couple of times, so it's accepted that he's her boyfriend. That's for you to find out. Something else. Not too many weeks ago she came on duty with some heavy bruising to her face, which she said happened when she tripped over at home, which wasn't believed. That might fit in with the nasty temper you mentioned.' She frowned. 'Remember, George, I got this in confidence from a friend of mine and I don't want you broadcasting it.'

'And the nurse's name?' he asked. Putting to one side her expensive feeding habits, he felt a warm glow for her.

She shook her head. 'No must do. You can find him easily enough without her.' She returned her attention to her eating as if that was that.

'No I can't,' Rogers said, the warm glow fled. 'Hanging around the hospital occasionally doesn't mean he's going to be there today, tomorrow or even next week.' He stopped as the waitress appeared at his side and placed a beautifully smelling coffee before him. When she had gone, he spoke with a mock toughness. 'Heavy official threat, Morag. No name, no hold back on heavy footed coppers taking Outpatients' department apart.'

For a moment he thought that she was going to be angry, to unleash the smouldering Celtic darkness in her that could wound with cutting words. Instead, she looked at him as if weighing up a patient for signs of rabies and said, 'You wouldn't, would you?'

He was serious, his eyebrows down. 'Yes, I would. I'm investigating an unlawful killing and I can't give a damn who I upset in doing it. I try not to, but it doesn't mean I won't. Her name, Morag, and where I can contact her.'

'You are a bastard, aren't you,' she accused him, then shrugging her shoulders. 'I don't know why I have anything to do with you.'

He hadn't angered her, knew already that he could be a bastard and that, despite it, she was now going to tell him. He smiled at her, wisely keeping silent.

'All right,' she said, having considered it. 'She's Nurse Killick and a Miss. You won't have to go to Outpatients to see her, she'll be finishing her duties at six-thirty this evening.'

'That'll suit me. How shall I know her?' He sipped at his coffee, keeping his eyes on her and thinking how very sexually attractive she was. And, as with his smoking, addictive.

'You shouldn't have any difficulty,' she said. 'She's short and dumpy and has lately been wearing a red coat. And she usually cuts through Maggits Piece to catch a bus home.'

'You had it all ready for me, hadn't you, Morag?' He would always acknowledge that he could never understand the workings of a woman's mind, glad now and then that he could not.

113

'You can guess, I imagine, that she was probably one of Ungrish's one- or two-nights' engagements?' That, he realized too late, had been a descriptive blunder considering his own visit to her last night, but there was no sign that she had applied it to herself. Or even to himself, he thought ruefully.

'I don't wish to know about it,' she said firmly. 'I've only told you because of him. And you did say she wouldn't be brought into it.'

'That's true,' he admitted, 'and so far as I know at the moment she won't be.' He drank more coffee as he watched her eating. There were other matters he wanted from her and knew that he would have to get there with an unaccustomed subtlety. 'I'm worried about Mrs Ungrish,' he said at last. 'I've seen her twice and she seems to be under a more than the usual strain expected at losing a husband.' He paused, thinking bugger the subtlety, he would go the whole hog. Or some of it. He could trust her were she as guarded at the hospital as she was with him. 'She knew he was tom-catting around with other women; well, certainly with one woman in particular. She works in the hospital and I do know who.'

Morag's interest was concentrated on her food and he couldn't see whether she knew or cared. 'I hope that you're not going to tell me,' she said.

'Not her name, no. Only that she's not one of yours, but is a somebody on the administrative staff. You knew that, didn't you?'

'Yes,' she agreed, unsurprised. 'It's been going on for months.'

'But off and on.' He made that a statement.

'Why do you say that?'

'Ungrish used to do his tom-catting out of town in a cottage he'd rented. Last August, the long-haired man we've been discussing was surprised by a very reliable witness peeping through the window of it. As his actions on discovery weren't those of the usual peeper it wouldn't be unreasonable to suppose that he was trying to see whether his nearest and dearest was in there being overly chummy with Ungrish.' He cocked his head. 'Somebody like Nurse Killick?'

'And that's what you wanted her name for?' She sounded ready to leap on him.

'Only peripherally,' he assured her. 'I don't think it's a criminal offence yet to have a gynaecologist as a part-time lover. As I said, I'm more interested in her boyfriend. Does Nurse Killick being there surprise you?'

'Nothing surprises me any more,' she said, 'but if we're talking about the other woman, she was in a nursing home in August.'

'The administrative one?' Seeing her nod, he said, 'That rather explains matters, doesn't it? Under the care of Ungrish?'

'Certainly not.' She was definite, but smiled briefly. 'She had minor surgery for haemorrhoids, which would hardly be something he'd deal with. Or that she would particularly want him to know about. I only know that because the one who told me attends there.' She smiled broadly then. 'The one you wanted God to rot last night, George.'

'I withdraw that now,' he said, having a professionally detached approval of garrulous boyfriends. 'Just so long as you don't confide to him anything about me.'

Morag had finished her crab salad and had nodded to her waitress. 'You'd like something more?' he asked her, wondering at his financial recklessness and remembering the two cheese sandwiches he had eaten for his own lunch.

'It's already ordered; profiteroles with hot chocolate sauce and clotted cream.' She gave him her ward sister's look. 'Don't change the subject, George. I've told you things, so tell me about Isabel knowing that her husband was sleeping with that woman.'

'She didn't know,' he said amiably, realizing that she was femininely curious after all. 'At least, she said she didn't know who she was, and that's reasonable enough.'

'Was she upset about it?'

'She didn't like it, naturally. Her pride was hurt, as I suppose any woman's would be.' He blocked her questioning with his own. 'You suspected that she knew, didn't you?'

'I'd thought about it. I knew there was something wrong because . . . you won't ask her about it if I tell you?'

'No, not unless it's something unlawful,' he promised.

'Just see that you don't,' she warned him, 'or I shall never forgive you. And I mean it. I'm not that close to her, just friendly, although I only see her when she visits the wards with the book trolley. Over the past few months I've noticed that she was losing weight. She hadn't much before, so she wouldn't have been on a diet. It wasn't that so much as her being so highly strung on occasions and looking as though she had something eating her inside. We used to have occasional little chats in my office when she'd finished the ward, and I did get the impression that she was desperately unhappy at home. It wasn't from what she said, but what she didn't. Knowing about him, that didn't surprise me.' Morag was working herself into a little passion. 'Other times in between she would be bright and cheerful and acting as if she hadn't a care in the world.' She grimaced and added, 'Much too bright and cheerful, I sometimes thought.'

The waitress appeared with the profiteroles and Rogers waited. Her attentions weren't helping continuity of thinking and he had to hide a growing exasperation. Too, he wasn't very impressed with what Morag was telling him, mostly confirming what he himself had seen in Isabel Ungrish. With the waitress gone and Morag forking into the gooey mixture, he said, 'Isn't that how you'd expect a woman with a known philandering husband to act?'

'To a point, yes. But not as she did a month or so ago. She was sorting out the books for the patients as if she didn't know what she was doing, muddling them together and dropping some on the floor.' She paused, dabbing chocolate from her mouth with her napkin and clearly thinking out her words. 'When one of the nurses went to help her, she left the trolley where it was and came rushing into my office. She was dreadfully pale and perspiring and holding her stomach. She almost fell into a chair and I said to her "What on earth's the matter, Isabel?" and she said that she thought she was dying. She hadn't meant precisely that and I didn't believe it anyway. When I said that I'd call a doctor she got frantic and said no, she wouldn't allow it and that she would be all right if she could have a drink of water and sit still for a moment. When I insisted, she said she would leave if I did and actually tried to do so. So I didn't. I asked her how exactly she felt and she said she must have eaten something that disagreed with her and felt faint, that she would go home and rest. She'd been a nurse herself once, so I considered her as good a judge of her own condition as I was. In fact, in about ten minutes she had recovered completely. Then she apologized quite unnecessarily and I went out with her to her car. She left after I'd satisfied myself that she was quite capable, not that she would have let me to do anything about it had she not been. I phoned her at her home later to see that she'd arrived safely and she had. She said then that she was completely recovered.' Morag shook her head slowly when she had finished and said, 'Silly woman.'

'So you're not all that happy about it?' Rogers asked, reading behind what she had told him.

Morag pursed her lips. 'I'm not happy that it was a stomach upset. That doesn't generally clear itself within a few minutes, although there could be exceptions. Neither could I fit it in with fainting, or with the mental distress she'd obviously suffered about him.'

'Then I'm not really much better off for knowing, am I? You've no idea at all? You've not asked for a doctor's opinion?'

'Of course I haven't,' she said tartly. 'She wasn't a patient, it wasn't any of my business and I'd have looked a bit of an idiot into the bargain.'

'The last time I saw you,' he said carefully, 'you said something about closing the gate on one's husband and opening it to someone else. Now don't shut up on me, but have you heard whether she was doing that? Possibly, probably if you like, with somebody from the hospital? Of professional standing?'

Morag narrowed her eyes with suspicion in them. 'I also remember saying that if she had, she'd be more clever at keeping it quiet than her husband was. Which means, no, I haven't heard and I don't think I'd have believed it if I had. Who was it?' she demanded.

'I don't know,' he said. 'It's why I'm asking you. Tell me of any male she had contact with while doing her thingy with the books and I might be able to make a good guess.'

'Idiot!' she said witheringly. 'As she visited every ward in the hospital on every Wednesday, you could say she would meet the lot.'

Rogers was grateful that he had a fairly thick skin. 'But not, I imagine, with anybody from the non-ward departments?' He wanted to dispel his unworthy suspicion that Twite might be Mrs Ungrish's so-far-anonymous friend but, since he was the only doctor in the pathology department, was unable to be specific.

'Of course not,' she retorted. 'The books are for patients. Are you going to tell me who he is?'

'On what you've told me, it would only be a guess,' he said mildly, 'and that wouldn't be right.' He saw that her plate was empty. 'Will you have something more?' he asked, believing that there was nothing much more she could tell him, or eat.

'Only coffee,' she said, staring at him as if to convey a message, and then an enigmatic, 'Don't forget, George. If you want anything in this world badly enough, you have to ask for it.'

'Being flawed *Homo sapiens* and willing to admit it,' he said amiably, 'I undoubtedly will.'

After he had paid the bill – as hefty as he had feared and not saying much for the gratitude of the manager as Morag's ex-patient – he left her, having sworn on a hypothetical stack of bibles that the origin of what she had told him was to be held with all the inviolability of a confessional.

Going out through the hotel's lobby, his attention was caught by a gilt-framed reproduction oil painting he had not noticed in entering. It was in the French Impressionist style and signed with what he had difficulty in deciding was Paatss or Hoolff. It showed a garden restaurant at night with a sombre indigo background of narrow houses in a tree-lined street. The central figure was a late nineteenth-century, black-bonneted, black-dressed woman seated at a circular table with a pink surface. Her hand held a glass of amber-coloured liquor, the bottle from

which it came standing at her elbow. A waiter in a dark jacket
and an ankle-length white apron, a tray held under his arm,
stood at one side. The woman was attractive, had a sad and
lonely expression and was obviously waiting in vain.

Waiting for a not-able-to-come Rogers-type lover, he con-
cluded glumly. It wasn't a picture he had found pleasure in
noticing, and wished that he had not; but admitted guiltily to
himself that he had given no thought to Katherine for the past
few hours. Certainly less than he had given to his consideration
of a possible further approach to Morag when not buttoned up
in her ward-sisterly starchiness.

20

Leaving his car on the forecourt of the Headquarters building,
its architectural austereness looking less like an immense cell-
block with the smouldering crimson sky reflected from its
windows and its ashen masonry tinged pink, Rogers shivered in
the thin chill air of the dying sun. Lingard was back, his green
Bentley, its canvas hood down for its seemingly windproof
owner, parked along the line of departmental cars.

In passing along his corridor, Rogers put his head through
the doorway of his second-in-command's office and said, 'See
me, David. I'm in need of some investigational brilliance.' He
noticed that at some time Lingard had changed his shirt and tie.
Which made him feel even more bedraggled.

In his own office he turned on the radiators, having remembered, as he seldom did, the Chief Constable's economy-
minded order for autumn; *All personnel on leaving a room
unoccupied for lengthy periods will switch off lights and heating.*
Keeping on his coat until it warmed up, he looked through
papers left in his tray in the hope that either Hagbourne or
Millier had hit some sort of a winning button. Which, if they
had, hadn't yet reached him.

Lingard, following in a few minutes, sat down, produced his

snuff box and said, 'Nothing to stir your blood, George, so don't get too delirious.'

'I won't,' Rogers assured him dourly. 'I don't think I expected anything. Have you any religious or moral objections to having a tiny drop of the malt before the sun goes down?'

Lingard inhaled snuff elegantly, sniffed vigorously and flapped away loose grains with his green handkerchief. 'I most certainly do,' he murmured, 'but I've just overridden them.'

Rogers tugged open a bottom drawer in his desk and, without lifting the bottle into the view of any chance caller, poured whisky into two sherry glasses that he would always assert just happened to have been in there. They represented his progression from the soft to the hard stuff. He passed one to Lingard and drained his own with a 'Gesundheit', putting it back in the drawer. 'Dear God, but I needed that,' he said. 'Tell me whatever it is you've got.'

Lingard, drinking his, handed the glass back. 'I needed it too. Don't ever detail me to interview a dead gynaecologist's nurse again. She's a Miss Beatrice Abercrombie, knocking on fifty with a moustache nearly as lush as Hagbourne's and, no argument, an archetypal ironclad no-go area who managed to scare me rigid. The consulting rooms were closed, of course, and it was hard work finding out who was employed there, let alone running her to earth when I did. She was serving tea and sandwiches to the more elderly at a Silver Threads Club soirée and refused to speak to me until she'd finished. A waste of time, George,' he added with disgust.

Rogers was reaching dismissively for the pending-tray and a report he had waiting for Lingard's attention. 'If she hadn't, David, if she wasn't, then leave it. I think I've found the lady we're looking for.'

'Dammit, no,' Lingard said, baring his teeth. 'You sent me, and I suffered. You are going to take your share of it. Put me down as a pusillanimous coward, but I could no more ask her if she'd dallied with her boss than I could ask the Chief if he smoked pot. Take it as read that she hadn't, that she wouldn't and probably couldn't. I sounded her out about his goings-on and she shut me up almost as soon as I'd got started. Blasted me, in fact; made my ears ring. She'd heard rumours, she said. Filthy lying slanders about a gentleman *par excellence*, about a man of the highest professional probity and honour. Absolute rubbish and people spreading it should be prosecuted, hung, drawn and quartered, etcetera. And we wretched police for whom, until then, she had had the highest regard should be ashamed of ourselves for listening to them. In short, George, we should be,' he said ironically. 'He was apparently kindly, generous, compassionate and well-loved by all; destined for a tomb in Westminster Abbey.'

'She sounds as if she's his mother,' Rogers said drily. 'At least she's one who doesn't think him unmitigated nastiness, and I suppose that'll help him wherever he is at the moment. Is that the lot?'

'No. Something a mite more interesting. I think,' Lingard qualified. 'Once she'd got started she wasn't all hero-worshipping. Not about Mrs Ungrish, that is. Apparently the good lady would ring him up at his consulting rooms every other five minutes. An exaggeration, I suspect, but I know what she meant. It apparently upset friend Ungrish and he eventually gave instructions to Miss Abercrombie to say he was out, or tied up with a patient. It didn't stop Mrs Ungrish telephoning, but I gather she had little luck in getting to speak to him. Tone of voice only, but I gathered that Miss Abercrombie thoroughly disliked his wife and thought him a saintly sort of character for putting up with her.'

Rogers still couldn't believe that whatever it meant advanced his thinking to any significant degree. 'Probably the jealousy of the uptight virgo intacta, David. That'd be a normal reaction to the wife of a man you'd put on a pedestal. Wives are never considered good enough for them. It isn't important now, but did you ask her if he'd ever slept there?'

'I did. On only a very few occasions that she knew about.'

'Good,' Rogers said. 'Leave her with her tea and sandwiches and let me get you up to date with the lady who does matter and a few other things happening in the outside world.' When he had finished, he handed Lingard the copied Occurrence Book entry. 'I think we'd better have Gillard down here for a chat,

David; he isn't likely to be too forthcoming on his home ground. Thumping Ungrish, who then makes his wife look a fool covering up for him, means that they both had something to hide from us. I don't want to pile any more worries on her, so take him out without any fuss if you can.'

Rogers was about to start writing up notes of his interview with Morag, a part of his brain wondering not too optimistically whether he could claim the cost of her crab salad and profiteroles as a working expense, when his telephone bell rang.

'Froude here, George,' the voice said, light-heartedly enough to presage bad news. 'Depending on how you look at it, I've problems for you. Enough, I fear, to give you a headache.'

'Good for you, Charles.' Rogers knew Froude well as a principal scientist at the Forensic Science Laboratory. 'It's just what I wanted to hear. Break it to me gently.'

'Your Sergeant Magnus caught me at the right moment with my alchemist's kit all set up for a cocaine analysis for Customs and Excise. I don't seem to do much else these days so, when I'd finished with my first come first served customer, I gave yours a couple of tests and there it was. For you, George, I even put a drop on my tongue to check on desensitization. Good stuff too, I'd say. The whisky, I mean.'

Rogers was surprised. 'You mean there's cocaine in it?' His thinking was already worrying at that and not coming up with anything.

'I certainly do. It'll dissolve quite readily in it, although why anyone should want to spoil a good whisky by doing it, that I don't know. The problem is I've not so far run across anybody getting his fix of it in solution. And certainly not with what's in that bottle.'

'You're about to make life difficult for me, aren't you?' Rogers said with feeling. 'Why not?'

'It's difficult already, isn't it, with a couple of dead bodies on your hands?' Froude was enjoying his gentle baiting. 'While I haven't yet worked out the precise concentration of it in the solution, I'm as certain as can be that it's going to be a lethal one. Of course,' he qualified, 'it depends in the ultimate how idiosyncratic or not a person is to it. But, approximating it for you, and definitely subject to errors minus or plus, I'd say there could have been two grammes in the full bottle. Believe me, that would knock down an elephant and a half, and no user who hadn't a death wish would touch it. If it's any comfort to you, fatal poisoning by an overdose of cocaine could fit in nicely with Dr Twite's diagnosis. And when I get around to doing your dead man's stomach fluids and what not – which won't be today because I'm about to go home – I'll let you know all on paper.'

'Charles, I'm grateful,' Rogers said, 'even though you're quite right about it giving me a headache.'

Replacing the telephone after exchanges of mutual esteem, he saw that the colour of the sky had darkened to a deep purple. That being, he considered, so appropriate. In his mind's eye he could see the soaking-wet housebreaker Pring hanging his pathetic deadness from the cottage window. Poor bugger, he thought. Drinking on the job from a brew probably organized for Ungrish; that is, should he have been a whisky, and not a vodka, man. And, possibly, by somebody with an unauthorized access to the cottage. Which could be so with the two keys to it accounted for; one in Ungrish's possession when found dead, the other in his Mercedes. The two grammes of cocaine worried him. If Froude was right, and Rogers was prepared to bet money that he was, that was a massive amount of a dangerous drug and suggested a deliberate intent to kill, apart from being a horribly costly way of doing it. It also put a different light on the violence that did eventually kill him. And, as much to the point now that he was considering it, could Ungrish's mistress have been the intended victim? Or Isabel Ungrish, drinking a less than lethal amount and suffering only the symptoms described by Morag? Or, wildly surmising, with the number of bottles available in the cottage, had it been a liquid form of Russian roulette, Pring being the involuntary and unlucky loser? Although, like Froude, he had never encountered a drug addict who launched into his or her fantasies with a mixture of whisky and cocaine, he couldn't rule it out, for nothing about transmogrifying one's brain with narcotics was too far-fetched for him to believe. Not when he knew that some male addicts injected themselves either in their genitals or in the tips of their noses. 'Please God or whoever,' he said with exaggerated irony to the featureless white wall facing him, 'if you're ever going to be on the side of the good and the unflawed, it'd better be now.'

Filling and lighting his pipe, he opened his pocket-book and reached for a pen. Making notes – not in erasable pencil, which judges frowned on – was an official requirement; adding below them his own non-evidential comments and opinions, before they pupated into clumsy moths and flew out of his skull, was his own discipline. After he had written for the official record, he added the table of what he needed to encapsulate and remember – errors and omissions always excepted when he did so.

UNGRISH, Simon. Rumoured divorce action. Grounds? Petitioner him (ex. Dr Twite) or her (ex. M. Kelf)? Cocaine addict? Whisky drinker?

UNGRISH, Isabel. Motives: rumoured divorce, killing cat or liaison with unidentified professional man.

KELF, Marian. Motives: jealous or dispossessed mistress of Ungrish, involvement in criminal offence and deception and possible threat of disclosure to employers/police. Use of car to cottage? Not taxi? Whisky drinker?

GILLARD, Obadiah. Quarrel, unknown cause, with Ungrish. Mrs Ungrish know/concerned?

LONG-HAIRED MALE. Possessive jealousy, Nurse Killick? Violent temper (ex. Revd Dodson). Car?

KILLICK (Nurse). Ungrish's mistress? Past/Present? Associate of above (ex. Sister M. Anderson). Motive, jealousy if discarded. Car?

UNIDENTIFIED MALE. Lover, Mrs Ungrish? Doctor from hospital? Motive: need to dispose of Ungrish, unknown reasons?

TRANSPORT OF BODY. If taken from cottage to rail crossing in Cambridge (after 10.09 pm), second car necessary for journey to cottage and from crossing to —? Clarify one/two cars heard, Revd Dodson.

COCAINE. Check known local sources. Drug Squad. Laboratory check on remaining bottles.

That done, he could now see more clearly how, so far, foggily unclear everything was. It confirmed only what he had always known; that *Homo sapiens*'s built-in mechanism for procreating his species was as much a source of unprayed-for trouble as was his unquenchable greed and itch for power. He said, 'Sod it!', put his pocket-book away and concentrated on reading what his text books had to say about cocaine.

When he had finished the few pages dealing with it, he understood more about the agreed physical symptoms its addicts suffered, less from the differing opinions offered on the psychopathic behaviour that could arise from its use. One he would remember was that, apart from cocaine being a short-lived supercharge to a transcendental self, it was also a powerful aphrodisiac. As well as increasing erotic tension it could also remove normal inhibitions, not unusually resulting in sexual perversion in the male when potency, if not desire, had diminished.

Putting the books away, he reached for the telephone and dialled the number of the pathology laboratory. Being told that Dr Twite was then operating in the mortuary, he asked to be put through to him. 'Wilfred,' he said, 'would it be convenient for you to do some quite minor surgery on Ungrish? If I come down to you now?'

'It's never convenient when I'm on something else, old chum.' It was Twite's standard reply when asked for something to be done immediately. 'What is it?'

'A face job. It wouldn't take you more than a few minutes.' He was not particularizing because he didn't want Twite doing it before he got there.

The pathologist was thinking about that. 'You're on to something more than I found?' he said at last.

'Yes, but in a way it's likely to prove negative and nothing for which you'd have needed to look. I'll be there in a couple of minutes and explain all.' He had pressed his finger on the disconnect button before he finished, cutting off any protestations Twite might have been about to make. Not that he would believe him, but he could always blame it on to a faulty connection.

125

21

A cold grave excepted, Rogers was convinced that there were better places to be than in a mortuary smelling of dead flesh, formalin and scented cigarette smoke. Twite, his fatness made fatter in a loose green gown and plastic apron, was working on the ravaged body of an old woman laid out on one of the necropsy tables and already subjected to the indignities of his scalpel and rib shears. Nothing, Rogers knew, would be spared in a search for the hole through which death had entered. Not even his own sensibilities which, prompted by such horrors, pushed him into murmuring to himself *Gather ye rosebuds while ye may* and thinking of missed opportunities of gathering them with women like Katherine and Morag as he did so.

Twite, on Rogers's entering, dismissed his brown-overalled attendant with an 'I can manage now,' laid down the saw he had been about to use and stripped off his smeared rubber gloves. 'You're a bloody nuisance, old chum,' he said amiably enough, although with something that might have been irritation showing in his eyes.

Rogers, soft-centred about the dissection of old ladies, averted his gaze from the table. 'I am, aren't I,' he agreed. 'I thought you'd like to know about our housebreaker. You're a clever fella, Wilfred; he did die from a vegetable poison. An overdose of cocaine in the whisky he drank at the cottage.'

'Ah!' That had pleased the pathologist. 'So who'd do a damned stupid thing like that? And why ask me to do whatever it is you want me to do on Ungrish?'

'Because it's a fair bet that it was meant for him,' Rogers said, pointing out the obvious. 'Or, possibly, the woman he happened to be entertaining at the time. There's a limiting factor, of course, and it'd help considerably if we can satisfy ourselves that Ungrish was, or was not, a cocaine addict himself.'

'It's daft, and I've never heard of anyone lacing his whisky with it,' Twite objected. 'And I'm sure that even if he had, neither I nor the laboratory people would be able to isolate what might be left in him.'

'No, let me make my point,' Rogers said. 'There was a lethal dose in it, so he wouldn't be drinking it even were he a cocaine-in-solution addict. I'm thinking that if he used cocaine, say by sniffing or by hypodermic syringe, it would at least prove its origin. And, if he did, he'd probably show the signs of it. You know, needle marks in the arms, ulceration or perforation of the nasal septum.'

'Who needs a pathologist when there's Detective Superintendent Rogers to tell them what's what?' Twite said with amiable mockery. 'The needle marks I've done already. It's a routine pathological check and there aren't any. The nose I haven't done because it isn't and nobody told me anyway. What was your lethal dose?' He moved to his working top, put a cigarette in his mouth and lit it, then took fresh rubber gloves from a cardboard box and began pulling them on.

'The laboratory says probably two grammes,' Rogers told him, following his example and lighting his already filled pipe, mainly because of the mortuary smell and not because his nervous system was calling out its usual distress signals.

'God Almighty!' Twite said fervently. 'Do you know there's about fifteen grains in one gramme and, give or take a tolerance to it, a very few grains would be more than ample for a fatal dose?'

'I know,' Rogers assured him. 'Apparently two grammes would knock over an elephant and a half, although which half of an elephant it does it to is a problem. Not that our housebreaking friend drank that much, but being only halfway out of the window he seemed to have died remarkably quickly. Is that what you'd have expected him to have done?'

'I certainly wouldn't be surprised. There'd be this sort of sequence following his drinking it. His breathing would become rapid as paralysis of the respiratory centre took effect, he could experience nausea, convulsions and possible fainting. He could, in fact, die within a very few minutes, and probably did in his reaching the window to get some air in his lungs.' The cigarette in his mouth, waggling as he spoke, dropped un-noticed ash on to his tie. 'While I don't pretend to a specialized knowledge on what his mental condition might be at the time, it must have been grossly chaotic. While absorption by the brain of small amounts of cocaine might be a stimulant, larger amounts could produce a mental confusion of terror, panic, an alienation from reality and, most probably, hallucinosis.' He shook his head and more ash fell. 'It doesn't bear thinking about, and I rather think that I'll stick to my nicotiana taba-cum.'

He moved to the instrument cabinet, selected a scalpel and led the way to the Body Room. 'I hope that I'm going to waste my time, old chum,' he said. 'I'll be very surprised if poor old Ungrish did take the stuff, for it wouldn't mix at all well with obstetrics and gynaecology.'

In the room, the bank of refrigerated drawers hummed and vibrated, retarding the decomposition of their contents in a temperature close to freezing. While Twite could regard them dispassionately as filing cabinets, Rogers saw them as metal coffins containing unsettling reminders of his own mortality. He noticed that *UNGRISH, S. (MR)* had been substituted for the original *JOHNSON, D.G.* on the card, and that *PRING, N.* was in unhappy juxtaposition at his side.

Twite pulled out the drawer containing Ungrish – chilled now to a pale yellow marbling – exposing his body down to the waist. Despite his earlier confidence that there were no needle marks, he examined at length the skin of the arms, shaking his head and muttering inaudible words to himself. When he started cutting at the side of the nose with the scalpel, Rogers moved so that the adequately bulky mass of pathologist was interposed between himself and what he quite definitely did not wish to see.

While Twite worked in silence, Rogers felt, or imagined that he felt, Ungrish's presence. Although he neither believed nor disbelieved that it could actually be, he had sensed this sort of presence before when with the violently dead, usually accepting with reservations that the unverifiable entity was urging him to get on with it, adding to the burden he already had of bringing

128

to justice whoever had brought death to its physical body. Now he felt no such urging, rather the impression of a posthumous whatever it was taking an interest in what Twite was doing to its earthly nose. He shrugged away what was probably mere fantasizing and thought about more pleasurable physical matters such as, given the merest opportunity, of manoeuvring himself again into Morag's bed.

Five minutes later Twite said a satisfied 'Ah', slammed the drawer shut and turned to Rogers, his expression that of a man delivered from error. 'As I was convinced,' he said. 'He wasn't. No perforation, no ulceration and no inflammation. You were barking up the wrong tree there, old chum.'

'A half-hearted bark, Wilfred, and I'm quite happy I was wrong.' Rogers had noticed his relief. Having originally failed to identify a colleague, it would have been embarrassing to have also failed to diagnose in him an addiction to cocaine. It reminded him. 'Our friend's face is now in a terrible mess, don't you agree?' he asked. 'What with the train going over it and now your having cut his nose about, we've rather gone over the top for him being recognizable. He hasn't been formally identified yet and I don't propose that Mrs Ungrish should do it, even if she could. She's in a bad enough state already and it wouldn't be kind. Would you do it when you give your evidence of the cause of death?'

That didn't please Twite. 'It's a bit unusual isn't it? Can't you get somebody else?' With a fresh cigarette in his mouth, he was dropping ash down the front of his gown.

'Who, for example? I don't know of any relatives of either of them. I couldn't ask a woman to do it anyway.' He chose his words carefully, watching for Twite's reaction. 'I suspect that Mrs Ungrish has in tow a male friend or lover, possibly a medical man. If he had known Ungrish, as he probably had, he might be able to do it. That is, of course, if I can find out in time who he is.'

The only reaction visible to the detective was a jerking of his head in guileless surprise. 'Good Lord!' he said, 'I'd never have believed it. It just doesn't sound like her. Don't tell me who, but you're sure?'

'No, I said suspicion only.' Rogers felt that he should eliminate Twite as her possible lover, feeling a little shame-faced that it had ever entered his mind to consider him as such. 'Will you do the identification?'

Twite grimaced his unwillingness. 'Reluctantly, old chum, but I will.' He smacked his hand against the metal of the drawer. 'If we've finished with him, I've the poor old dear to get on with.'

'A couple of questions only, Wilfred. And not in there.' Rogers indicated the door into the mortuary, thinking of the meal he would need to have soon, knowing that already his clothing would be pungent with the smell of formalin and repellent for eating in. 'Is cocaine used in the hospital? And if so, where is it kept? Who has access to it and why?'

Twite shook his head emphatically. 'You're wasting your time if you think your stuff came from here. Bulk cocaine is stored under lock and key in the hospital pharmacy. As the staff's required to keep a record and monitor all supplies used or issued, any improper outgoings would be known. The pharmacy itself is barred and padlocked at night and no doubt checked at intervals by the hairy-chested security men we have floating about. No chance at all,' he said decisively. 'It's as safe there as if it was in the vault of a bank.'

'We've had a few banks lose money from their vaults,' Rogers pointed out. 'Is the pharmacy under the control of the Chief Administrative Officer?'

'Yes, it is, and he's a good reason for knowing that there couldn't be any fiddling.' Twite was obviously anxious to defend the purity of the hospital's management.

'I'm sure you're right,' Rogers said, straight-faced. 'What happens to cocaine when it's handed out? Does it go to the wards?'

Twite frowned. 'I know what you're thinking, and you're wrong. We're now talking about cocaine being used in minute quantities in preparations for the patients. They're issued to authorized persons only and when they reach the wards are kept in locked drugs cupboards, accessible only to the medical and senior nursing staff.'

130

'Would there be any cocaine not in preparations? In the wards, I mean.'

'I'm sure not. And if there were, certainly nothing like two grammes of it. Are you satisfied now?' Twite asked, smiling genially and shuffling his feet in wanting to go.

'I think so,' Rogers conceded, knowing inwardly that he was not. 'The second question. Would stomach pains, perspiring and pallor of the face suggest anything particular to you?'

Twite raised his eyebrows. 'As you describe it, old chum, and with my not being there to see for myself, yes. Bellyache from any number of causes.'

'Question wrongly put,' Rogers said. 'I'll rephrase. If an unaddicted person were given a less than fatal dose of cocaine in solution, would you anticipate those symptoms?'

'Ah, we're back to that, are we?' Twite thought about it. 'It could, but it needn't. It'd depend on the amount taken and the physiological reaction of the person taking it . . . obviously.' He shook his head and pursed his lips. 'You won't get an offhand answer to that from any doctor but his own; there're too many variables.' He had plainly a medical man's caution in not wanting to know to whom the detective was referring. 'If you've finished, perhaps you'll now get out of my hair and let me get on with something useful.'

It was dark when Rogers reached the outside air and the mist had thickened into a fog. It was also chilly and smelt strongly of meals being cooked in the hospital's kitchens, though not strongly enough to dispel the reek of formalin he carried with him like an off-putting body odour. For all that, it hadn't by any means been a waste of time for a detective superintendent who already had very little regard for the trustworthiness of either Marian Kelf or the administrative department's records.

22

With less than fifteen minutes to the time of Nurse Killick's leaving the outpatients' surgery, Rogers walked around the rear of the hospital, through the parking lot, and stationed himself at the entrance to Maggits Piece.

Long ceasing to have been a piece of anything, it provided only a lengthy and narrow alley between a stretch of medieval town wall and the blank brick backs of warehouses. Used infrequently, an economy-minded local authority had provided it with a light at each end where they were least needed. Blanketed by the dank fog, the light under which Rogers stood was the burnt-orange of a miniature sun dying in darkness. It was quiet but for the muted growling of traffic passing the far end of the alley. With the fog damp on his skin, Rogers was considering that given a hansom cab or two and a couple of gas lamps, this could be a suitable milieu for Jack the Ripper; a dismal enough place and fit only for throat-cutting.

With his hopes for a solution to his investigation centred for the moment on Marian Kelf, he felt in his bones that Nurse Killick and her bad-tempered boyfriend were going to be a waste of time, an enquiry that had to be furthered if only to eliminate them from his thinking.

When two women approached the entrance from the direction of the hospital, neither answering to the description given of Killick, they skirted wide of him, warily and with eyes averted, their footfalls echoing between the walls as they quickened their walking. It had to be, he mollified his wounded *amour propre*, the hazy illumination and dark shadow that had made him appear a figure of apparent menace.

When she came, suddenly looming out of the fog and easily recognizable in her scarlet coat, she started in apprehension when he spoke to her. 'Miss Killick?' he asked. 'It's all right, I'm a police officer.'

It didn't seem so all right to her, but she did halt, though out of his reach. 'What is it you want?' she said in a voice that shook.

'A few words about Mr Ungrish.' He reached his hand into a pocket of his overcoat. 'Would you like to see my warrant card?'

She had moved closer and was staring at his face. 'I don't have to,' she said. 'I've seen you in the hospital. Why do you want to see me?'

Her voice had a nasal squeak to it that he knew would put his teeth on edge should he have to listen to much of it. Obviously Ungrish had been made of sterner stuff, as well as possessing a catholicity of taste in the shapes of the women he seduced into his cottage. She was definitely dumpy and, although with a loose coat on, manifestly top-heavy with her breasts. She couldn't yet be twenty and hers was an immature prettiness with her wide ingenuous eyes only just clear of an overhanging fringe of straw-coloured hair, a small pert nose and a pink mouth that even in repose left her uppper teeth showing.

'I waited here, Miss Killick,' he said, 'because I assumed you wouldn't wish to be seen by me where you work. We can go somewhere else, if you'd prefer.'

'No, there isn't anywhere, but I'd like to get away from the light.'

He thought he understood why and looked around him, seeing a deep doorway in the side of the warehouse wall, heavily shadowed and out of the view of any passerby, but from which could be seen the nearest cars in the park.

In there, his feet among discarded cans and paper rubbish, he was unable to see a lot more than the pale disc of her face. That near, she smelled strongly of iodoform. Believing that restraint and subtlety would be wasted, he said, 'I take it that you know Mr Ungrish has been found dead on the Madbrook Farm rail crossing, that we're enquiring about the women he is alleged to have slept with at different times? You were one of them, weren't you?'

'Yes,' she replied softly with no trace of an objection to his question in her voice. 'But I wasn't . . .'

'Yes you were.' He cut short whatever she was about to deny. 'I know, so please don't quibble. You went to his cottage at

Alwick in his car on one or more occasions. You were obviously not there for an all-night nursing session on a gynaecological case, so we can assume you went there to go to bed with him. Your boyfriend – the one with the long hair – knew it, and when he thumped you in the face it was probably because of it. Is that so?'

She didn't speak, but he saw her nod her head.

'If that's all there was in it so far as you are concerned,' he said, 'I'm not interested in doing anything about it. And I certainly wouldn't pass it on.'

She surprised him. 'I don't really mind. Most everybody knows something about it. Except my mum and dad, though.'

Rogers had trodden on a step that hadn't been there. She sounded as though it were something to be proud of and, from her point of view – a trainee nurse being the mistress, even a temporary one, of a senior gynaecologist – it probably was. He said, 'I'm glad you're being frank with me. It was in August, wasn't it?'

'Yes.'

'Several times?' She wasn't, he thought gratefully, going to be difficult at all.

'Yes.'

He could see, although only vaguely, that she was arching her body from the door against which she had been leaning. Although he chose to see only an unconscious suggestiveness in the way it was being done, it could be that a dark doorway and a man within grabbing distance was a turn-on for her.

He edged a little further away from her and cleared his throat. 'Did your boyfriend follow you out to the cottage?'

'Yes, he did. The last time I was there.'

'Tell me what happened when he did.'

'He hit me, like you said, when he met me the next day.' So far as he could read into her words, it hadn't been too uncommon an event.

'No, I meant what happened out at the cottage.'

The gloom could not conceal the surprise in her face. 'Nothing. I didn't know he'd followed me until he told me.'

'You don't live with him then?'

'No, I don't.' She was offended, her voice's squeakiness more apparent. 'I live with my mum and dad.'

'Does he follow you often?' He was only curious now.

'I think so. I don't always know when he does.'

'And when he sees you with another man he hits you?'

'He gets very angry,' she said evasively.

Having allowed Ungrish to make love to her and being unlikely to have refused a similar concession to her forceful boyfriend, he didn't put the question to her, but asked, 'What is his name?'

She hesitated, then said, 'Harold Crutcher.'

'His address, please.'

'Number 7 Huish Road at Blackfell.'

That rang a quite clangorous bell in the detective's recollection. 'He's a friend of Neville Pring's then?'

'I don't know. Is he?'

'You haven't heard his name mentioned?'

She shook her head. 'No, he's never said.'

He knew he could be misled but, despite her initial attempt at it, she had impressed him as a girl naively honest enough not to lie. 'What does Crutcher do for a living?' he asked.

'He's a tree surgeon.'

It was a pretentious title for a man who felled and trimmed trees and, until thinking better of it, he had felt tempted to comment ironically that she appeared to confine her favours to the medical profession. 'Do you know if he ever met or spoke to Mr Ungrish?'

'No. He wouldn't. He wouldn't dare.' She had straightened her body as if wanting to leave, turning her head to look towards the entrance to the alley.

It could have been her demeanour that triggered it, but he thought that he was being watched, feeling the frisson in him that could result from the unseen and intense regard of another. 'Do I take it that you are not all that fond of him?' he said.

'I don't think so.' She was hesitant. 'He won't leave me alone.'

'And you're frightened of him?' She was, he guessed, weak

and silly-minded enough to eventually submit wholly to a man who refused so resolutely to take no for an answer.

'Yes, I am.' Tears suddenly glistened in her eyes. 'Please let me go,' she pleaded. 'I have to go home.'

He put a comforting hand on her shoulder. 'Don't cry about it,' he said, worried that she would do so in full flood. 'I've nearly finished. Are you thinking that he's watching you now?'

'I don't know; he might be.' She wiped her eyes with the tip of a gloved finger.

'Don't let it worry you,' he said reassuringly. 'If he is I'll deal with him, and make sure he doesn't hit you again. Were you with him last Wednesday evening?'

'Wednesday?' she said blankly. 'I was home.'

'You didn't see him or hear from him?'

'No. He doesn't come there because dad won't have him.'

'Has he ever . . .'

She had stiffened, looking away from him in the direction of the car park. An incongruously long-haired Crutcher in a sheep-skin-collared bomber jacket was walking stiff-legged towards them. As short as Rogers had imagined him, his lack of height was compensated by a burly sturdiness of body. He carried in one hand a short length of branch, and if a man's intent could be projected by his carriage and gait his was shown as a furious bull's need for charging violence. It carried to the detective a message that there would be no exchange of civilized words, that if he didn't wish to have his skull badly dented then he had better be prepared to do something about it. It had, he now reflected ruefully, been a mistake to go into the doorway with Nurse Killick.

He stepped out into the open as Crutcher came at him with a rush, his teeth bared, the club in his hand held shoulder high and swinging. Rogers heard the girl behind him screaming 'No, Harry!' and got no more words out of his mouth than 'I'm a police off . . .' before the club hit numbness into his uplifted arm. In an immediate response he sunk his knotted fist hard into the belly carelessly exposed to it, stopping the man abrupt-ly as if he had run into a wall. Dropping the club, his mouth gaped and he made a hoarse whooping noise, his eyes squeezed tight in anguish. With his face suffusing to the colour of an old brick, he pressed his hands to his belly, dropping slowly to the asphalt on his knees and vomiting.

Feeling his arm to be jellied and beginning to hurt, Rogers was not disposed to feel sorry for him. He was getting too old for brawling with unreasoning primitives and it went ill with his rank. He picked up the piece of wood and flung it into the darkness, hearing hurrying footfalls from the alley as he did so. The doorway was empty and Nurse Killick had fled; wisely, he thought.

Crutcher, wheezing his distress, had finished vomiting – it had been all liquid and smelled repulsively of sour beer – and Rogers grasped one-handed the sheepskin collar of his jacket, hauling him to his feet. 'Now listen,' he growled close to his ear, not releasing his hold on him. 'I'm a police officer and I was questioning Miss Killick. We were in that doorway because she was frightened she would be seen with me. Frightened of a lout like you who's now going inside for a talk. Do you understand?' He shook him to emphasize it.

Whatever fighting aggression had been in Crutcher was now withered, although he was by no means cowed. 'How was I to know?' he muttered. 'I thought you was screwing her.' He grimaced. 'You hurt me hitting me low like that.'

Rogers took his hand from his jacket collar, concealing the fact that his arm felt as if it were about to drop off. He had sized him up as a brainless rough-house tough with the misfortune of possessing a frail stomach and he expected no further trouble. 'Where's your car?' he asked him.

'In the park. It's my truck.' He was doing his own sizing up of Rogers with eyes that still watered from his vomiting and, whatever intent he had formed, the time for it didn't appear to be now.

'Lead on,' Rogers ordered him. 'You can give me a lift to the police station.' He added without rancour, 'If you make any more trouble, I'll hit you again. Bloody hard this time.'

The truck, parked close to the spot from which Crutcher had appeared, was a muddy-brown open flat-back, old and decrepit, and carried a half-load of tree cuttings. It sagged on worn-out springs as Rogers, following Crutcher, climbed into the passenger seat. He kept his damaged arm clear of the side framework as the truck jolted and rattled out of the car park and into the street, the dense oily smoke spluttering from the exhaust adding to the fog through which traffic crept and in which buildings were swallowed up.

Rogers wasn't complaining about it, but in an uncharacteristic dog-in-the-manger attitude was hoping that the fog also covered the airport, and that it would persist long enough to ground Katherine and the 10.30 a.m. flight to Paris. At least until he had cleared up the killing of Ungrish and those crime files waiting for him in his office cupboard.

23

Rogers, steering a glowering Crutcher along the corridor to his office, sat him in the visitors' chair. He had spoken only to give him directions during the short journey, a silence deliberately imposed to give Crutcher time to consider his position and to worry about it.

Rogers took his own chair, immediately picking up the internal telephone and dialling the number of Sergeant Magnus's office. 'Sergeant,' he said, staring at Crutcher to note his reaction, 'there's a truck parked at the back near the garages. Drop whatever you're doing and do an immediate check on it. The usual things; driver's cabin, engine, documents and the load-bed contents. Call me back with the result.'

He had replaced the telephone without seeing any significant change in Crutcher's expression, and that was what he expected from his type. In the unflattering fluorescent light of the ceiling tube, Rogers was able to read him with more certainty. Framing a heavy-boned face, his hair – there were grains of sawdust in it – had obviously been bleached for he had thick black eyebrows and a dark beard stubble on chin and jowls lumpy with muscle. His pale-blue eyes were bloodshot and set too close together to suggest the likelihood of amiable frankness, his thin-lipped mouth, clamped shut, showing a clear distaste for the detective. His jacket was stained with green smears and he wore torn flannel trousers tucked into turned-down wellington boots. He was, as Morag had said, scruffy and distinctly unhandsome. Rogers, not overly concerned how he looked or was dressed, considered him only just short of being an aboriginal throwback.

'We've a lot to talk about, haven't we?' he said comfortably, leaning back in his chair as if it weren't very important and that they had all night to do it in.

Crutcher wasn't worrying himself sick either. 'I told you,' he said, his words coming in the fumes of stale beer. 'I didn't know you was a copper. I thought you was one of them doctors messing about with my girl. That's fair enough, ain't it?'

'Oh?' Rogers was excessively surprised. 'I'm not concerned about *that*, it's only common assault anyway. I was thinking more on the lines of incitement to commit the crime of burglary. Although, for all I know, you might have been there yourself.'

Crutcher looked at him as though he were mad. 'What're you getting at?' he said, an edge of anger in his voice. 'Are you trying to balls me up or something?'

'I was wondering how you felt about Neville Pring?'

Crutcher blinked and his forehead, not too visible behind the hair, creased. 'I don't feel anything. Why should I? What's he got to do with me?'

Rogers was chancing it, but Crutcher hadn't apparently heard of his death. 'The cottage at Alwick,' he said. 'Didn't you tip him off about it? It'll certainly be called incitement by the judge who'll put you down for it.'

'I don't know what you're talking about,' Crutcher grunted, although his eyes had said that he did when the cottage was mentioned.

'But you do know Pring?'

'Yes,' he replied reluctantly.

'And you know the cottage I'm talking about? The one where you threatened to hit the vicar – and to kick his dog, for all I know – when he caught you looking through the window. Back in August, if you'd like me to be more specific.' When there was no answer and he could almost see Crutcher's slow-moving brain working that out, he said, as if doing him a favour, 'We can line you up on an identification parade if you think it'll help you to remember. I've no doubt the vicar has a good memory for a face with hair hanging all over it.' Rogers suspected that he wore it like a woman's so that he might force a fight on anyone incautious enough to jeer at it.

He thought about that, too, sucking at his scarred knuckles with unease in his expression. 'That weren't nothing. I was looking for my girl.'

Rogers left the unfortunate Pring lying in his refrigerated limbo, his connection with Crutcher unlikely to throw any light on who killed Ungrish. 'So I understand,' he said. 'And she was inside with Mr Ungrish?'

'She were.' There was a sort of satisfaction in the way he said it.

'Which would make you angry with him? To make you want to put the boot in, so to speak?'

Rogers was expecting an occasional no-answer when a question touched on fact, and he got one. 'All right,' he said curtly, 'I'll take it that you would have if the vicar hadn't come along. When was the next time you went there? Last Wednesday? The night Mr Ungrish was killed?'

Crutcher's lumpy jaw dropped and the brick colour flushed his face. 'Killed!' he managed to get out. 'Who said he was killed!'

'I did. When somebody hits you hard enough it's not un-known. Somebody like you, for instance.'

There was a longer silence then, with heavy breathing, and it was Crutcher who broke it. 'I ain't standing for that,' he said angrily. 'I want to see a solicitor.'

'Of course you do,' Rogers said. 'It's a sure sign of guilt about something. Do you have one?'

'No.' He seemed to be having second thoughts after Rogers's ready acceptance of it.

'I'll send for the list and you can choose who you want. I have to tell you, though, it doesn't stop my questioning you.'

140

Crutcher did more of his thinking, his thick eyebrows hard down, and finally muttered, 'No, it don't matter. I ain't got nothing to hide.'

'Good,' Rogers said. 'I'm pleased to hear you haven't. So now you won't mind telling me where you were on Wednesday evening. Say, between seven and eleven o'clock?'

'I wasn't there. I was out with one of my mates.' His face lightened, his manner seeming to say that this could rock the detective back on his heels.

'Doing what, and where?'

'We was out in different places looking for dead trees to buy. I do loads of logs as well.'

'In the dark?' Rogers was feeling more comfortable, less tempted to bite off Crutcher's head now that his arm had given up its complaining twinges of pain and was contenting itself with a sometimes forgettable throbbing.

'It don't make no difference, I can see them.'

'What's your mate's name? Trotting around in the dark looking for dead trees needs a bit of corroboration to be believable.'

Crutcher's features were heavy with outrage. 'You ain't dragging him into this. He ain't nothing to do with it.'

'A commendable sense of loyalty,' Rogers said ironically. 'Was your anonymous friend with you when you smashed up Mr Ungrish's car and sprayed *Leave Her Alone* all over it? Presumably meaning leave Miss Killick alone?'

That had been a hit, awareness showing in Crutcher's eyes. He had started perceptibly, holding his body rigid. Then he relaxed, his face wooden. 'I don't know what you're talking about.'

'Nor when I say that you telephoned him at his house and threatened him? Told him that he would pay for what he was supposed to have done?'

Not so evident a hit there, but one all the same and evoking the same response. 'I don't know what you're talking about,' he said, though beginning to look defensive, the muscles in his jaw working hard. 'I didn't hit him. You got no right to say I did. I never even saw . . .'

141

The telephone bell had interrupted him and Rogers lifted the receiver. It was Magnus and he said, 'All right to speak, sir?'

'Without shouting,' Rogers told him, keeping his eyes on Crutcher who was apparently deep in his thinking again, and worrying about it.

'A piece of sacking in the back under the brushwood,' the sergeant said. 'It's soaked in blood and still tacky inside the folds. Dried blood in the floorboards – at least, it looks like blood. Quite a lot of it, too. Is that what you wanted?'

'It surprises me.' He couldn't say with Crutcher in earshot that it didn't fit Ungrish's death, or express his bafflement too obviously. 'Anything else?'

'The Road Fund Licence was issued for somebody else's Ford PLG, and the registration number altered to the truck's.'

'That should shake him,' Rogers said sardonically. 'The lot?'

He closed down on Magnus's 'That's all, sir,' and forced Crutcher's attention by staring hard at him and tapping a pencil on the desk. 'That was bad news for you,' he said, sternness in his face. 'What's your explanation for the blood in the back of your truck? And don't dam' well tell me that you cut yourself shaving.'

Crutcher's eyebrows beetled and he made a not very convincing show of being shocked into anger. 'That ain't right,' he said, his voice rising. 'I didn't know.'

'And you may also not know how many times that's been said to me.' Rogers frowned at him. 'Somebody else you wouldn't know put it there, did they?' He paused and visibly came to a decision. 'I think a cell's the best place for you while I find out more about it.' He reached and lifted the telephone receiver.

Crutcher half-rose from his chair. 'No!' He had trouble in getting it out. 'It was rabbits. I've been shooting them.'

Rogers replaced the receiver. 'Sit down,' he told him sharply. 'It couldn't have been, there's too much of it. It's much more likely to have come from Mr Ungrish's body. You took him to the Madbrook rail crossing and dumped him there, didn't you?'

That was as astonishing to Crutcher as the detective had expected it to be, but as a serious accusation on an unwarranted assumption it had the effect of galvanizing him into disclosure.

'I didn't,' he cried hoarsely. 'God help me, but I didn't. It was a deer and I can prove it.'

'Prove it then.' Rogers had added 'You cruel sod' under his breath, disliking him the more.

Crutcher had seen the anger in his eyes and it put urgency in his words. 'I was with my mate like I said. He did it with his crossbow. I was only watching.'

'Watching? You were more likely cutting the poor thing's throat. You'd be the sort to do it, wouldn't you? And you certainly provided the transport. When?'

'When you said, on Wednesday. We was out all evening.' There was eagerness in him to explain now, and he was sweating with it.

'Where?'

'Gryke Moor, near the woods. I thought he had a licence.'

'You're a liar,' Rogers said tersely, still unprofessionally angry. 'There isn't such a thing. Give me his name.'

There was no resentment and only a token resistance. 'Do I have to?'

'Not if you want to stay inside for a long time. Longer than you need while I find out if he actually exists. And,' he added, 'whether it was on Wednesday evening.'

'Willie Doust,' he said grudgingly, 'but don't tell him it was me.'

Rogers knew Doust as a convicted poacher who would deny his own existence until blue in the face should it suit his purpose. 'Until I get something from him,' he said to Crutcher, 'you're going to be detained on charges of deer-stealing and the theft of a Road Fund Licence which just happens to be exhibited on your truck.' He leaned forward, his gaze hard on him. 'Don't go out of here thinking that I'm satisfied you know nothing about Mr Ungrish's death; I'm not. I *am* satisfied that you threatened him over the telephone, that you wrecked his Mercedes and that you put young Pring on to breaking into his cottage; and all because Miss Killick showed some good taste in preferring him to your unsavoury self. It'll take a few hard facts to convince me that you didn't finally kill him for it.'

When Crutcher started to protest, he stood and walked

around the desk to him. 'One other thing,' he said grimly, imposing his physical presence on him. 'When you get out – *if* you get out – and I hear the merest whisper that you've laid a hand on Miss Killick once more, I'll forget I'm a policeman and come looking for you.' It was a threat he wouldn't and couldn't follow up, but the best he could do for her.

With an apparently fatalistic Crutcher, charged and lodged in a cell – more docile about it than had been anticipated – Rogers returned to his office and gave instructions to one of his detective sergeants to look for and find Doust. When he had, he was to invite him to an obligatory conference with Detective Superintendent Rogers who now accepted that Crutcher, like Pring, amounted to no more than a damned nuisance, impinging his grubby misdemeanours on an investigation in which he was not criminally involved, giving Rogers both a sore arm and a load of useless work in trying to eliminate him from it. Although Crutcher was temperamentally capable of using severe violence and had something of a reason for inflicting it on Ungrish, his truck – which Rogers had examined cursorily on arrival at Headquarters – failed to fit in with the theory he held so tentatively.

The only thing of which he was quite certain was that when Crutcher appeared at court, the blow with which he, Rogers, had stopped him from bringing lumps up on his skull would command more attention than the offences charged. He could conjure it up now. Allegations would be made by a persuasive and indignant defence lawyer that, concealed in a dark doorway, he had made a sexual advance to Nurse Killick and had struck the first blow against an understandably outraged Crutcher intent only on defending his sweetheart's honour. It would be hackneyed and a policeman's routine court crucifixion, but it could work.

24

Rogers stood in the corner of the Traffic Department's workshop, now empty of the civilian mechanics who could finish happily at five o'clock and go home to put their feet up, looking intently at the wreckage of the dead Cambridge. The post-mortem examination of its rusty carcase, the ripping open of its crushed-in shell with chisels and metal cutters had done little to give it back its shape as a car. That there were no signs of possible evidential material on the upholstery mattered little now. Nor, with the metal and plastic interior fittings still damp from the rain and condensation, was there any prospect yet of a fingerprint examination. And that, even when done, might still not determine the identity of whoever it was who had driven the dead Ungrish to the rail crossing.

Rogers's main interest was in something else, a something else that could possibly be identifiable to Ungrish's death, and in this he had to accept that he could either eliminate the Cambridge from his thinking or discard a newly-formed theory proving to be as wet as the car.

He was still worrying at it when Hagbourne came in. 'They told me you were here, sir,' he said, standing at his side and joining him in staring at the Cambridge. There was a jaundiced melancholy about him and his moustache drooped. 'Nothing from the taxi business, I'm afraid. Nobody seems to have collected a fare, female or otherwise, from Alwick that night. Or any other night lately, according to their records.'

'You're sure?' Rogers asked, not sure himself that it had been the answer he wanted, and allowing for Hagbourne's pessimism anyway.

'I don't know,' he said cautiously. 'I didn't go all that much on the office paperwork and half the rank drivers were out on jobs, so I wouldn't swear to it on oath. Bearing in mind there's always somebody on the thievish make, it's no more than a fair bet that she didn't order a taxi at all. There're nothing but local hirings in the fares book and the woman I spoke to who was on duty Wednesday night said definitely not. On top of that the meters would have to agree mileage readings at the end of the day. I spoke to as many drivers as I could find, and the same result. That'd have to be if they didn't want to be sacked for fiddling an unbooked fare. If your woman lied about telephoning the rank office, there is an alternative. She could have used one of the independent cruisers, although I don't know how she'd contact one. They don't have an office for a start, and if any of them stays put on the end of a telephone I've yet to know of it.'

'So have I.' Rogers accepted that Kelf had lied about the taxi as she had lied about other things. He gave the Cambridge a last look. 'Inanimate and insentient as cars must be, Thomas,' he said, 'don't you think there's something pathetic about one that's been smashed up and discarded?'

Hagbourne clearly did not, and replied, 'Only in terms of how much I could screw out of my insurance company for it.' ·

'You're a bloodless philistine,' Rogers said amiably. 'I advise you never to say that in the presence of Mr Lingard's Bentley. Or in mine, if it comes to that, and which is now standing unattended outside the mortuary.' He gave Hagbourne his car keys. 'Get one of the better drivers in the department to collect it for me straight away, will you? And then I want you to stand by in your office. I could have another little job for you in the offing.'

In his own office, against his need to be out and doing things, his requirement for more and more information seeming to be a tethering rope that jerked him back into it, he took papers from his neglected In-tray. The only one of immediate significance was a preliminary report from Sergeant Magnus. Among the finger impressions he had found with his powders and sprays in the cottage were several he considered had been left by a woman. Comparing them with the fingerprints developed from Rogers's visiting card, he had identified two of them as having been made by the person handling it. An impression taken from the top surface of the sideboard had been made by a left index finger with an ulnar loop, and contained eleven matching ridge characteristics. An impression taken from the rim of the bath-room hand-basin was made by a left thumb with a twin loop pattern. It contained sixteen matching ridge characteristics which, unlike the sideboard impression, would make it accept-able as evidence in a court. Having been engaged on other duties – Rogers read into it a reproof that his visits to the mortuary and the Forensic Science Laboratory had been valu-able investigative time wasted – he had not yet had an oppor-tunity of comparing the remaining finger impressions with those of Ungrish and Pring. The absence of these latter com-parisons and identifications was not, at the moment, any hin-drance to Rogers's scheme of things to be done and he thought he might bear it with some stoicism.

A further harvested result from initiated enquiries came from the attractive Sergeant Millier who knocked at his door as he was about to make a telephone call. She laid the plastic-bagged nightdress she had brought with her on his desk, giving him one of her beautiful smiles which must betoken something achieved.

'Sit down, sergeant,' he said, 'and tell me.' One day, he reminded himself, he would find the courage to suggest to her that the discreet but heady scent she wore wasn't quite discreet enough for the peace of mind of any male colleague with whom she worked. But definitely not on an occasion when, no nose-gay himself, he was giving off far from heady waves of the mortuary's *Eau de Formalin*.

'I made my enquiries about the nightdress,' she said, 'on the basis that it was thought to be stolen property and that we were trying to trace the loser, who we believed to be a Miss Kelf. I thought that you'd prefer it that way?'

'And so I do,' he agreed. 'You've identified the purchase?'

'Yes, from Bellinghams. Four under that label were bought on the third of August on a credit charge in the name of Marian Kelf, her address in their records given as 41A Cumberland Crescent, Abbotsburn.' She raised her eyebrows. 'Four of them! That's going it a bit expensively, isn't it?'

'Not ever having to buy them for myself, I wouldn't know,'

he smiled. 'She did go into a nursing home about then for an operation, so they could have been thought necessary. Have you anything useful about the wig?'

'No, sir, not yet,' she said, shaking her head, her blonde hair swinging. 'Some of the salons were closed by the time we got around to them. Do you want me to see the owners at their homes?'

'I don't think so. You've got me what I really wanted. A nightdress laid out on a man's bed should be a sufficient indication of a prearranged get-together for me to work on.' He gave her a lopsided grin. 'Or am I being filthy-minded? And that doesn't require an answer,' he added hastily.

When she had gone, he reached for the telephone again and dialled the number Marian Kelf had given him. Although the voice answering him only said 'Yes?', he recognized it.

'Rogers here,' he said, not too loudly. 'Are you able to speak?'

Not surprisingly, he wasn't the most welcome of callers and there was a fraught silence before she managed a strangled 'Yes, I am.'

'I have to see you, Miss Kelf,' he said in what, to her, must have seemed a doom-laden voice. 'As you don't wish me to call at your house, I'd like you to come here to my office. Within the next half-hour, please.'

There was more silence and, until she spoke, he thought she had left him with a dangling telephone. '*Please*,' she said at last with none of the clenched teeth arrogance he had suffered earlier. 'Not there. I'd be seen . . . somebody would know me. I . . . I . . . *please*.'

'I have to see you, Miss Kelf.' He was stern, unwilling to be cozened by her transformation into frightened feminity. 'If not here, where?'

'W . . . Will you come here?' she asked. 'My mother is out and won't be back until after ten.'

'I'll be there in twenty minutes or so,' he promised, closing down on her.

He couldn't imagine it happening but, acknowledging the unpredictable perversity of some women, he used his internal telephone to reach the waiting Hagbourne. 'Thomas,' he said urgently. 'Cumberland Crescent straight away. Park there and watch 41A. If Miss Kelf comes out – she's thirtyfive-ish with a slim build and grey eyes and freckles if you get near enough – stop her from going wherever she might be thinking of going. Arrest her on suspicion of something or other if you have to. She's probably got her car parked outside so don't give her too much leeway. I'm due there in twenty minutes. She knows it and she has reasons enough not to want to see me.'

He disconnected, satisfied that if running was her intent – something of which he wasn't sure, but giving her the opportunity of doing so and exposing whatever guilt might be provoking it – Hagbourne would, unless she was doing it already, be there in time to chop it short.

25

Carrying his briefcase and leaving the Headquarters building for an outside darkness chilly from the wet grey fog, Rogers was ready to set fire to somebody were his car not returned and standing where it should be. It was and, as he reached it, Lingard, his yellow hair adrift, drove in from the street and turned his Bentley on to his reserved hard-standing. With its canvas hood being still folded back, Rogers saw his passenger to be a sullen Gillard, wearing his leather hat and being immediately chivvied from his seat and up the steps into the building by Lingard. Rogers knew that his second-in-command had seen him and, although impatient for his can-opening interview with Marian Kelf, he waited. Fortune might at last have delivered an unexpected something of astonishing importance into Lingard's hands.

That, he discovered unastonishingly, was not to be. When Lingard came out and joined him, he said sniffingly, 'The tightest-assed bugger I've met in years, George. And he's made my cockpit smell like a damned stable.'

149

'Force him into drinking cups of canteen tea,' Rogers advised him genially, getting into his car and starting its engine with the key left carelessly in the ignition. 'If that doesn't open him up, nothing will. I'll be back in an hour, so stick with him until I am.'

The tall terraced brownstone buildings of Cumberland Crescent, their roofs unseen in the fog, were big-windowed and each with a basement area and a porticoed front door. Probably early nineteenth century, they had been built without any forethought that garages might one day be needed. Rogers, prepared to double-bank if he had to and to hell with obstructing the highway, found a rare and only just big enough space for him to squeeze into the line of cars parked along its curved length.

His soft-soled footfalls sounding his approach, Hagbourne loomed out of the darkness as Rogers started his search for 41A in the fog-dimmed illumination of the road lights. 'You passed it, sir,' he said as if he thought his senior needed a guide dog. 'She's still in there and her curtain's been twitching back and forth since I got here.'

This fell short of what Rogers had half-expected, her waiting his coming suggesting that she had less than the ultimate to fear. 'Lead me to it, Thomas,' he said and then, seeing that Hagbourne looked chilled, droplets of moisture bedewing his eyebrows and moustache, added sardonically, 'Slope off once I'm in there to whatever it is you'd rather be doing. I think I might manage her on my own. She can't be much more than eight stone.'

In the portico, having pushed on the bell-tit, his impassively held features were subjected to a scrutiny by Marian Kelf's grey eyes through the gap in the safety-chained door. He said nothing and neither did she as he was allowed in and through the hall into her sitting-room.

It was a room of feminine delicacy, neatness and warm comfort; of graceful mahogany furniture and frilly flowered chair coverings, green velvet drapes with gold-coloured tasselled cords and ivory-shaded wall lights; a rosewood escritoire with a white telephone, a gate-leg table with tidily arranged women's magazines on it, a huge floor-standing brass container of dried flowers and seed capsules, and a wall cabinet of engraved goblets and cordial glasses. It lacked conspicuously – probably without any feeling of deprivation – anything suggesting a man's occupancy. Not a room into which to bring the ugliness of bloody death, the eroticism of sexual galumphing, it made the detective conscious of his own masculine coarseness and of the hard-nosed attitude he was so often forced to adopt in doing his job.

Marian Kelf stood herself in front of the brass-canopied coal fire, waiting for him to speak. With her hair still tied back and wearing the plain grey dress with its immaculate white collar in which he had seen her that afternoon, her neat features were pale and set in resolution, obviously having dredged from her fears a sufficiency of defiance in coming to terms with Rogers's visit.

'I'd be obliged if you'd sit, Miss Kelf,' he said. 'This may take some time.'

She nodded and said 'Of course' in a steady voice, sitting with a slow and cautious folding of her body into an easy chair at the side of the fire. Rogers, keeping on his overcoat and rejecting the conducting of an interrogation made sloppy by easeful relaxation, ignored its companion and drew up a wooden straight-backed chair, sitting opposite her and laying his brief-case on his lap.

'We had a reasonably useful talk this afternoon,' he started, modulating his voice to that of a not very bright and slightly nonplussed man faced with ambiguities, 'and I thought we had more or less sorted out the details of your visit to Hidden Cottage.' When she made no reply to that, but held him with her stare, he snapped open his briefcase and withdrew the nightdress, putting it on the arm of the easy chair close by him. Her lips had thinned momentarily when she saw it, her eyes following its placing. 'I was hoping that you'd recognize it,' he said diffidently. 'It is yours, isn't it?'

'No, it certainly is not,' she retorted firmly. 'Is that all you've come here for?'

'Bellinghams,' he said, allowing his expression a show of

hesitancy. 'I was told that you had bought some of these in August. Surely you remember that?'

The freckles showed clearly as she frowned and thought, her mouth pursed. 'Yes, I do remember. But they weren't white, because I never wear white. They were blue.'

'This one was upstairs in the bedroom.' He shook his head and grimaced. 'It must have been left there by someone else then?'

'I don't like your insinuation that it was mine, superintendent,' she said tartly. 'I told you exactly the circumstances of my only visit, and what happened.'

'So you did,' he agreed docilely, wondering if she really did believe him stupid. 'You were only there a very short time, you didn't move much from near the front door and you left after a few minutes because of Ungrish's sexual advances.' He paused, allowing the silence to lengthen until she must begin to wonder what next. 'That's so, isn't it?' he asked.

'Yes.' She was plainly wary now, but not losing command of herself.

'It's very odd, don't you think? The someone else who left the nightdress on the bed must have also left one of your fingerprints in the bathroom.' He shook his head again. 'No doubt about it, and that isn't anywhere near the front door, is it?'

Suddenly, as though an inner substance had been sucked from her, she looked smaller, her eyes widening and her mouth dropping open. 'No,' she whispered. 'You can't say that.' She looked down at her hands, clenching and unclenching them. 'How can you?'

'I can and I do.' Rogers discarded his put-on expression of puzzled diffidence. 'You left your prints on my card when you wrote out your address for me.'

His words put something of a fighting spirit back in her. 'That was contemptible . . . despicable,' she said fiercely. 'It was wrong.'

'You think so?' He thrust his nose at her, his voice implacable, his expression stern. 'Wrong in dealing with a woman who conspired criminally in her position of trust to steal the documents and identity of a dead man? A woman who is undoubtedly involved in the killing of her adulterous lover? A woman who has lied to me from the very beginning, and is still doing so? A woman knowing that her fingerprints could be used to prove her a liar and who would certainly have refused to give them to me had I asked? Who then, Miss Kelf, is the contemptible one? The despicable one?'

His uncompromising accusations had shaken her, and through them had been trembling-mouthed denials he had ignored. 'I swear I had nothing to do with his death,' she choked out, desperation in her words as her eyes sought for escape from his. 'I really and truly didn't.'

'If you're going to convince me,' he said, softening his voice, 'you had better try telling the truth about what did happen. You've heard of Jeremy Bentham? Jeremy Bentham the philosopher?' He feared that her agitation would change to an unmanageable hysterical weeping and that there would be nothing he could do about it.

She pressed a clenched hand to her mouth, shaking her head dumbly.

'It doesn't matter. It's what he wrote that's important, and it applies to you. It was to the effect that innocence demands to be heard, while guilt chooses to remain silent. Do you understand that?'

'You'll arrest me . . . my mother will know,' she whispered around the hand at her mouth.

'I shall certainly be forced to in the absence of a believable explanation from you about what you actually did in the cottage,' he assured her grimly. 'If you are innocent of any connection with Ungrish's death, you should tell me now.'

On this occasion, obviously more harrowing to her than before, she didn't ask him for time to think, but took it, staring into the fire and biting at her bottom lip as she brought herself under control. Whatever decision she was making, she was making it now.

Rogers waited, aware from his experience with harder, more criminous characters that a tension-filled silence between two people in dissension was the most effective purgative for a flow of words. He was as relaxed as his hard chair would allow him, content to give her time to think out what she was going to say while worrying herself sick about how much he knew. He would have been more content could he have smoked his pipe, even if only to disguise the mortuary smell he felt must still be clinging to his clothing. But it wasn't that kind of a room, or an appropriate occasion.

Because he was looking abstractedly at her very attractive body, his thinking had strayed peripherally to a pleasant contemplation of an *affaire de trois* involving unknowingness on the parts of Morag and Katherine, interrupted when she stirred and spoke. 'I'm sorry,' she said humbly, 'I've been a silly little fool. Will you help me?' Her expression was soft and appealing and it irritated him, suspecting that she was about to use a self-seeking female-in-distress attitude when he knew that her true feelings towards him as a police officer were of arrogance and dislike. But not, he guessed, now of contempt.

'I am not here to help you, even if I could,' he said bluntly. 'I'm here to find out the truths I haven't so far had. Are you now prepared to give them to me?'

'Yes, I am,' she answered in a subdued voice. 'But *please*, you won't write it down?'

That appeared to be a no-option handicap and not one he liked, although one he could later remedy if what she admitted justified it. 'Not if that's your wish,' he conceded, 'but I shall certainly remember what you say. Now tell me what happened on Wednesday.'

Her hands lay passively on her lap and she inclined her head in looking at them, foreshortening her features against his steady gaze. 'I would like to say first that what I said about Simon in the cottage was completely untrue. It has worried me since that you should have the wrong impression . . . he was none of those things I said.'

'If you mean that absurd filthy beast part and you defending your virtue,' he said drily, 'not to worry. I didn't believe it for a moment. Start with your going to Alwick.'

Before speaking, she had glanced at him with a glint of resentment at his derisive remark. 'I really am telling you the truth now,' she said. 'I met Simon in the Centre car stack where I park my own car and we drove to the cottage together. As we weren't going out to eat until later on we had time to sit down and rest. We hadn't been there long when we heard a car – I think it was a car – stop outside. That was unusual because we were at the top of the lane and it doesn't go anywhere else. Simon got out of his chair and looked through the curtains to see who it was. His face changed immediately and I'd never seen him look so absolutely furious. He said to me, quite angrily, "Go upstairs, Marian, and stay quiet. And for Christ's sake don't show any bloody lights." He doesn't . . . didn't often swear, but he did then. He was quite upset and livid with temper.' Her expression changed to one of sadness. 'I didn't know then, but those were the last words I heard him say, and I shall always remember them . . .' She trailed into silence, her eyes blinking and reflecting moistly the red glow of the fire.

When Rogers remained silent she continued. 'We had been listening to Scarlatti on the radio when this happened and even then I couldn't bear not to hear it to its end. I turned it down low and took it with me to the bathroom because that is at the back of the house. Then I bolted the door in case it was somebody who would come in and look for me, although I couldn't really believe they would with Simon there. In my mind I half-thought it might be a divorce detective trying to get evidence against us because Simon had warned me that it could happen.'

'Is that the reason why you disguised yourselves when you went there? Wig, false moustache and things?'

'Yes, always, although we took them off when we were inside.'

'I'm sorry to have interrupted you. Please go on.'

'I think I expected Simon to come up quite soon and tell me when whoever it was had gone, but he didn't. It was cold and dark in the bathroom – I felt that I was going to be left there all night – and I began to be very worried. I opened the door and crept to the top of the stairs and listened. I could hear nothing at all, so I went back to the bathroom and waited again, wondering what had happened and thinking silly things like had he gone away for some reason and hadn't been able to tell me. I was also feeling humiliated at being made to hide and becoming a little angry myself. It never entered my head . . .' Her throat jerked convulsively behind the white collar and she began kneading at the grey fabric over her thighs. 'I came out of the bathroom again and listened, and when there was no sound of anything I came downstairs.' She gave a tiny moan and shook her head despairingly. 'He was lying on the floor near the door and I thought he had fallen over and knocked his head, or fainted. I went to help him, asking him what had happened, and then I knew that he was dead. I was terrified then, not knowing what was happening or what I could do. I wanted to run away, not to be involved in what would be a dreadful scandal. I couldn't have done anything, could I? I would never have harmed him . . . you must believe me. We . . . we were awfully fond of each other and it was understood that we would be married when he eventually divorced Mrs Ungrish. So I wouldn't, would I?' She looked him directly in the eyes. 'That's the truth and I'm terribly, terribly sorry that I didn't tell it to you before.'

Even if it were, and a not too impressed Rogers could not be sure of it, it wasn't nearly enough. 'How did you know he was dead?' he asked. 'That's a condition not always easy for a medical man to determine.'

She shook her head, anguish in her face. 'He wasn't breathing. He looked dreadful . . . as if he had suffered. I just knew.'

'You were shocked, I'm sure,' he said. 'Did your finding him like that cause you to scream?'

'No, I'm sure not. Should I have?' She obviously felt that he was being critical of her reaction to it.

'I thought not,' he said, satisfied. 'Having diagnosed him dead, Miss Kelf, would you know or care to guess how he died? Or was killed? I did tell you that he was probably murdered, didn't I?'

'You told me, yes, but I hadn't any reason to think so then. There was no . . . no blood or anything. Nothing. Please . . . I didn't.'

He put disbelief into his voice. 'You just thought that he'd died? Like that? A presumably healthy man doing nothing

156

more than possibly opening a door to somebody who had made him angry by stopping outside his cottage?'

She made the small moaning noise again. 'I couldn't understand . . . he didn't look like anything I'd seen before. There was nothing I could do to help him.'

'Such as getting a doctor to him?' he said, keeping the distaste he felt for her selfishness from his voice. Expecting no answer and getting none, recognizing a dead-end when he was in one, he changed direction. 'You didn't hear the car leave? Or look to see if it had?'

'No, I was completely shattered. I couldn't think properly and all I wanted to do was to get away before anybody came.'

The black marble clock with the hollow ticking on the mantelshelf began striking the time and he waited for it to finish. 'Didn't you hear voices? Downstairs, or outside?'

'I wouldn't be able to in the bathroom, and I had the radio on for most of the time.'

Rogers thought that he detected relief at his getting away from the subject of a dead Ungrish, perhaps understandably. 'Did you take it downstairs with you?'

Her forehead creased in attempted recall. 'I can't remember, but I probably did. I think I would have.'

'Before you went upstairs, had either of you taken a drink?'

'No. Simon would never drink spirits if he was going to drive, and I don't if I'm to drink wine.'

'What do you drink when you are at the cottage?'

'Vodka.' Puzzlement overlaid the tenseness in her face. 'Why do you ask that?'

Interrogation rarely demanded the answering of questions and he ignored hers. 'Whisky as well? Or just him?'

'Just him. I don't like it.'

'Did he bring those drinks from his home?'

'No, from the off-licence in Aylmers Road.'

'He told you that?'

'Yes, but I was with him once when he collected some. And he said on one occasion that he kept no drink other than wine in the home because of Mrs Ungrish.'

'A warning, Miss Kelf. If I'm not satisfied with your reply to my next question, I shall take steps that will definitely not be to your advantage.' Watching her intently, he paused and then shot the words 'Do you use cocaine?' at her.

Her suddenly opened mouth, the stupefaction in her face gave him the answer even before her cry of 'No! What are you saying? What do you mean?', her words finishing on a rising note of distraction.

'It's all right,' he said reassuringly, making his mental reservation that it might not be so. 'It was something I had to know. You had your wig on when you left the cottage, I assume?'

His sudden changes of subject were keeping her off-balance, giving her deliberately little time to prepare a lie or an evasion, and she said 'Yes' apprehensively.

'And you wore it in the taxi that nobody remembers driving to Alwick to pick you up?' Then, leaning forward and demanding sharply, 'Is that so, Miss Kelf?'

'I'm sorry,' she faltered, shifting her gaze from his to her folded hands. 'I did go into the kiosk to telephone for one, but while I was looking for the number a bus drew into the stop and I caught it.'

'And you knew I could check the time you left Alwick if you told me,' he said. 'So it couldn't have been ages before eight when you arrived, could it? What time did you leave?'

'I don't know, I honestly don't, but I think it was about nine or shortly after when I got off the bus.' She knocked her forehead with her small fist and screwed her eyelids shut in her recalling. 'But I didn't go home then. I was too upset and I had to think about it. I wanted to tell the police . . . it was the thought of Simon lying there on his own and perhaps not being found for days, but I couldn't bring myself to do it. I went into the terminus café and tidied myself in the toilets, had a cup of coffee and then collected my car from the stack. I'm sure it was ten o'clock when I arrived home.'

'Was your mother surprised? You had intended spending the night with Ungrish, hadn't you?'

'My mother knows nothing about it and she mustn't. She's been staying with her sister and comes back tonight. That's why I was able to go.'

'How much was the bus fare?' he asked casually.

She stared at him for long seconds, her expression suggesting a mind working frantically at providing an answer. 'I can't remember. Truly I can't. But it was under a pound because I gave him a fifty-pence piece and some other silver. Would that be right?'

He gave her a sceptical smile which must have looked to her like the baring of a hungry piranha's teeth. 'It sounds a pretty wild guess to me,' he said, 'and it leads me to question your statement that you returned by bus at all. Wouldn't it be more likely, more convenient, for you to have driven your own car to Alwick and met Ungrish at the cottage? Aren't you lying about the bus as you lied about the taxi?'

'*No!*' she cried out vehemently. 'It's true! I've never been there in my car. Never!'

He shrugged his doubt. 'I can get that checked if I have to. What car do you have? Give me its make, colour and registration number, please.'

'It's a dark-blue MG-BGT, registration B2175KLG, and I swear I didn't drive it there.'

'Even if you didn't, I shall still want to see it,' he persisted. 'Where do you garage it?'

'It's outside in the road. You aren't taking it, are you?' She was agitated. 'Please – I need it to meet my mother off the train. That is . . . I mean, if you are going to let me.'

'Don't excite yourself, Miss Kelf,' Rogers said mildly. 'I said I only wanted to look at it. When you ran out from the cottage, how did you leave the door? Unlocked? Open?'

She knocked her bent thumb against her forehead, closing her eyes and biting at her bottom lip. 'I don't know. You're confusing me. I think I must have closed it. I would have had to take the key outside if I had locked it and I'd have remembered that.'

'Yes, I imagine you would,' he agreed. He regarded her speculatively, wondering if she really was confused, or a woman

159

with enough gall to persist in her lying to him. 'Did Ungrish wear his spectacles for reading?'

'Yes.'

'And he was wearing them in reading his newspaper?'

There was total incomprehension in her face. 'Of course,' she said. 'Why?'

'Why not? Asking questions is why I'm here. You are still insisting that you went to Alwick in the Cambridge, are you?'

'I swear I did.'

'Where was it parked when you arrived?'

'At the rear of the cottage. Simon always did that.'

'Understandably discreet under the circumstances,' he murmured. 'Something puzzles me about that, Miss Kelf. When you found the body and wanted to run away, wouldn't it have occurred to you that you could take the Cambridge to get back to Abbotsburn? Ungrish, being dead, would hardly want it, would he?'

'No.' She was back to gnawing at her underlip. 'No, I didn't. I told you, I was terrified . . . I couldn't think.'

His eyebrows were down. 'Assuming that you didn't take your own car, it seems to me to be a strong probability.'

'*I didn't! I didn't!* I never thought about it.' Her eyes glistened in the emotion of her denial.

'All right,' he said soothingly, 'I'm only asking. There's something you mentioned about Ungrish divorcing his wife. Previously you'd said it was Mrs Ungrish who was divorcing him and that you were frightened it was a divorce detective outside the cottage looking for evidence. Would you like to make up your mind which it is?'

'It's true,' she insisted. 'She was. Simon was sure of it because he had heard that she had been to see a solicitor. He told me later that he was going to get there first, that he had good grounds for accusing her of sleeping with a man while he was away. He said that he meant to be the plaintiff and not the defendant.' She added nastily, 'Not that he cared how much she slept around.'

'He could hardly care or complain if she did,' Rogers commented drily. 'Did he say who?'

'No, he wouldn't. He called him a filthy toad, if that helps, and told me the less I knew about him the better.'

Rogers stood from the chair whose hardness had numbed his buttocks and left furrows across the backs of his thighs. Having been watching and listening to Kelf for nearly an hour, he now knew that behind the coldly severe and bureaucratic persona that was the top dressing for her doing things in the administrative department of the hospital, there had skulked a sexuality repressed into spinsterhood, possibly by an over-dominant and clinging mother, which had found its late and calamitous flowering in the bed of a womanizing gynaecologist. It was this, although recognizing that her emotional reactions to his questioning might have been simulated, which decided him not to disclose to her the taking of Nurse Killick by her faithless lover to the cottage while she had been in a nursing home. Should she have had a serious thing about Ungrish, he couldn't feel it in himself to destroy it.

'I'll leave you now,' he said. 'There may be further questions when I've checked on what you've told me and possibly further action in connection with your being an accomplice to Ungrish's deception and theft. You understand?'

She rose from her chair, her manner more composed, less apprehensive, as though she had weathered his interrogation better than she had anticipated. Her eyes, too, although she was possibly unaware of it, had ceased concealing her distaste for him. 'Please,' she asked softly, her voice supplicating, 'you do believe me, don't you?'

'Not happening to be God, I can't see into your mind,' he said unbendingly, refusing her any easy comfort. 'You've already lied to me comprehensively and in cold blood. It leaves you in my book with a suspect record for telling the truth about anything, and I neither believe nor disbelieve you.'

Being let out through the door and into the road, he was filled with his usual niggling suspicion that there had been other questions he should have asked, fancying that even now Marian Kelf would be doing a dance of thankfulness and relief at his departure, quite certain that she could watch him die a painful death without too much grief. But he was philosophical enough about it when, after lighting his pipe and getting his deprived nervous system back in order, he found her car and studied it in the not very helpful foggy darkness with a fair degree of profit.

26

Rogers, on his return to Headquarters, found Lingard in his own office. Smaller than his senior's, it illustrated his level in the constabulary's hierarchical strata. A shorter length of blue carpeting (as Rogers's was shorter than *his* immediate superior in rank) with a probably less dense pile, two drawers less in a smaller desk, only one telephone, one starkly uncomfortable visitors' chair and one window overlooking the rear of a scrap dealer's yard were all a material impetus to hoped-for promotion. On the emulsioned wall behind the desk were coloured prints of the *Cries of London*, a steel engraving of the Royal Crescent at Bath and a drawing of Beau Brummell, the dandy whose foppishness Lingard copied as far as acceptability by the Chief Constable and twentieth century fashion would allow him. There were two framed photographs on his desk. One, of his cherished Bentley with a blond long-nosed Afghan hound sitting upright in the driver's seat, uncannily resembling Lingard himself; the other of a remarkably beautiful woman who had signed it 'Nancy'. She was long dead, but the ghost of her still exorcised any attraction the elegant detective might have felt for any other woman.

'Gillard's down in the waiting-room,' he said to Rogers, 'and let me tell you he's as cunning as a hungry polecat. He isn't amenable to friendly persuasion either, and I didn't spend too much time on him in case I spoiled him for you.'

'You couldn't, David,' Rogers assured him. 'About the only thing that interests me is why he walloped Ungrish. Fetch him up, will you?'

He sat in Lingard's chair to wait, looking at the photograph of the dead Nancy Frail and remembering back to the problems she had brought on her besotted lover's head. When the once-besotted lover came in with Gillard and steered him into the visitors' chair, sitting himself on the window-sill, Rogers was smoking his pipe, feeling starved and grubby and wondering when he could do something about it.

Still with his leather hat on – nailed to his head, Rogers guessed – Gillard wore a blue cloth lumber jacket over a dirty tee-shirt with a Marilyn Monroe print on its chest and narrow skin-tight jeans that left little of his pudenda to the imagination of even the least curious. He was sullen, suspicious of what was happening and manifestly unloving of policemen.

Rogers said, 'I assume that you now know Mr Ungrish was found dead in a car on a rail crossing?'

Gillard looked at Lingard, then back at Rogers. 'She tol' me. She 'ad to, 'adn't she?'

'And presumably it was a surprise to you?'

'Course it was,' said sneeringly. 'I already told 'im.' He looked at Lingard again.

Rogers rose from his chair and walked around the desk to him. He put his finger under the brim of the hat and lifted it, exposing Gillard's face to the light and scrutinizing its olive skin, high cheekbones and the black eyes that slanted to give his features a faun-like cast. For all his scruffy uncouthness, he would, Rogers judged, cut a dash with those dizzy-brained females not objecting to filthy fingernails and the smell of horse manure. And also, his past experience told him, as a young gypsy likely to draw to himself those homosexually inclined males preferring the rough trade. Gillard had flinched momentarily, but no more. 'What're you looking at?' he demanded.

Rogers returned to his chair and sat. 'I was looking for the bruises,' he said mildly. 'You know? Those you had fighting Mr Ungrish. He beat you up, didn't he?'

If anything, the youth had male pride. ''Im!' He snorted his derision. ''E never did. 'E couldn't.'

'It was you who hit him then?'

He was contemptuous. 'I could easy, I could eat 'im. But I di'n't.'

And, Rogers believed, so he could have. Young as he was in years, he was physically mature and whatever it was between him and Ungrish must have been a half-hearted affair. 'What was your quarrel about?' he asked.

'There weren't no quarrel either. I never 'ad any reason.'

'Was it about his Mercedes being smashed up?'

Gillard's face showed anger. 'I don' know what you're talkin' about.'

'It was vandalized in the Arts Theatre car park a few days before Mr Ungrish was hit in the face by you.' Rogers was stern. 'It seems to me quite logical that he could have suspected you of doing it, accused you of it, and you hit him. Of course, I'll accept that he could have hit you first if you say so, that you hit him in self-defence.' That he had believed Crutcher had done it was beside the point. He didn't *know* and accusation could often bring out the truth about something else, although understandably a lesser something else.

'I di'n't! He di'n't either! It was . . .' He stopped short, sullen but still angry.

'It was what?' Rogers urged him.

'Nothin'.' That had been a door to something now firmly shut. ''E never tol' me anythin'.'

'You must have noticed that he wasn't driving the Mercedes for a couple of weeks.'

'It weren't to do with me. All I knew 'e was driving 'er car for a bit. Tha's all I know.'

From his perch on the window-sill, Lingard gave Rogers a brief quirk of his lips as if to say 'What did I tell you?', then inhaling generously of his snuff as if to anaesthetize his nose against Gillard's growing smell.

Rogers changed tack, not recalling any instance of a gypsy admitting anything to his disadvantage, and half-believing him anyway. He said flatly, 'You didn't like Mr Ungrish.' It was an accusation, not a question.

Gillard hesitated, then went through the motion of spitting his contempt.

'Why not?' Rogers asked, as if merely curious.

'I jus' di'n't.' He stared straight at the detective. 'No more'n I like you. Or 'im,' he added, including Lingard.

'No doubt we'll manage to bear up under it,' Rogers told him cheerfully. 'Mr Ungrish died at about eight o'clock on Wednesday evening. It could be interesting to know where you happened to be then.' The stables, he guessed to himself, with a couple of conveniently mute horses as witnesses to it.

Gillard surprised him. 'It would an' all, would'n' it.' He bared his teeth in aggressive triumph. 'I was in the Colefax Arms.'

'With anybody?'

'I don' 'ave to be, do I? Ask the lan'lord. Me an' 'im was talkin' about 'orses an' I 'ad me supper there.'

'What time in? What time out?'

'I went in about seven, an' came out about 'alf-past nine, per'aps later'n that,' he said with the promptness and indefiniteness of the truth.

Rogers spoke to Lingard. 'Do you mind, David? Will you do a check with the landlord straight away? And call me back.' He had looked hard into Gillard's eyes as he said it and if they could ever show an unworried guilelessness, they showed it now.

With Lingard gone, he asked, 'What did you do after you'd come out?'

'I went 'ome, of course.'

'You mean the stables?'

'I tol' you, yes.'

'What do you know about cocaine?' he said, watching him unblinkingly for a sign that his words were hitting at something vulnerable.

Gillard, who had been probing in his ear with a finger, scowled his incomprehension. 'I don' know what you're on about, mate.'

Rogers, feeling that he had yet to talk to anyone who did, said, 'Whatever it is, I'd prefer you didn't call me mate. You know what cocaine is?'

'Course I do.' He was taking it lightly enough to decide Rogers that he could be wasting his time.

'So? Have you ever used it?'

Gillard snorted derisively again. 'Yes,' he said, 'I 'as it for breakfast every mornin'. 'Eaps of it.'

Not having expected to chisel much from the youth's stubbornness, Rogers was not particularly disappointed with the possibly useful little that he had. 'If there's nothing more you're going to insist on telling me,' he said with amiable irony, 'perhaps you wouldn't mind waiting until Mr Lingard calls back.'

Withdrawing his pocketbook and ignoring the sullen and untameable Gillard – he hadn't tried too hard to tame him, anyway – he wrote down the notes of his interrogation of Marian Kelf. Then, chewing on the stem of his pipe and leaning back in the chair, he pictured in his mind the sequence of events at the cottage. That might, he thought with a forced optimism, tell him something that he had not already considered.

He had no difficulty at all in visualizing Kelf and Ungrish sitting in their chairs before the electric fire, reading the newspapers they had brought with them and listening to Scarlatti. Then the sound of a car drawing up outside, although it need not have been a car. That had to be only supposition and it could have been anything less than a bus or an articulated lorry. Whatever it was, its arrival was unusual enough for Ungrish – Rogers had problems in picturing him alive other than in the black and white of his press photograph – to leave his chair and look through the curtains into the darkness of the lane. Although he hadn't chosen to tell Kelf who or what outside he had been able to see, it had angered and frightened him enough to send her peremptorily upstairs. Was he expecting whoever it was to come in? Probably not, if the still visible evidence of two newspapers was anything to go by. So why the panic and the hurried dismissal of Kelf? Logically, it had to be somebody who knew or suspected the reclusive Johnson to be Ungrish. Or, not so logically, somebody looking for Kelf. An unknown somebody rampantly jealous? Why not? She was an attractive woman should she ever choose to smile, and certainly one with a penchant for having it off when her mother happened to be away from home. It couldn't have been the divorce detective she had feared, for Rogers somehow didn't think that the battering to death of a surveillance subject would come within the terms of his employment. And Kelf, by now in the bathroom, a bleak enough place to sit and wait out whatever was happening, said that she had heard nothing. Even over the Scarlatti music to which she seemed so attached, it should have been possible to hear the words that must have been spoken, for they had to be angry ones. Given that the vicar, not a hundred yards away, really had heard Ungrish's dying scream, and not the mating call of a vixen, shouldn't she have heard it too? Or, ten minutes or so later, the sound of the car or whatever being accelerated at a fair old lick along the lane?

Rogers scratched the stem of his pipe against the now emerged stubble of his jowl in thinking about that. Was the car connected with the eight o'clock death of Ungrish? It had to be, or the whole thing was going to fall apart. However it was, its going appeared to have left an undiscovered Kelf, a dead Ungrish and the Cambridge all at the cottage. And Kelf, a car driver, with access to the Cambridge's ignition key. So, could he believe what she had told him? Assuming that Ungrish *had* been killed while she sat unwittingly in the bathroom and that she had discovered his body as she had alleged, might she not have felt that she would be incriminated by its being found in the cottage? Or, assuming her complete innocence, that she could be implicated in a scandal damaging to her reputation and employment? Either, he supposed, could give her the desperation and courage needed to do something about it other than to run. Not too hefty a man and not yet stiff from *rigor mortis*, it was reasonably possible that she could get his body into the Cambridge and drive it to the rail crossing, a not-too-far eight miles away. But necessarily later than ten o'clock, when the earlier train went through without incident. That would mean at the least a two-hour gap between the death and the Cambridge being placed on the rail crossing; at the most, just over three hours. So, should she be the disposer of the body, what could she have been doing during the intervening hours? Not, it was certain, removing traces of their visit there. The fire had been left on, her nightdress left on the bed and the newspapers lying where they had been put down; all suggesting that she had gone either in a blind panic or in a state of shock. Perhaps she hadn't been in either, that those matters didn't concern her, that she had spent the time in doing some deep worrying about what to do with Ungrish's body. Further, he argued with himself and harking back to the rail crossing, on her own she would have no transport back to Abbotsburn. She could have walked the six miles. That would be nothing for two healthy legs and an overriding fear of being found out. Or, as seemed more plausible, there could have been an accomplice with a car. The man who had killed Ungrish? Given the circumstances, that wasn't too outrageous a theory, but certainly of the sort that could, tied to Kelf, fall apart in intensive thinking.

The damned cocaine that nobody knew anything about. As Ungrish had held the two keys to the cottage, how could anybody dose his whisky with it and not leave evidence of their breaking and entering the cottage to do it? By somebody professional enough to be able to pick a mortice lock? By Kelf, already having access and not drinking the stuff herself? That was going to be difficult to believe unless she had put it in as an aphrodisiac and had wildly overdosed on the assumption that the more of it the better the effect. The only alternative to that was that somebody with access to the cottage wanted, or needed, to kill him. And, not succeeding in that, did it in another way. So far as that was concerned, he had satisfied himself with only . . .

The telephone bell ringing cut short his inner arguments. It was Lingard calling from a kiosk and Rogers pressed the receiver close to his ear to prevent Gillard overhearing. 'We've a dead end, George,' he said. 'However chummy's involved, he's clear for Wednesday evening. The landlord knows him well. He says he goes there nearly every evening to scoff his two pork pies and bacon-flavoured crisps, and he remembers Wednesday even though he's a bit dodgy on the times. He says that as near as dammit he was in the spit-and-sawdust bar from about seven-thirty to nearly ten. He knew it was a longish time because he had his ear badly bent from listening to what was apparently an endless monologue on horses and motor bikes.'

'How sure about the day, David?'

'I couldn't shake him on it. He doesn't like chummy anyway, and I'm certain he wouldn't cover for him.'

When he closed down, Rogers spoke to Gillard. 'You can go now,' he said, 'but don't think yourself off the hook, because you're not. I'll get a car to take you back.'

Gillard stood, his expression revealing nothing. 'You can stuff your car, mate,' he said sourly. 'Jus' show me 'ow to get out of this bloody place an' I'll go on me own.'

Seeing him off the premises before returning to his own office, Rogers thought about him. He realized belatedly that there could be an unlikely but possible situation involving Gillard which might explain Ungrish's quarrel with him. That he had thought of it at all, he blamed on a mind conditioned to focus on the incontrovertible presumption that, faced with temptation, *Homo sapiens* would almost always make the easy descent into lechery.

27

Rogers believed he needed what he called a breather; a respite from hearing his own voice growling out the same old questions and listening to answers that ran the gamut from shifty evasion to barefaced lying. The day could come – 'I should live to see it,' he told himself – when somebody would say after the first question, 'I did it, and I want to make a completely honest statement admitting it.' While it gave him a feeling of scrimshanking on the job to take his breather in the middle of a murder investigation, he mitigated his doing it by convincing himself that he did no credit to the British police service by walking around smelling like an overcrowded mortuary.

Void of a loving wife, even of the unloving one who had left him, his house was nothing to go home to. Its dusting and vacuuming was done by a woman he paid (exorbitantly, he considered) to come in three mornings a week. When she didn't come, it wasn't; and it showed. In between he had developed a talent for occasionally washing accumulated dishes without smashing too many of them, for making his bed with a time-saving single lifting into place of its sheets and blankets, and in opening the refrigerator for a frozen-solid convenience meal. He considered that it all added up to a justification for his intermittent forays into the open market for agreeable women with whom to share what his discomforts had made of him.

He switched on a few lights to make the place look lived in, congratulated himself on having had the foresight to turn on the central heating, and climbed the stairs to the bathroom. Doing a necessary run over his chin stubble with an electric razor, in front of a dusty mirror and allowing himself a little exaggeration, he judged that the day's efforts had aged him to not much short of sixty years. His nose definitely looked longer, and there were the beginnings of pouches below his eyes. Eyes, he was certain, that had probably seen things his brain had not yet wholly evaluated. Such as the injuries that had caused Ungrish's death. Twite had said that he had done his bleeding internally and that would certainly rule out his body gushing blood in the back of Crutcher's truck, even had he accepted against the evidence that it had been involved in his actual killing. In him, he had clobbered a contemptible deer-slaughterer, a thuggish woman-batterer, and that was all, wasting so much time in clearing dirt from the picture that should by now be showing the truth. Ungrish's external injuries, those which had appeared to have bled, posed a suggestion of what might have happened, compounded although they had been by those sustained on the rail crossing. It left him with conjecture only, and that based solely on Twite's not infallible opinion. And, despite the same man's opinion, had Ungrish been a cocaine addict? Subjecting himself not only to its aphrodisiacal effects, but also to its degenerating propensity for sexual perversion?

Which reminded him. There were gaps to fill. He had done nothing yet about Marian Kelf's presumed access to the hospital pharmacy, a source of cocaine if there was ever one. Nor had he done anything yet about identifying Mrs Ungrish's professional and high-standing lover, if lover there were. And she

170

was hardly someone he would care to browbeat about that. 'Turn it off, Rogers,' he said to his reflection. 'You're supposed to be taking a breather, not flogging your brain with what you're paid to do in the office.'

Showered and smelling of *Locker Room*, a pungent so-called man's soap which had done nothing for an arm displaying the handsome purple bruise given him by Crutcher, he dressed. With three of his suits uncollected from the dry-cleaners and most of his shirts still with the laundry, he was forced to wear what he believed to be a shade too gaudy a combination of a pheasant-brown suit, a pink shirt and a red tie. It took away, he was sure, some of the gravitas of his persona.

In the kitchen he loaded and switched on the coffee percolator. Then he prepared himself a meal of warmed-up steak-and-kidney pie he had been trying to finish for nearly a week, worrying for a few seconds about dying from botulin or salmonella poisoning and having the slap-dash Twite dismantling his entrails for the information of an inquisitive coroner.

It was while drinking his coffee and doing some unbidden thinking about the uncommunicative Gillard that the situation crossing his mind earlier became significant and applicable, and the probable answer, if not to Ungrish's death, to the later disposal of the body. It needed corroboration that would not, he guessed, be obtained by treading heavily or using hard words. It was a reasonable enough theory for him to decide that he should have Gillard back inside. And reasonable enough – although one aspect of it disgusted him and was difficult to believe – to call himself a bloody idiot for not having considered it before.

He telephoned Headquarters and spoke to Lingard, giving him the bare bones of his thinking and asking that he and Sergeant Millier stand by to await his return. Then, with a confidence he hoped was not misplaced by self-deception, he telephoned Katherine. God, fog and a bit of luck permitting, he told her, he would be at the airport at the appointed time, ready to help with her in-depth research into the life and times of Gustave Flaubert.

28

Before leaving Headquarters, Rogers did a satisfactory and a hoped-for final check on a Rover patrol car under repair in the Traffic Branch's garage. It was something he should have done earlier and, while it didn't give him hot flushes with its confirmation of his theory, he did feel that he might not be as feather-brained as he had been imagining himself to be.

With Lingard and Millier in the Bentley and tight up against his exhaust pipe, he drove in second gear at a hearse-like crawl through the muffling fog, his dipped headlights never picking out more than two cat's-eye markers at a time. Stopping his car short of the gates to Capstone House and thinking that Isabel Ungrish's accusation that he had done so previously might have a touch of precognition in it, he climbed out and walked to the now hooded Bentley pulling up behind him.

'Egad, George,' Lingard said ironically, opening the passenger door for Millier to get out, 'reckless driving'll be the death of you. We're not going in?'

'Only on our feet, and you're going to the stables to collar Gillard. If he's not back yet, the Colefax Arms seems indicated. I think we might make a charge of impeding the arrest of an offender stick.' Rogers smiled. 'If I'm wrong, all he can do is to sue you down to your last shirt for false arrest.' He turned to Millier who was wearing a belted camel hair coat with a silk scarf knotted around her throat and looking far too attractive to be out in a murky fog that was glistening its droplets in her blonde hair. 'You come with me, sergeant,' he said, 'and see that I say all the right things to a not very grieving lady. My attitude towards her wasn't approved of the first time I came here.'

It wasn't until they had passed the damp and dispirited silver birch trees that the house emerged from the darkness, a narrow crack of yellow light showing through the drawn curtain of one of the groundfloor windows. Standing in the arched porch with Millier close enough behind him to smell the disturbing scent he knew he must have outlawed, Rogers tugged at the bell-pull and waited. He hadn't heard it ringing but was hearing, not too distinctly, a woman's voice raised in an ululating wail. It wasn't unlike an oriental lament for the dead, and there was a tonality in it that the darkness exaggerated into weirdness.

He tugged the bell-pull again and this time heard the remote sound of its ringing blend in with the continuing ululations. When it became obvious that his calling was being ignored, he said in an unnecessarily low voice, 'I don't like it, sergeant,' and pressed down on the iron door handle. Unlocked, the door opened to his cautious pushing and, with his head around it and into the dark hall, he listened. The ululating, louder now and recognizably in Isabel Ungrish's voice, came from the sitting-room he had previously visited. Nothing about it seemed right.

He pulled a questioning what-the-devil's-happening face at Millier and walked soundlessly through the hall to its inner door. He opened it slowly and stepped through, prepared to apologize effusively if necessary, but realizing when he saw her that it would go unheard.

Wearing a dressing robe of cobalt-blue satin, she sat in the wing chair nearest to the blazing logs in the fireplace with her knees widespread and her feet tucked awkwardly beneath her, her hands folded on her lap like a gaunt female Buddha. Her hair was tousled and her pared-to-the-bone face bedizened with make-up. Patches of rouge blotched her pale cheeks with feverishness, scarlet lipstick was smeared messily around the mouth still wailing its eldritch lament and her huge deep-green eyes stared lost in some inner world, her expression of one experiencing a sensual bliss.

Rogers stood inside the door with Millier at his side. Isabel Ungrish was manifestly oblivious of their entering the room and there was nothing he could do but wait, to suffer the embarrassment of intruding on a woman's emotions. He had rarely felt the degree of pity that he now had for this gentle ravaged woman he thought needed the help that was not in his mandate to give. Although no judge of what appeared to be a psychopathic condition, he knew that if this were to be proved so, then whatever she said in answer to the questions he had intended putting to her would almost certainly be argued as being inadmissible in evidence.

When, after several minutes, she trailed off her singing and her eyes lost their transfixed stare, she looked at him and said softly, 'I knew you would come.' Then, turning her gaze from him to Millier, added more forcefully, 'Why did you bring her with you?'

'I'm sorry to have barged in like this, Mrs Ungrish,' he said, ignoring her question and crossing the room to stand near her. 'When you didn't answer the bell I thought you might be in trouble. How did you know I was coming?'

The only light switched on in the room was parchment-shaded and immediately behind her, leaving, as he had seen it before, her face illuminated by the flames licking around the pyre of logs. It was enough for him to see her smile when she said, 'Shouldn't I have?'

'I suppose you would,' he agreed, though still wondering why. 'I do want to talk to you about your husband's death, and Sergeant Millier is with me to give you help should you need it. As did the other policewoman.'

She stared at Millier and flicked her head. 'No. I don't want her here. Send her away.'

Rogers, while still discerning the gentleness behind the grotesquery of her make-up, could also accept the resolve in her words. Speaking to Millier, he said, 'Perhaps you'd wait outside in the car, sergeant.' With his head turned away from Isabel Ungrish, he mouthed silently, 'The hall . . . door open . . . take notes.'

'I understand, sir,' Millier said ambiguously, glancing at the seated woman and frowning as though to pass a message of warning to her senior before leaving. Please God, not another Sergeant Jarvis, he complained to himself.

He said, 'May I?' and sat in the chair at the opposite end of the vast fireplace. There was an undercurrent of something he couldn't quite resolve in Mrs Ungrish's attitude towards him that he would rather not face alone, particularly not when he

174

noticed, and could not have avoided noticing, that she was a pallid nakedness beneath the blue dressing robe. And that, even to the extent of her not wearing her chains and bracelets; nor, his nose told him, her overpowering scent.

'I'll come straight to the point,' he said, hoping fervently that he wasn't about to shoot himself in an over-zealous foot, although encouraged somewhat by her bizarre behaviour. 'We haven't so far got around to discussing how much you really know about your husband's cottage at Alwick, and the woman he was taking there.' He paused, seeing no significant reaction other than, he believed, her looking at him as if he were edible and sweet-tasting, and that there was somehow an understanding between them. 'Are you going to help me?' he asked quietly.

'Yes,' she said calmly. 'Of course I am. Did you come here to ask me if I knew who had killed Simon?' She did an oddly affected backward jerk of her head as though flicking her hair in place.

She had surprised him and he abandoned his opening gambit. 'Do you know?'

'Yes.' There was an air about her of being in control, a different woman from the one he had previously seen.

'Are you going to tell me?'

'I'll tell *you*,' she said, giving him the meaning look again. 'It won't make any difference to us, will it?'

She was puzzling him with her odd remarks, but he kept to his purpose. '*Who* killed him, Mrs Ungrish?'

'Gillard, my groom,' she said. 'You didn't know, did you?'

'No,' he admitted, frowning his disbelief because that hadn't changed his mind about anything. 'How did you know?'

'I made him tell me. I said that I would call the police if he didn't.' She shifted in her chair, her robe falling sideways and exposing a stringy thigh until she readjusted it.

'And when he did you still didn't call?'

'No,' she said. 'It wasn't necessary. God will punish him.' Astonishingly she giggled, looking up at the ceiling as she did so.

Rogers stared at her blankly, not following her change of

mood at all. 'How did he kill him?' he asked when she had finished and had returned her gaze to him.

'He didn't tell me,' she said, her features composed. 'And I didn't ask. I couldn't, could I?'

'This was when, Mrs Ungrish?'

'The next day. Simon was killed on Wednesday.' She said it as if he hadn't known.

'Did he drive your car that night?' His arm was beginning to throb and, so near to the fire, he was feeling uncomfortably hot. Apparently unnoticed, he unbuttoned and opened his overcoat.

'Yes, he did. How did you know? He asked me if he could borrow it and I said he could.' She was reaching behind her and apparently scratching her back, beginning to fidget. The hand left in the dark-blue shadow of her lap was clenched as if she held something small in it.

'He spent that evening in the Colefax Arms,' he said, feeling his way carefully, 'and that's only just down the road. Would he borrow it for that when he has his own motorcycle?'

'No, he shouldn't, should he?' Her expression of euphoria had been fading, a haggardness and a dulling of her eyes supervening as though vitality were draining from her.

'Possibly he hadn't used it at all? And if he was in the Colefax all evening – as he was – it'd be unlikely that he killed your husband. Would you agree?'

'Yes,' she whispered listlessly. There were swallowing movements in the long throat that looked longer for the absence of the chains she had earlier worn around it. 'I don't know why I said it and I don't care any more. I'm so tired and I'd like to go to bed.'

He searched her face. Until the last few minutes there had been a certain liveliness in her manner, and the sudden deflation of her mood baffled him. 'I don't think that would be a good idea,' he said, putting firm refusal into his words. 'You must bear with me for a little while yet.'

'I have to go.' Her words were barely audible. 'I must.'

She could, he reflected, need to use the bathroom and that was something he could not refuse. 'For a few minutes then,' he agreed. 'But only if you have the policewoman with you.'

'No, I won't have her.' She spoke louder and was quite definite, her head doing its odd jerking. 'You wouldn't stop me?'

'I'm afraid I'd have to.' He hoped Millier, whom she appeared to dislike, was taking all this down. Were he wrong in his supposition he could himself be badly exposed to a complaint of unlawful restraint.

Her hands were moving in the shadowed cleft of her thighs, her fingers manipulating the small object she had held hidden from him. Then, so quickly that he could not have prevented her even had he known what she was about to do, she put her closed-together finger and thumb to her nostrils and inhaled sharply. Looking at him as if to see what he would do about it, she pushed what he now saw to be a tiny enamelled pill-box under her robe and back between her thighs.

He had started convulsively from his chair before accepting that what she had done was now a *fait accompli*, made a decision to call in Millier, changed his mind about that and sank back to resume his sitting, angrily aware that his interview was even more of a non-starter.

'That,' he said to her, 'was a dam' silly thing to do.' He leaned forward and held out his hand. 'Please give it to me,' he coaxed her, knowing that where it now rested was as much out of his grasp as if it were in the strongroom of a bank.

She shook her head. Incredibly, she was changing as he watched her, her eyes brightening beneath half-lowered lids and an ecstatic orgasmic expression showing in the gaunt face flushed on one side from the flames of the fire. She pulled in her stomach, her breasts becoming prominent beneath the tautened robe, and began breathing deeply.

Rogers, though believing he need not be in the room for all that she was aware of him, said, 'Can you hear me, Mrs Ungrish?'

She had closed her eyes fully, reassuming her Buddhaesque pose as she retreated into her inner world, but her head lowered fractionally.

Praying fervently that she wouldn't start her ululating lament, Rogers asked her, 'Can you speak?'

177

As she sat motionless, he heard the easily recognizable throbbing of Lingard's Bentley being driven away from the gate. Which probably meant that Gillard was in the bag or, if not, promising to be hauled out from the bar of the Colefax Arms.

When she opened her eyes, luminous in the firelight, she said, 'I am perfectly capable,' the words coming carefully articulated from the smeared mouth. Before he could say anything, she spoke again. 'You may, you know. I've found you such a beautiful and understanding man.'

He groaned inside himself, hoping that it was said in mockery, for he was recalling what he had read about cocaine's effect on the libido. What the hell was Millier thinking about what had been said? And she would be writing it down in her unarguably competent shorthand. Keeping his voice expressionless, he asked, 'Have you been taking cocaine long?'

'Of course. Shouldn't I?' She seemed almost with him again and, although the ecstasy had gone, her face held in it a calm tranquillity. 'It's the only time that my life has not been dreadfully unhappy. Is that so wrong?'

With no ready answer to that, he said, 'Did your husband know?'

'Yes, but then he would, being who he was.'

He felt that unless he kept feeding her questions she was going to revert to her contemplation of whatever wild fantasies were inside her head. He said, 'But *he* didn't?'

'No.' She sniffed loudly. 'My nose has gone cold.'

That, too, anaesthesia of the dermis, he had learned from his text books. 'Did you put cocaine in his whisky to poison him?'

'Of course not, but I had my reasons.' She hadn't visibly resented his accusation.

'Your reasons must have been serious ones. He could have died from it.'

'Could he?' That hadn't appeared to worry her. 'I didn't believe so, and it wasn't my intention.'

Rogers was thinking that this interview had a weird out-landishness about it; his questioning of a near-naked pigmented woman sitting in a more than less yoga lotus position – if that was what it was – with a pill-box of poisonous cocaine concealed in the darkness of her thighs, stoned to the eyebrows from it and with the almost certain probability that what she was saying in her changes of mood could never be self-incriminating.

'How did you get into the cottage to do it?' he asked her.

She looked bemused. 'I didn't. It was in the boot of his car. I found the keys when he was in the bath.'

'*Why*, Mrs Ungrish? Tell me why you did it?'

'I tried to get it back later.'

She wasn't going to tell him and he said, 'From the car?'

'No.' She showed a touch of impatience as if he were slow of understanding. 'I went to the cottage.'

'How did you know about it?'

'I told Obadiah to follow him.'

'On Wednesday evening?'

'Of course not. That was when I went to get it back.'

It made sense now that he had her unquestionably at the cottage and he thought it out, uninterrupted by the woman who, closing her eyes, appeared to have dismissed him from her consciousness. Dammit! He had forgotten and she had slipped away. 'Mrs Ungrish,' he said loudly. 'Are you with me?'

She was, and said, 'Please go away. I don't wish to talk any more.'

'Were you at the cottage when your husband was killed?'

She didn't reply immediately and he waited. Then she said, 'It was an accident.'

'Tell me how it was.' He kept the tone of his voice casual and conversational and not very interested.

'I don't wish to discuss it now. Please come back later.'

'Perhaps I can help you,' he persisted. 'I'm sure you'll correct me if I'm wrong.' He paused to think her actions into the scenario of his supposition, having now to accept that Marian Kelf had finally told him the truth, or much of it. 'You went to the cottage that evening, you say to get the doped whisky back. If that is so, you presumably expected your husband not to be there. Is that right?' How she had expected to get into the cottage without a key was an unimportance he decided to leave for later.

With her eyes still closed, she nodded.

'But he was and he heard you arriving, had looked through the window and recognized you or your car. He was angry and decided to come out to you.' Rogers was watching her mouth closely, expecting a twitch or a narrowing of the lips when he hit a nerve or made a wrong guess. 'He possibly said insulting things to you and told you to go, which would make you angry also. You started to turn your car in the lane, having to reverse to do it.' He could visualize that clearly now, explicable from the twin tyre tracks in the flower border. 'Your husband was standing near the wall of the cottage, waiting for you to leave, to make sure that you did. You must have seen him in your rear-view mirror standing there behind you.' He waited, trying to detect a reaction from the features that reflected only an inner calm. 'Yes, or no, you reversed hard enough to crush him against the wall with the back of your car. He died then, didn't he? After screaming from the pain of it.'

There was no response from her withdrawnness, only the soft sizzling of sap in the burning wood and the pulsing of blood in his ears disturbing the mouse-like quietness. In his waiting he saw Ungrish, seconds from his horrible crushing death, dark against the pink wall and, surely, starkly visible in the reversing lights of the car.

Her answer came only after many dragging seconds when she opened her eyes and shook her head from side to side. 'It was an accident,' she whispered. 'I didn't see him.'

'In that circumstance, wouldn't you have considered it proper to have called an ambulance?' he said with nothing in his voice to imply disbelief. 'To report it to the police?'

She was forcing her attention on him now, the eyes fastened unblinkingly on his, the deep-green pupils almost hypnotic in their intentness. 'I didn't wish to. I knew he was dead, that I could do nothing and there were personal matters I had no intention of disclosing to others.'

'Are you going to disclose them to me?'

'No.'

'When you realized that he was dead you dragged him into the cottage, leaving him lying on the floor just inside the door. Is that so?' It was difficult for him to imagine this thin and gawky woman, desperate although she must have been, hauling at the dead weight of her husband; but it had to be so.

She lowered her head in agreement; an answer for him but nothing for Millier to record in her notes.

'Didn't you expect the woman he was associating with to be there?'

'Why should I? He told me that he was there on his own . . . just to get away from my company, he said.' There had been raw bitterness in her words and a brief bleakness in her expression.

God! Even though emotionally hurt, surely nobody could be that naive, he told himself, mentally raising his eyebrows. He said, 'You left in your car then, didn't you? Was that to get help in moving him from the cottage to the rail crossing? Help from Gillard?'

She was drifting off again, her eyelids slowly drooping. When she remained silent he knew he would have to jolt her to awareness with what must, he guessed, for a woman like her, be a corroding guilt. 'I know you asked Gillard to help you,' he said. 'And he did so because he was already your lover.'

He had misjudged her. There was a fleeting expression of what could only be lewdness, the garish make-up seemingly congruous for the first time. 'He forced me,' she said, as if it had been an act of which she was not now wholly disapproving.

Rogers had hoped that he had been wrong, not wishing one of his hardly-held beliefs about educated and cultured women to receive a bruising. Troubled and angry as he was at the confirmation of her copulating with the filthy and uncouth Gillard, it was mollified only slightly by his knowing that the cocaine she had been taking was aphrodisiacal, that it must have overriden her natural fastidiousness.

'I don't quite follow you,' he said as if he did not. 'Do you mean that he forced you to make love?' He swore to himself. Millier with her greater familiarity with the female anatomy should be probing the details of the rape she was alleging, for he was neither wishing nor intending to.

She bowed her head, looking down at her hands, now the

sensitive woman she must normally be telling reluctantly of her shameful ravishment. 'Yes. The first time . . . in the stables. He tore my dress . . . hurt me.'

But not hurt enough or objecting enough to complain about it, he wanted to say, but forbore. 'And later? You say that was only the first time?'

She was doing the odd backward jerking of her head again. 'What could I do? I was frightened of him.'

'Did your husband suspect that you and Gillard were lovers? Was that the cause of the quarrel when you sent for the police?'

'He didn't care. He hated me, he said so. That's why he killed Abigail. All he wanted was a divorce.'

She was being oblique in her answers and he was forced to continue with his guessing. 'Is it so that when Gillard returned here on Wednesday evening you drove him to the cottage in your car? That you put your husband's spectacles in his pocket, and after getting him outside and locking the door did the same with the key? You'd know he would have to have them with him, wouldn't you? That you and Gillard then loaded your husband's body into the car you knew to be there, and that he drove it to the crossing with you following in your car?'

He would have been glad had she denied being responsible for subjecting her husband, dead although he was, to the kind of mutilation he had suffered. But she did not, only shaking her head impatiently as if she couldn't be bothered with what he was saying. Then, with a mawkish slyness in her half-closed eyes, she opened her mouth and pushed her tongue forward in a sexual gesture. 'Why didn't you come in last night?' she said repoachfully. 'I know you wanted me, and I was waiting.'

Because he knew that any such suggestions could attract a belief that there must be something in them, because he felt irrationally the response he considered only an outraged virgin could have and that Millier would be scribbling it all down, he was angry and wanting to shout hard words. Instead, he said stiffly and loud enough to be sure that Millier heard it, 'Don't be under any misapprehension, Mrs Ungrish, and please don't be offended. I don't want you, and I have never said or done anything to give you that impression. I was neither here, nor near here, last night at any time or in any circumstances.'

He pushed himself out of his chair, deciding to finish his interrogation of her in his office when she was decently dressed and, more importantly, in a condition that could be described as compos mentis. 'I want you to get dressed now and come with me to the police station.' Turning his head to call in Millier, he saw in the periphery of his vision the quick movement of her hand to her nostrils and heard the sharp sniffing of inhalation. 'Goddammit, no!' he barked in exasperation and moved to her. 'Give it to me!'

She flinched and stared up at him with what he thought to be hurt in her eyes, then obediently held out the box on the upturned palm of her hand for him to take.

'Thank you,' he said, regretting his irritation with her and reaching to take it, seeing her other hand being withdrawn from between her hip and the arm of the chair. The grimace of sudden effort twisting her face and her lunge forward surprised him into seeing with a slowed-down clarity her body's movement gaping the dressing robe to show ugly red smears on the flesh below her tiny breasts, her bony fist holding gleaming broad steel that was, sluggishly it seemed, being pushed into his belly; then the fist was gone, leaving only a black handle protruding from the fabric of his trousers' front. Strangely disassociated from a body that felt as if it had been punched, he gasped in outraged disbelief that this was happening to him and lurched back on suddenly weakened legs. As he fell he heard his voice calling for Millier, chopped into silence by a jarring blow to the back of his skull that brought to it a lightning stroke of pain and then black unawareness.

29

Rogers opened his eyes to a white ceiling, a dangling lightshade
with its glaring electric bulb and, immediately above his head, a
clear plastic bag of fluid on a metal stand from which a tube ran
down to an unseeable somewhere at his side. Conscious that
there was an unwanted somebody in the room with him, he
reclosed them. His belly hurt, his arm hurt, he had a headache
and his mouth, tasting of warm metal, felt lined with sand-
paper. He couldn't think what time it was or what day, and he
couldn't be bothered to care. He was sure that he had been
where he was for weeks, and he didn't care about that either.
Otherwise his mind seemed to have pushed back its fogginess,
allowing recollection's impressions to return.

He could now recall his last moments of consciousness in
Isabel Ungrish's sitting-room, his falling and receiving a stun-
ning blow to his head, of confusion and cold air and being in the
rear seat of the Bentley, then soft bouncing into thick darkness
with Lingard cursing foully at him and the fog, pain growing in
his belly and his certain belief that he was destined for the
mortuary's necropsy table. A gap, and he was flat on his back on
a smooth-running trolley, hearing shouts, seeing the ceiling
lights of interminable corridors vanishing behind him, and
consciousness again ending on a table beneath a blinding light
as big as a dustbin lid. After that, only the bed in which he now
lay and a succession of periods of dreaming nightmarishly; of
waking in between and having only vaguely seen figures cluck-
ing incomprehensible words at him and pricking needles into an
arm that hadn't enough strength left in it to object.

The dreams, with one remembered exception, had been
terrifying and the worst happenings of his being here. The
exception had been embarrassing and only just adrift from
being a nightmare, but vividly pleasant and enjoyable in retro-
spect. Wearing only a much-too-short singlet, he had been

184

making leisurely love to Morag who, naked but for a blue dressing robe, lay on a small linen-covered table in a restaurant in a welter of broken crab shell and squashed chocolate profiteroles. The embarrassing part of the dream had been the solemnly interested spectators grouped around them. Recalling that nudged him into remembering a more solid and uniformed Morag looking down at him in one of his moments of waking and putting a warm hand on his forehead. He had tried to say something to her, but could only mumble and then she was gone.

Whoever it was he had heard in the room was still there, still making small sounds of sniffing and of clothing being rustled. He opened his eyes and looked down the ridge of his nose. Lingard was standing at the foot of the bed and watching him with a quizzical smile.

'I thought you never would, George,' he said, moving around to his side and sitting himself on a white-painted chair. 'Should I ask how you feel?'

Rogers moistened his lips and swallowed. 'Am I in the intensive care ward?' he asked in a voice not much more than a croak.

'No, and you're not about to die if that's what you're worried about.' Lingard sounded in good humour, at his most irritatingly flippant. With his overcoat open, his waistcoat colour of the day was an embroidered gold. 'How *do* you feel?'

'Bloody awful.' In turning his head to look at Lingard he could see an intravenous needle and tube fastened to his forearm with pink surgical tape, and that didn't make him feel any better. 'She stuck a knife in me,' he said as if he couldn't believe it possible.

'So she did. Force of habit, I imagine, and you were lucky at that. Don't let on you already know when your vet gets around to telling you things, but you've had what I'd personally call an unsuccessful kitchen-knife appendicectomy. I got back to the house just as Sergeant Millier, bless her, was having thirteen different kinds of fits about what to do about you and your lady friend both together. Weeping, she was; Sergeant Millier, I mean.' Lingard wagged his head, then opened his ivory box, pinched snuff and inhaled it, a man hiding things up his sleeve. 'You were bleeding more than somewhat and not with us in spirit due to your having banged your head on the fireplace. What with pumping out your life's blood and the fog slowing up everything, I decided not to wait for an ambulance and we hefted you into the back of my true and only love and brought you here at a fair old rate of knots. For all of which I've been given a couple of steamy wiggings by the hospital's head wallah and our genial chief.' He smiled mockingly. 'He, by the way, sends you his love or whatever and promises to come and see you when he's not bogged down with reorganizing the force in your absence.' He was serious for a moment. 'I thought you'd had it, George. I honestly did.'

'I'm not so sure I haven't, the way I feel,' Rogers said morosely. 'What have they done to me?'

'I quote the vet, more or less verbatim. He said that bearing in mind you were bleeding badly, that the knife was still in you and that a stab in the belly could bring on a nasty case of peritonitis, not to mention any influx of streptococci – whatever they may be – they had to open you up instanter without too much time given to thinking about it. The good news is that the blade just missed slicing a hole in your abdominal artery – you'd have been a goner then and there if it hadn't – the bad, that it didn't miss one of the big veins running from it, and that it finished up going through a bit of intestine and digging into a bone in your pelvis. They had to pump gallons of blood back into you, and if you manage not to get something catching from it you should be tottering around in pyjamas in a month or so.'

'Thank you, David,' Rogers said sardonically, 'you've cheered me up no end. How long have I been in here already?'

'Since last night.' He looked at his wristwatch. 'Twenty-three and a half hours to be exact. Just about the same time that I've been keeping your chair warm as acting detective superintendent.'

'God help the bloody department,' Rogers grunted. 'So tell me what you've done about Mrs Ungrish.'

'She's safely inside charged with attempted murder – that's yours, George – and murder.'

Rogers frowned. Even in hospital his authority wasn't to be wholly supplanted. 'You've presumably read Sergeant Millier's notes of what she said? While she could certainly be lying about the killing of her husband being an accident, there isn't any evidence, apart perhaps from the cocaine business, that it wasn't. I'd have thought an arguable charge of manslaughter unless you know more than I do.'

Lingard fed his nose with more snuff, his blue eyes mischievous. 'I shouldn't worry you with it in your state of health, but when you sent me off to collect Gillard I was wasting my time. He was with you.' He paused, waiting for comment from Rogers who, knowing his second-in-command's quirkiness well, refused to oblige by expressing his surprise. 'Ah!' Lingard said. 'I can see that you're baffled into silence. I charged Mrs Ungrish with murder because Gillard was upstairs and most bloodily dead in her bed. And I couldn't believe *that* was an accident.'

This time Rogers was visibly astonished, lifting his head from the pillow, wincing from the pain of it and lowering it again. 'Christ!' he muttered, recalling the smears of blood he had seen beneath her dressing robe. 'She must have been insane.'

'Either that or so stoned that she didn't quite know what she was doing,' Lingard agreed. 'She'd obviously used the knife she later carved you with, stuck it in his side and *didn't* miss the artery.' A spasm of make-belief distaste showed in his narrow face. 'It was done in the most unedifying of circumstances and you were certainly right when you said they could be lovers. He was naked and had lipstick all over his kisser, so he presumably died reasonably happy and on the job, so to speak.'

'I'll bet you a pound he was still wearing his hat.' That was a reflex remark on the part of Rogers not wishing to believe it of her, or to think about it.

'You've lost,' Lingard told him. 'I found it and the rest of his clobber in the bathroom, Apparently he was required to scrub himself down before she allowed him into her bed.'

'That's something in her favour, but not much. Personally, I'd have preferred one of the horses. Which reminds me, you'd better find somebody to look after them now that he won't be there.' Rogers wanted to close his eyes, to forget it and sleep for days. 'Is that the lot?'

'Apart from finding five or six grammes of cocaine in her bedroom and passing it over to the drug squad, yes, it is. No, it isn't,' he immediately contradicted himself. 'There're two other minor matters. You were going to tell me why you thought it had to be Mrs Ungrish who did the dirty on her husband.'

Rogers managed a tired smile, and that only because he had been proved right. 'I decided eventually that the injuries that killed Ungrish might have been caused by a car's bumper pinning him against a wall or some such, with the radiator simultaneously crushing his belly. That didn't explain the gouging of flesh on his right shin, so I changed ends and had the car's boot reverse into him, realizing then that the stuck-out end of an exhaust pipe could do it.' He smiled again to indicate that not all his words were to be taken seriously. 'Working that out with slide rule and calculus, it seemed probable that the exhaust pipe had been on the off side of whatever car had been used to do it. Most cars seem to sport them on the near side. Of the cars I got around to examining, only the Traffic Department Rovers had off-side exhausts. Mrs Ungrish's car is a Rover, so I was rather forced to start leaning in her direction. No problem, David,' he said misleadingly. 'It only took up time. Now you can bugger off, I'm tired.'

'I did say two matters,' Lingard reminded him. 'When she was charged with attempting to murder you, she said, "I only did it because he didn't want me any more." That, I'm afraid, was written down and signed by the duty chief inspector as a true record. *I* know it isn't so,' he added hastily as Rogers scowled, his face darkening. 'Nobody else would think so either, but if she does come to trial it'll be bound to come out in evidence.'

Rogers had thought about it and was certain – almost certain – that with the existence of Millier's notes to support him, it would be accepted as the drug-induced imagery it had to be. But it wasn't anything likely to make him happy. 'She said as much when I interviewed her,' he replied with as much indifference as he was able to summon, 'and I'm not going to worry myself sick about it.'

'Good for you, George,' Lingard said with all the cheerfulness of a man neither involved nor lying trapped in a hospital bed. 'And neither would I. I'll say have yourself a nice night now, and I'll keep in touch.'

When he reached the door, Rogers called out. 'Now that you're acting detective superintendent, David, there's one little load you can take off my mind.'

'Of course, I'm all eagerness.'

'And I'm glad to hear it. You'll find the best part of forty crime files in my cupboard that I haven't yet got around to reading. You wouldn't want me to see them still there when I got back, would you?'

He turned his head and closed his eyes. His belief was that even the darkest night had a bright star somewhere in it, but there had only been that lacklustre one for him. Just about now – had she managed to get away – his luscious and literary Katherine would be sitting at her café table in the *quartier Montparnasse*, resentful and fuming about his non-appearance the airport and vulnerable prey for that sod of a Frenchman even now possibly ordering the cognac which could so easily unbutton any of the inhibitions she might have brought with her.

As he drifted into sleep, he thought drowsily of Morag. Perhaps he would dream about her again – preferably, this time, without an audience – and that, a warming possibility, would be infinitely better than nothing at all.